Road to Thunder Hill

ALSO BY CONNIE BARNES ROSE

Getting Out of Town

Road to Thunder Hill

A NOVEL

CONNIE BARNES ROSE

inanna poetry & fiction series

INANNA PUBLICATIONS AND EDUCATION INC.
TORONTO, CANADA

Canada Council   Conseil des Arts   ONTARIO ARTS COUNCIL
for the Arts   du Canada   CONSEIL DES ARTS DE L'ONTARIO

We gratefully acknowledge the support of the Canada Council for the Arts and the Ontario Arts Council for our publishing program.

We are also grateful for the support received
from an Anonymous Fund at The Calgary Foundation.

This book is a work of fiction. Names, characters and incidents either are the product of the author's imagination or are used fictitiously, and any resemblance to actual persons living or dead or events is entirely coincidental.

Cover design: Val Fullard
Interior design: Luciana Ricciutelli

Library and Archives Canada Cataloguing in Publication

Rose, Connie Barnes [date]
          Road to Thunder Hill : a novel / Connie Barnes Rose.

(Inanna poetry & fiction series)
ISBN 978-1-926708-28-7

          I. Title. II. Series: Inanna poetry and fiction series

PS8585.O72544R63 2011   C813'.54   C2011-905665-8

Printed and bound in Canada

Inanna Publications and Education Inc.
210 Founders College, York University
4700 Keele Street, Toronto, Ontario, Canada M3J 1P3
Telephone: (416) 736-5356 Fax: (416) 736-5765
Email: inanna@yorku.ca Website: www.yorku.ca/inanna

For Eric, who holds my heart.

PART I

1. We Need to Talk

FOR AN OLD DOG, Suzie's ears are still pretty good, given she can hear a car downshift out on the highway before it even turns down our lane. She's barking at the window now, her long snout pushing aside the curtain, her paws up on the windowsill.

The pillows fly off my head, and here I sit up with the heels of my hands planted on the mattress hoping they'll ground me. There is something familiar about that wallpaper ... and what about that wall calendar with the picture of Peggy's Cove above the words, "The Four Reasons Gas n' Stop?" There's no mistaking that place. Alana's Danny, in a drunken moment of creativity, had come up with the name way back when. Now my life can slide into place. Apparently, the year is 1994, the month is April, and I'm home in bed. I'm all alone except for that old collie barking her head off.

I go to swing my feet out of bed but they're so snagged up in the sheets I feel bound as tight as a mummy. I struggle to untangle myself and make it to the window where I grab onto Suzie's ruff. Who needs to lock their doors with a watchdog like her?

I pull up the window blind and cannot believe what's happening out there in the yard. Snow! The blowing, biting kind of snow you expect to see in January, not April. Especially since only yesterday ground water gurgled from every possible hole in the yard and the first crocus buds had popped up. Whoever it is out there in the yard must have parked up close to the door. That rules Ray out. Ray parks his truck in exactly the same spot, rain or shine, right next to the linden tree across from our bedroom window. Excuse me, *the* bedroom window.

For some time I thought things between Ray and me would be okay. I went so far as to fantasize about some cold winter night when, all snug and safe in our bed, one of us would say, "Remember that year you moved out? Remember how freaked out we both were?"

And the other would say, "Yeah. But think of the fun we had finding each other again."

"Fun? You call what you put me through, *fun*?"

The fantasy ends there. The cold floor under my feet is all too real. Last night, I turned the oil furnace off thinking spring had come and besides, I had to be tough. Ray would laugh at that. He thinks our problem is that I'm *too* damned tough. My toes are freezing as I search for wool socks.

Now a cheery voice drifts upstairs. "Hello. Hello, it is I."

"I" would be Olive, my so-called half sister. I forgot she was coming over this morning. She'll be carrying the book-of-the-month in her satchel, as well as some yummy treat to go along with our meeting. I'd like to dive back under my covers.

"Patricia?" she says, her voice coming up from the bottom of the stairs. "Are you okay?"

Okay? "Yes, I'm okay," I say, stumbling into jeans. "I'll be right down."

I've given up on getting her to call me Trish, like the rest of the world does. Olive seems to think people should be called by their proper names. I've noticed that with some people she asks if they mind if she uses their real name. Not me though. She insists on Patricia.

"I'll put on the tea," she calls up.

Heading for the door I catch myself in the mirror above the bookcase. Two words spring to mind. *Tired. Sad.* But hey, thinner! Just the other night Alana pointed out that I'd sure lost a pile of weight since Ray left last year for the job down in Newville.

"We need to talk," Ray had said.

Isn't that what a woman typically says to her man? The tone should have tipped me off, but I was still so mad at him. Our daughter Gayl had just declared her sixteenth birthday to have been the absolute worst in her life. Nobody else's parents got into a fight in the middle of their daughter's party and nobody else's father stormed off to town to get drunk. At least, that's where everyone figured he'd gone. But soon after everyone had left the party, he'd come back sober. This fact should also have twigged something in my brain, but I folded my arms anyway. "Talk away, Mister."

He let out his breath like he'd been holding it in since he walked through the door. "Where's Gayl?" he said.

"She went into town with my mother."

"She hates us, doesn't she?"

"Us? Am I the one who stormed out of here?"

"No. You're the one who threw a can of tomato juice at me, remember?"

Many times since then, I've cleaned up this scene in my memory. What I should have said was, Hey, we both messed up. Maybe it was wrong to fight on Gayl's birthday but we're not perfect parents, either. This kind of talk could have saved the day because there was a time when Ray believed in me.

But what I said was, "I'm sick of how you embarrass our daughter."

He mumbled into the kitchen sink and then looked into the mirror above it. Something about his face in the mirror made me rush to him. Ever since my father died of heart failure I'm pretty sensitive about faces that suddenly turn grey.

"What's wrong?"

He shuddered then, and still speaking to the dishes in the sink, said, "I'm taking that job down in Newville."

We had talked about this job, just the week before. The salary for driving a Payloader in the salt mine was pretty decent. But it meant he'd have to board down there and drive two hundred kilometres to come home on weekends. We had decided, he had decided, he wouldn't want to be away from Gayl and me so much. To think I'd even made a joke about him giving up an opportunity to find a new family down in Newville, one whose daughter could pick up after herself. Why, perhaps he'd find a woman who'd provide him with stews and cookies and blow jobs on demand. We'd laughed at the very idea. We must have thought we were still in love that day.

No jokes on this day though. In the past, we may have flirted with the idea of putting an end to Trish and Ray, but as many times we'd fallen safely back into our lives together. This was the first time I felt weak in the knees. In less time than it takes to draw a breath, Ray was telling me he was leaving.

Turns out the big fat fight we'd had there in the kitchen in the middle of Gayl's party was all the excuse he'd needed.

"Don't you own an electric kettle?" Olive asks me now.

"Oh, probably, only don't ask me where it is." I pull the remaining pieces of birch from the wood box and stuff them into the stove. "Anyway, the stove will be hot soon enough."

The stove will be hot soon enough because at some point last night I had a dream about Ray getting that very service we'd joked about. What I remember about the Newville woman in the dream was that she had no teeth and Ray was groaning as if this was the best he'd ever had. The dream woke me up so I went downstairs to shake it off and walked over to stare out the back porch window. The moon was full and there was a big orange ring around it. On my way back to bed, I'd refilled the wood stove, which is why the coals are still hot this morning.

"Amazing that your coals are still hot!" Olive says, holding her hands together like in prayer, her chin resting on the tips of her fingers. I've come to know this pose. It's all about prying, not praying.

"I was up earlier to pee," I say with a yawn. "So I filled it then."

"I see." She has that thoughtful look which says she thinks there's much more to it. Ever since Olive moved to Thunder Hill almost two years ago, I've discovered what it's like to have an older sister. Correction. Half sister. Correction. Not even. Olive also seems to be the only person on earth who believes we share the same father.

She says, "I thought Ray was supposed to come home last night."

"He was, but he got overtime work. So now he's coming today."

I set the kettle on the stove. Drops of water fizzle and pop across the stovetop. "He's been working a lot of overtime," I add.

"He hasn't been home for a few weekends now," she says. "I wouldn't think there'd be such a call for rock salt in April. Mind you, it certainly doesn't look much like April today, does it?"

"Nope," I say, rubbing my hands together to warm them. Out the window, I can see that the snow has clumped around the corn stubble in the field next to our house. Snowy Saturday in April. Olive in my kitchen. Ray gone. No wonder everything feels so cold today.

Wanting to avoid gossip, I'd said to Ray, "We need a story. Just in case."

"In case what?" he'd said, knowing I meant in case he came back. The story that we made up for the rest of the world was that Ray needed the work, and because of the distance, we decided he should take a room down in Newville. The move was a drag, but temporary, and as soon as Ray made his hours he would move back home and things would return to normal.

Most people bought the story. I could tell by the way they'd say, "Heard you shipped Ray off to the salt mines," or, "How's Ray making out down there in Newville?" If they'd known the truth, all the talk would have swerved around Ray like a dead skunk in the road. The thing was, I wasn't sure how long I could go on pretending things were normal.

That was almost a year ago. Ray had been gone for only two days when Olive showed up in my kitchen with her satchel full of books.

"Everybody needs a book buddy!" she'd said, unloading the books onto my table. "And now that you're on your own, come over to Kyle House if you ever get lonely."

Before I had a chance to protest by saying that it wasn't like I was really alone, with Gayl here and Ray planning to come home most weekends, she'd also handed me an extra reading list for when I finished with Jane Austen, Alice Munro, and some Russian writer named Nabokov.

To be polite I told her I'd been thinking of getting rid of the TV anyway.

But secretly I meant it. Things were going to change around here. No more wasted evenings under a blanket in front of the television. I'd do all the things I used to dream about. I'd join the theatre group in town. I'd read important books!

Under a ticking clock in my kitchen, I'd begun to read. But my mind would drift to things like the talk we had just before Ray left and how I even agreed that we'd run out of room to grow together and were starting to suck each other dry like raisins. I'd even said, "If you think you'd be happier by leaving, then you have to do it."

It was a bluff, for sure. I'd expected him to drop his bag at the door so we could begin Trish and Ray all over again. But when he put his hand on the doorknob, I'd said right out, "Okay, Ray, you can stop running away from home now." He stopped for about five seconds, his shoulders hunched, his bag looking too heavy.

I stood heartsick at the door, and watched him drive up the lane, away from our little home tucked in the hollow below Thunder Hill. I kept watching until his truck was well out of sight. He didn't even toot his horn when he turned onto the road.

I decided not to chase after him, to test the old "set him free" approach, but how long was a person supposed to wait for her lover to return? While I waited I read and sometimes stuck my foot out to rub Suzie's head. Thank God for Suzie, who is content to curl up on her rug near my feet. Ray had often said that I'd be happier if I could keep *him* tied to a leash.

Every so often, Carrie the cat, asleep with her white front paws tucked neatly under her chest, opened one eye to stare back at me. The house was so still. Gayl was spending more and more time in town with my mother and I thought about how strange it felt to have both husband and daughter out of the house. I tried to look at it in a positive light, so I'd keep reading, but the ticking clock kept putting me to sleep and I'd wake up at midnight with a sore back and barely a chapter finished.

For that entire month of May last year I tossed and turned and stayed awake every night until it was time to go to work each morning. I thought about taking time off from the factory so I could stay in bed just to catch up on my sleep, but I needed my job now more than ever. One night I couldn't wait any longer so I phoned Ray at his boarding house. I held my breath through five rings before he picked up.

"Hello?" I said.

"Trish?"

I could tell by the huskiness in his voice that he'd been asleep. "You were expecting someone else?" I tried being my usual snarky self, but ended up swallowing too hard right after "expecting."

"I was kind of hoping it was you."

I stifled the urge to say, "you were?" Other than when he'd first moved to Newville and he'd put an end to our calls we hadn't spoken to each other except when he'd phone for Gayl, and the time he asked if I'd paid the oil bill.

"So," I said, trying to hide my surprise. "How's life at the boarding house?"

"Oh, it's there I guess," he yawned. I pictured him lying on his back, his fingers pulling at the triangle of dark hairs on his chest. "You know, I was wondering what you'd think about me ... about me coming home this weekend. To visit. Would that be wrong?"

I think I coughed. "Wrong?"

"I'd understand if you said no."

I didn't answer right away. I was too busy trying to breathe. "Um," I finally said. "I suppose Gayl might like to see you. I guess Suzie and Carrie would like to see you, too."

There was a long silence before he said, "I was hoping you might like to see me."

I felt something huge lift off my heart. Maybe our break-up had just been one of those fights that had gone too far. Now, he was asking if there was anything I might need him to do when he arrived home.

"Hmm," I said, like I was giving it thought. "Well, there is something I might need you to help with in, um, the bedroom?"

"Don't tell me the ceiling's leaking again. Shit, I thought we'd solved that problem."

"Well, actually the problem I'm thinking about has more to do with our bed."

"What, the mattress?"

"You're getting closer. Here's a clue. Remember that time with the blindfold?"

I guessed from his silence that he was remembering.

"And your bathrobe belt?" he said.

"Yeah. That too."

"Um," he said, "then I'll see you Friday night?"

"Okay."

After we hung up I went downstairs. I sat out on the back steps and cried so hard it hurt. I kept it up until that hurt stopped feeling so good. Ray was coming home.

I must have looked a nervous wreck that first weekend he came home, the way I kept going to the porch window to see if his truck was heading down the lane. I'd been practicing what to do and say, including a sappy run into his arms, but when he stepped through the door, we both acted like he'd gone no further than the Four Reasons store for a can of beans.

"It's cold out there," he said, as he hung his jacket on the hook. He seemed thinner, and there were lines in his cheeks I'd never noticed before.

"It got cold overnight," I said, as I filled the kettle under the tap. I peeked at my own reflection in the mirror to see if the new wrinkles I'd discovered around my eyes were obvious.

At first we were like strangers, the way we kept sneaking looks at each other over Suzie's hysterical barking. But then the more we looked, the more we smiled and when he raised his hands like he was asking what's next, I did the sappy run thing right into his arms.

For supper I made my famous fish chowder and as we sat around the table as a family, I was shocked at how Gayl said, "Please" and "Thank you," and didn't tip her chair legs back. In all the time he'd been gone she hadn't once said she'd missed her father.

Still, Ray and I treated each other like polite strangers all the way to bedtime, but as soon as we started licking and sucking and fucking everything felt right again. Then we were kissing and hugging and stroking and pressing together, even in our sleep, which made it almost worth the shit we'd gone through.

The next day almost felt like normal except for one thing. Gayl was still acting way too helpful and considerate. She cleaned up her room. And, she kept asking Ray geography questions, one of his favourite subjects.

"Dad?" she said, "Where exactly is Mozambique? I have this paper for school."

"Let's look it up together." He opened his atlas on the dining room table and they hovered over it. "Here it is in southeast Africa. Now you know if it ever comes up again in your life." She was being the child he'd always wanted.

We stayed on our best behaviour and Ray started coming home every weekend. I took to cooking roasts and casseroles to celebrate his Friday night arrivals. He mowed the lawn that was beginning to qualify as hay. He'd given me an antique weathervane three Christmases ago and that first weekend he stuck it up on the peak of the barn. We touched each other a lot, and fell in love again. And when our friends complained about us smooching in front of everyone, we hammed it up, just to prove that Ray's working down in Newville was the best thing to have ever happened.

We got so used to the routine of Ray coming home on weekends that by the end of last summer, this new way of life felt normal. I actually enjoyed having the entire week to myself, and maybe was even a bit resentful when Ray came home on Friday night. For one thing it meant I had to keep on top of the housework, because if I didn't Ray would haul out the broom and dustpan and start sweeping not only the floors but the walls and ceiling too. It drives me crazy when he does that because he always finds stuff I missed, even when I've gone over it twice.

Gayl went back to being normal too, as did her room with its explosion of clothes. Once again, her answers became grunts. The lawn turned into a field full of timothy straw. Friday night supper meant scrambled eggs.

Sex also became routine and sometimes I wondered if it even mattered if I was awake. Once, after he came, and I wasn't even close to coming, he whispered, "That was incredible."

"Oh, sure," I said, sure he was being sarcastic.

He nudged me. "You didn't enjoy it?"

"You did?"

"You were amazing," he sighed.

I almost said, well, I might as well have been in a coma, since I hardly moved a muscle! I didn't, of course. There are some things in life a man should believe in.

Olive now plunks this month's book on my kitchen table. While she rummages in her satchel for pencils I look out my window towards Thunder Hill. The snow is coming down so hard I can hardly see the base of the hill, even though it rises straight up from my back yard. On a clear day, smoke from Bear James' chimney drifts up over the spruces. But today I can barely make out my own barn. And the kitchen is gloomy, in spite of the big new sliding window we'd finally put in, right beside the table.

"I hate days like this," I say to the window.

"Really? I love stormy days. They're so dramatic," says Olive. "We can't expect every day to be sunny, now can we?"

"No-o-o," I say slowly, turning to face her. "But we shouldn't have storms in April either."

Yesterday, the same snowy yard had been bursting with spring while robins hopped around looking for buried worm treasure. It was so warm that Carrie the cat, who lives for birds and mice, barely lifted her head from her sunny spot on the picnic table.

Yesterday was a hopeful day and not just because of the weather. Three weeks ago, Ray and I had our first big fight since he'd come back to me. He hasn't been home since, and I've been going around telling everybody that the company has given him a lot of overtime. The truth is that one night I had too much to drink and I went a little nuts. Earlier, I'd come across an acorn in one of his pockets and when I asked him about it, he'd said, "Search me," with this weird guilty smile on his face so, naturally, I got it into my head that he'd had a fling in Newville last year because first of all we don't have oak trees in Thunder Hill and secondly, if I looked at it hard enough I could make out what looked like a little smiley face drawn on the thing. And Ray's not the sort of guy who puts things like acorns in his pocket unless someone was to give it to him. He kept saying he had no idea how the acorn had gotten into his pocket. Well, I pushed and pushed until he got mad and the madder he got the harder I pushed. Finally, he threw up his hands and shouted, "What if I told you I did have a *hot one,* as you say, down in Newville?

Would that make you feel better? In fact, I don't think you'll be satisfied unless I *do* tell you that."

I dropped the subject like a lit match had burned my fingers and went up to bed, slamming the door on the way. He'd ended up sleeping on the couch that night. In the morning he was gone, and I haven't seen him since. It killed me to swallow my pride and call him at the rooming house last week. I said that I believed his story about the mysterious acorn and apologized for not believing him in the first place. There was a long silence on the other end of the phone, as if he was deciding what would be the smartest thing to say. That was when he said he would come home Friday. The relief I felt was almost as keen as it was the first time he came back to me.

Since the Foghorn Pewter Company closes at noon on Fridays, I drove home with yard work on my mind. Just like the robins, I couldn't wait to expose what was under all that winterkill. The smell of spring reminds me of Ray, so that's why all day Friday I went around thinking we were back in business. I managed to rake the entire yard before the sun went down behind Thunder Hill.

Olive sits straight in her chair. With her reading glasses and her wiry red hair swept up in a loose bun, she looks like a school-teacher from pioneer times. My father always denied she was his child, but if she had been his, he would have approved of her posture. My own slouch had always bugged him. As a kid I'd been sent away from many a meal for refusing to sit properly in my chair. Sometimes, to be a brat, I'd sit up straight, but at the same time, tip my chair onto its back legs. It's odd that tipping chairs is something my own daughter seems to have inherited. I'm glad my father lived long enough to witness how this drives Ray and me crazy.

While Olive arranges her notebook and pencil, I notice that my hairbrush rests next to the honey jar on the table. All I need is for Olive to see that. She's had three kids, but her house is forever tidy. In her house, hairbrushes would be in the bathroom and not dripping with honey on the kitchen table.

The hairbrush was a gift from Bear James, Ray's closest friend. And next to Alana, I guess he's my best friend, too. The gift was for my birthday, but as soon as my family realized how nicely boar bristle rakes through hair, it became the family brush. Bear used to say the colour of my hair reminded him of Kraft caramels. I think that was the nicest thing anyone ever said about my hair. Now, with all the grey, my hair reminds me of dirty sand. Olive thinks I should dye it back to my original colour, but I never much liked the idea of cheating on nature.

Crammed into the bristles are a lot of family hairs like the mess of long blond hairs belonging to Gayl. If the brush hasn't been cleaned in a while, which is very likely the case, then a few of Ray's dark strands may also be twined around the bristles.

Last night I shouted at Gayl to come down and take it off the table.

"If you're down there looking at it, then why don't you move it?" Gayl shouted back.

"Because it's your job to clean off the table!"

"Yeah, of dishes, not other junk!"

"You put it there!" I shouted up the stairs.

"Relax, Ma, it's a freaking hairbrush. I'll do it after."

I stood there feeling my back go up, but by the time I went upstairs she was asleep so I decided to go fall into my own flannel sheets. I pulled my quilts up over my head and reminded myself that some battles simply weren't worth the fight. Like how she calls me Ma when she damn well know knows I don't like it.

That's why the hairbrush is still sitting on the table this morning. As I grab it now, I discover yet another surprise. A piece of last night's roast beef stuck behind the salt shaker.

Can't hide from me, I think, as I snatch that up too. As I head to the cupboard to put the hairbrush away, I drop the beef on the floor in front of Suzie's nose. One thing about dogs, they never ask where food falls from; they simply accept what's offered. When

I come back into the kitchen, Suzie's old jaws are still chomping away. And another thing about dogs? They're clueless as to who might be watching them with a frown on her face.

"Poor Suzie," I say, making a big deal of rearranging the salt and pepper shakers. "She's getting so finicky she'll only eat table scraps instead of her food. In fact, when Gayl and Biz drive into town, they're supposed to pick up a bag of that special geriatric food at the vet's."

Olive glances out the window. "With the way this day is shaping up, I wonder if they should drive Billy instead of your car."

Olive insists on calling her SUV "Billy." And she doesn't stop there; she makes everybody else call it Billy too. I'm surprised she doesn't call it William when she corrects them for calling it a "truck." I refuse to call it anything but a "truck." As for my own Toyota, I can't resist saying, "That's okay. If Tercel can't make it into town, then they shouldn't be driving today anyway."

Olive looks at me like she's not sure if I'm joking. She holds a pencil over her notebook. "Well, then. Should we start?"

I stare down at the book I'd chosen mostly because the writer used to live around here. "I don't know. I guess I kind of liked it."

"Really!" Olive says, as if I'd said I admired Hitler. "What did you like about it?"

"I guess it sort of reminded me of…" What had it reminded me of? *Me*, I want to say, mostly because the main character grew up in a town like mine. The town had a DDT truck to fight off mosquitoes too. The writer got it right when she wrote that the DDT fog smelled exactly like WD-40. At the sound of that truck, every kid in town ran from the supper table to the street, just to run behind the fog spewing from its back. Once, after the truck passed, I squatted down to watch a bee wiggle its legs just before it died. That was the first time I'd realized that the poison could hurt things other than mosquitoes. But when I asked my father if the spray could hurt me too, he told me that next to a bug I was a giant, which meant I was safe. He said this rule covered just about everything in life; how survival was about being large enough to take on poison.

"I guess I could relate to the small town thing," I say to Olive.

"But did you learn anything from this book? I have to say, I found it disappointingly simplistic."

"Because it was easy to read?"

"No, because it didn't teach me about anything I care to learn."

Olive goes on about how it's a writer's responsibility to raise consciousness, to inspire change. It simply isn't enough to write without a reason. The same might be said about the importance of getting people to read more: to open their minds, to expand their worlds.

Before I had a chance to say that I thought this writer wanted to write about her own time and place in the world, she suddenly jumped up from her chair.

"I just had a great idea!" she says, her eyes wide. "We should get some of the farmers to join us, and then we'll have ourselves a real book club!"

"Hmm."

Olive insists on calling the local women "farmers." I once tried to explain that calling a woman a "farmer" is almost an insult, since this is the word they were teased with all throughout high school. Besides, some women would rather be called housewives than farmers. But Olive seems to think she knows what's best for them.

"You don't think that's a good idea? Asking the farmers?"

"Sure, why not? I'm just not that optimistic about it."

Truth be told, I can't picture sitting around a living room with Midge Hutchins or Jean Bradley, let alone talking to them about books. I've also tried to explain to Olive that there are invisible barriers in Thunder Hill. That to the locals, Ray and I will never truly belong.

"But you and Ray are from here!"

"No, Olive, Ray and I are from town."

"But you spent your childhood in Thunder Hill."

"Only the summers. It's not the same, trust me."

"But our father is buried here."

I don't bother to correct her about the fact that Bernie Kyle was *my* father alone, and that *her* real father was some veterinarian her mother had had an affair with while she was married to my father. I keep my mouth shut because she seems to have no clue of this fact and has been living her whole life thinking she had an absentee father who sent her mom cheques and sometimes small notes when she was young and that except for him having left her Kyle House for some odd reason, wanted nothing more to do with her.

"True," I say. "But that's because my father was too ornery to be buried with the rest of his clan on the bay side of Thunder Hill."

"I don't get it. His grandfather built Kyle House, so doesn't that make us all locals?" she says. "How far back do you have to go to be considered a local around here?"

"It's not how far back that counts, it's where you live most of the year that counts. Other than during the summers, our family didn't live out here."

This is just one more thing Olive doesn't get because she's from Toronto. That while I'm happy to drop by my neighbours to trade eggs for honey, I wouldn't dream of stopping in at Christmas.

So about the book club, I say, "I don't think they'd have the time, you know. They're so busy."

"They still manage to find time for quilting clubs and cribbage tournaments. Think how a book club might expand their thinking. You even said yourself that nobody around here talks about anything except each other."

"I don't remember saying that."

"Well, you did. We were sitting right here at this table and you called Thunder Hill 'Dunderhill.' Remember?"

A prickly feeling travels up the back of my neck. I guess I must have been drunk one night when I confessed to Olive that I was dying of boredom here in Thunder Hill, because, "Between you and me, Olive, they're all a bunch of dunderheads."

Dunderheads? Where had that come from? I could have said, "There are *some* dunderheads," but no, I had said *all*. All would have to include Alana and Danny and Bear and, for all that matters, my own family. And me? My one year in Toronto happened almost two decades ago, yet over a bottle of Olive's wine she'd insisted that this somehow gave me a certain sophistication that my neighbours lacked. I had laughed at this and said I hardly thought one year away could qualify.

"Now Patricia," she said, "Surely that one year in the city must have felt like a lifetime."

Yes it had, I admitted to that, but I also said I've never regretted moving back to Thunder Hill.

"Because like Alana's always saying," I tell her, "Thunder Hill is the most fucking beautiful place in the world, man."

We laughed because that is something Alana does say a lot. And maybe it's because we drank two more bottles of Olive's wine, that I had started in about my neighbours, saying all those things I felt so ashamed of the next day. I felt like calling Olive up just to say, "In spite of what I said last night about the people who live around here, the thing I like the most about them is that they are real people." But of course I didn't, because I've learned to be careful not to say things to Olive I might regret later. And now she wants to start a book club with these people I called a bunch of dunderheads. I just don't get her.

When the phone rings I jump because it might be Ray. He told me he'd call this morning, before he set out from Newville.

But where's the phone? Ever since Gayl talked me into buying a cordless phone, I can never find it. Olive and I both head in the direction of the living room where Gayl's school papers cover the couch and floor. Just as I'm thinking I'll never find it in time, Olive reaches under the couch and pulls the phone out. She hands it to me with dust clinging to her sweater sleeve.

"Hello?" I say, while Olive plucks at the dust ball and I'm

thinking I'd better get to those before Ray comes home and makes a big point of pulling out his broom.

It's my best friend Alana on the phone, not Ray at all. "Hi Alana." I turn to look out the living room window. The snow is scuttling across the lane and beginning to drift along the sides.

Alana is saying, "Olive's there, isn't she?"

"Hmm. You must be psychic." This is a joke, since Alana is a certified psychic, with paying customers who come all the way from towns on the other side of Thunder Hill.

Olive asks from behind me, "What is our Alana predicting today, pray tell?"

Our Alana?

"Olive wants to know what *our* Alana is predicting for today."

"Let's see. She predicts you'll be a whole lot happier once Olive leaves your yard? How am I doing so far?"

"You've got that right."

Olive says, "What does she have right?"

"That we're in for a storm," I say. This isn't a lie. Last night, when Gayl and I finished getting our readings done by Alana, we stepped outside and Alana pointed to the moon and said, "Wouldn't be at all surprised if we got hit with a storm tomorrow."

Now Alana asks, "Did Ray get home last night?"

"No." I say, stifling a yawn. "In fact, I thought it might be him calling. He worked double time yesterday. But he's coming this morning."

"The roads aren't great," Alana says. "Weather report says it might turn to freezing rain. Are you guys still planning to come over to play cribbage tonight?"

"Hope so."

"And if you want to play 45s instead, you can ask Olive and Arthur over too. Oh, look, Bear James just drove up to the pumps. See you later."

I click off the phone and say to Olive. "Boy, it's really coming down out there. Maybe we shouldn't let those kids go into town."

It turns out that Arthur is away in Toronto, and even though he's due to arrive home tonight, he likely won't want to go out again so I don't have to feel guilty about not saying anything to Olive about us going over to Danny and Alana's later. As far as I'm concerned, it's just another sticky situation avoided. The last thing I need is for Olive to hear Danny teasing me about Ray and me living apart all week long. He usually starts by asking Ray about the so-called *hot one* he has down there in Newville. It's all meant as a joke, but no matter what Ray says to ward off Danny's teasing, it ends up backfiring on him.

"Don't worry," Ray said one time. "From what I can tell, the best-looking girls down in Newville don't have any teeth."

"All the better for, you know what there buddy," Danny said, elbowing Ray so hard he almost fell off his chair.

I said, "I never noticed any toothless girls the time I was there."

Well, I walked into that one alright. Danny smirked and said, "That's because they only take their teeth out at night when they go to work!"

I had to laugh too, knowing that both Alana and Olive would be watching me to see how I really feel about Ray living in Newville.

Maybe if they knew, they wouldn't make those jokes. Which might be even worse, I realize. So I pretended to pretend to be mad and said to Ray, "What I'd like to know, Buster, is how you noticed that the Newville women have no teeth?"

It was joking around kind of talk, the kind that puts to rest any social speculation. But like most joking around, in private, a person might take these things far more seriously.

Now I'm in the basement rummaging for stray sticks of wood. Upstairs, I hear the phone ring again. A chair scrapes on the kitchen floor above my head as Olive goes to answer it. I listen here in the dark. Yes, it must be Ray because he has this annoying way of making Olive shriek and snort with laughter. Ray isn't all that funny, but Olive thinks he's a riot. I spot some sticks of softwood behind the furnace. Winter has been long and nasty this year and I'm not the only one who has run out of wood. Olive's been telling the neighbours to help themselves to the birch from her neatly carded and plentiful supply. I'd sooner freeze than have Olive think I couldn't have handled this past winter on my own.

"Who phoned?" I ask, puffing from having lugged all this wood to the top of the stairs.

"Ray."

"Oh yeah? What was so funny?"

"Nothing, really. He said to tell you he'll be here by noon. Oh, and he said something about seeing Arthur and me tonight at the Four Reasons. I told him Arthur's due in from Toronto but that I hadn't heard about any plans for tonight." She looks at me in the same way Carrie looks at robins. "Did I miss an invitation or something?"

I shrug. "You know Ray. All talk. He'll be so wiped out from working all night he'll end up falling asleep as soon as he gets home."

"Oh, he's at work? That explains it then."

"Explains what?"

"Those women I heard talking in the background," Olive says with a wave of her hand. "I asked him who it was and he denied there was anyone close to resembling a female anywhere near him." She snorts. "That's why I was laughing. You know what a tease he can be."

Since when has Ray become a tease, I think, but I say to Olive, "He couldn't have been calling from work. He would have finished his shift at midnight."

"Oh well, maybe he worked right through? I heard all of these clanging noises in the background too."

I pretend to examine the draft lever on my stove. "It was probably his landlady you heard."

"I heard more than one and they sounded pretty young."

My mind is racing. As far as I know, there are no women working at the salt mine, so where the hell was he calling from? There used to be a time when I knew everything about my husband. At least, I thought I did.

Through the kitchen window I spot that cheery robin from yesterday, with feathers fluffed and now looking miserable on the crook of a branch. With one shudder his feathers are free of snow. Then he takes off, in search of a drier place. I sure do wish I could do the same thing.

2. The Deed to Kyle House

ONCE, A LIFETIME AGO, my father handed the keys as well as the deed to Kyle House to Ray and me. Later, when I told Ray that I had turned down my father's offer, he looked at me like a kid whose crayons had just been stolen. "How could you turn down the nicest property in the county?" I'd warned Ray about telling our parents that I was pregnant in the first place. But he'd wanted to do the right thing, so we'd driven the thirty minutes into town. My mother took our news in stride, meaning she poured herself a double shot of rum, but my father freaked. He went on and on about responsibility and maturity and all the other things we didn't have. Like real jobs. We told him we were getting married and that shut him up long enough to plan a surprise engagement party out in his back garden.

On the day of the surprise party, we were invited to what I thought was a simple brunch, but I realized I was heading into a trap when I spotted my Aunt Sybil and Uncle Lefties's car parked outside my parents' house, as well as about twenty others along the street. When I tried to do an about-turn there on the sidewalk, Ray grabbed my arm, whispered "surprise" and forced me up the walk, into the door, and "Surprise!" My biggest emotion was fury at Ray for being in on something he'd known all along I'd hate.

Later, on the back lawn, my father raised his glass in a toast to his fifty or so guests.

"The moment has arrived to toast the upcoming wedding between the love of my life — after my beautiful wife, of course — and this fine young man who'd better be worthy of my little girl."

As his audience laughed, my father clapped his arm around his future son-in-law, the same boy he had often referred to as "that girl," because of his long straight hair. Ray grinned ridiculously as my father held him in a tight grip, and I almost changed my mind about marrying him, especially when my father sprung the deed to Kyle House on "the couple who've decided to get a head start on our grandchildren." All the hand clapping startled a flock of starlings perched in the giant hackmatack tree. As the black frenzy whirred into the sky, I had a feeling Ray might throw his arms around my father and kiss his big bald head.

That's how I came to be sitting across from Ray at the kitchen table trying to explain, "I know my father better than you think you do, and he doesn't give anything away for free."

He sat there and had the nerve to say, "I've never figured out why you are so angry towards Bernie."

"Why do you suppose he gave us the house, Ray? Why?"

Ray opened his hands wide. "Because his daughter is getting married to the man she loves, and what was once the finest house in the county is sitting there rotting on the most spectacular point along the entire coast?" His voice rose here. "Maybe he thought that we'd be grateful? Which would have been true, at least for one of us."

"See, Ray? That's where you're wrong. He gave us the house for one reason. And that is so he could control our lives."

"For a free house, I'd be willing to let your father control whatever he wants."

"You say that now, but…"

"But nothing! You could have let me be a part of the decision."

Then Ray did what he always did when he couldn't get his own way. He took off to town to get drunk.

Alana, who has always been able to calm me down, drove me to the dump that very day. She'd heard there were boxes of giveaways lined up against the chain-link fence. People from town were opening their cottages along Thunder Hill Road and wanted to start the summer off fresh. While we rummaged, she said that the problem with men was that they saw only the big picture and never stopped to consider all the angles. Like my father assuming that because I was pregnant, I'd learn to live my life like everyone else. And the way Ray saw the mortgage-free house like a carrot dangling in front of him.

I said, "Ray was practically drooling!"

"But then again," Alana said, "there's something to be said for a free house." Then she gasped. "Hey, look at this, Trish. I have always wanted a juicer. I wonder if it works."

It's amazing what people throw away. Back then we furnished our homes with stuff from the dump. Every time my parents came for a visit, I'd show my father my latest find. I likely did this to annoy him, but over time it became a joke. The whole world knew my father would have bought me twenty brand new toaster ovens, if only I'd let him.

That day at the dump I said to Alana, "My father would want to control our every move."

"You'll think differently once you have the kid, and that's a fact," she said, and as if to prove it, she hollered, "Kim, get down off that fence! Hey look, Trish, here's a braided rug. And there's not a thing wrong with it. Kevin, you get down too! Except for this little hole, this is perfectly good."

That was the only time I've ever known Alana to be wrong about anything. Not about the rug, she was right about that, and all these years later it still keeps my back porch floor warm. But the part about me thinking differently? I feel the same way to this day. Ray and I managed to make our lives without my father's help. This drove my father crazy. Especially when it came to Gayl, who he adored. Every time she visited Gran and Gramper, as she called him, she came back with carloads of clothes and toys. There wasn't much I could do about it even if I felt back then that the fewer things in life a person could have, then fewer messes to clean up after. So we let them spoil her rotten, especially after my father almost dropped dead after a heart attack. He survived the heart attack but not the damage and his heart kept going out on him. He'd make a point of saying that what gave him the most joy the times he was out of the hospital was to take Gayl shopping.

It got so that we thought my father would live in a state of heart failure forever. He was in and out of surgery wards so often, he joked with the nurses about them keeping his bed warm until his return. When it actually happened we felt as shocked as if he'd died in a car accident. The only real thing about it was the funeral arrangements, which had been in place for well over a year. We were glad for that.

Two days before he died, Ray and I were at his bedside. We'd come so many times before, thinking he was dying, and just as many times he'd managed to fool everyone and had come back from death's window — the same window he'd blown his cigarette smoke out of — the whole time he was in the hospital.

That day, he exhaled towards the open window and said, "I used to think you kids were a couple of idiots, but I'll give you credit, you managed to do okay."

"Thank you Bernie," Ray said. "That means a lot to us. But we couldn't have done it without all your support over the years. Right Trish?"

He nudged me so I nodded, and when he nudged me harder, I looked at my father and saw his eyes were focused on Ray and not on me at all.

I said. "Yeah, thanks, Bernie. Dad."

I frowned at Ray and got up to smear some Vaseline on my father's lips.

I wonder what my father would say today about Ray moving out on me. Knowing him, he would have marched down to that boarding house in Newville to lecture Ray about everything he knew about women. He would have said something about women in general being more trouble than they were worth, but that wives, in particular, were necessary evils. He'd always considered himself an expert, since he had married two of them, my mother his second, and Olive's mother his first.

As for Ray, I doubt he'd have had the guts to leave me if my father had still been alive. It used to piss me off how they could talk for hours over a bottle of Scotch. My father never offered me any Scotch. When my father finally stopped drinking, because of his heart, Ray came up with the idea of the two of them building a boat in our barn — just a sturdy little dinghy, designed for fishing in the inlets. They didn't get far with it though, and its wooden skeleton gathers dust out there in the barn. Ray never wanted to touch it after my father died.

I realize that Olive has just asked me a question about sex, of all things, which snaps me right back to my kitchen. She is staring at me as if her life depends on my answer.

"I'm sorry, Olive. What was your question?"

"I asked you how your sex life is."

I'm thinking she can't be serious, yet she grips the edge of the oilcloth like my answer to her question is a matter of life or death.

"It's fine," I say, "considering Ray hasn't been able to get home much lately." Is that what she was getting at? I look around to see what could have possibly sparked this kind of talk but I'm not getting any clues.

"That's it? That's the best you can come up with?" she says, looking like she's bursting to tell me something.

I quickly get a feeling that this isn't about my sex life after all, which is a relief, so I ask, "And how about your sex life?"

"Our sex life?" Olive says, as if she has never considered this before in the twenty or so years she's been with Arthur. She closes her eyes and says, "Arthur is a wonderful lover."

"Really?"

Now, as far as I'm concerned, Arthur has all the appeal of an eel. Any time I've seen him in swimming trunks the sight has made me shiver. So what am I supposed to say to Olive now, congratulations?

"I am so fortunate. He is so..." Olive says, clasping her hands like she's praying. "Enthusiastic."

"Oh?" I say. I can't bring myself to picture Arthur in the act, let alone being enthusiastic about it. He looks so nervous, especially when he's around Olive. Plus, he has no chin. Danny once pointed out that Arthur's Adam's apple had to do double duty as a chin.

"Yes! He does the most amazing things!" Olive leans over the table and whispers, "The first time we made love was after an Egon Schiele exhibit."

"Who?"

"Arthur looks a lot like Egon Schiele, the artist. So we bought a book of his paintings. We like to look at it. *In bed.*"

"Oh." I can only imagine what these paintings are like.

"Sometimes Arthur pretends to be an artist and asks me to pose in some pretty erotic postures. Sometimes he paints me," Olive's voice drops to a whisper. "I mean, he literally paints me, with body paint or sometimes..." She blushes here, "he powders me with an especially soft and tickly brush."

"Oh really." I spy a cobweb hanging from the ceiling which reminds me of Ray so I go find the broom and get real busy sweeping it down. "To think I swept the ceiling just the other day!"

Olive steps closer to me. "Do you mind if I ask you a personal question?"

"Um ... you mean more personal than my sex life?"

"Do you consider Ray to be a clean person?"

I blink. "Why? Did he have dirt under his fingernails the last time you saw him?"

"Oh no, nothing like that. It's just that ... well, I wouldn't tell this to anyone but you, but Arthur has to be the cleanest person

I have ever met." She giggles. "Guess what he does the minute after we have sex?"

"I don't know, has a shower?"

"Close! He washes his penis in the bathroom sink! He scrubs it so hard I tease him it will fall off."

"Really!" I say, trying not to imagine Arthur's pale hands scrubbing away at his penis.

"Does Ray do that? Wash himself after?"

"Never!" I have to laugh. "He's the opposite."

"What do you mean?"

"I guess he doesn't think that sex is all that dirty. He might not think to wash for a couple of days after."

Olive's nose crinkles. "But don't you mind? I mean, doesn't he smell?"

"I don't mind his smell. I like it in fact. It's sort of woodsy."

"Oh really?" She raises her eyebrows. "Like, in a fresh pine sort of way?"

"No," I say, trying to match Ray's smell with a word. "More like in a rotted log sort of way."

Olive snorts and I'm wishing I hadn't said that. How does she get me to confess or admit to things I don't care to share with anyone, not even Alana? Even if Olive really was my half sister, it's none of her business how Ray smells! But here I am, trying to fix what I said just before.

"I mean in a healthy way," I mumble. "*Outdoorsy*, I mean,"

The tags on Suzie's collar jingle. She rushes to the door and lets out a volley of barks. I look out the porch window. A snow squall out there in my yard is so fierce I can't even see up my lane. Olive is standing beside me. It's getting whiter by the second. We can't even see beyond the first crab apple tree. So we're both squinting, trying to see the lane, and then clear out of the squall, Bear James's Rover comes barrelling towards us so fast that Olive and I scream and jump backwards. I even take an extra leap into the pantry because I expect to see the Rover coming right through my kitchen. But no, when I dare look out again, the Rover has come to a stop just inches from my front door.

The sheer size of Bear James takes up most of my doorway. Melting snow drips from a curl over his forehead and onto his nose.

"Man, that was wicked," he says, looking back out at the storm. In the time it has taken him to come into the house, the squall has moved on, so the lane is visible once more.

"How did you get through all that?" says Olive, who has perched once more on the edge of her seat, looking like one of the ravens who watches my every move from the top of the linden tree.

"Easy," he says. "Built-in radar. You don't drive down a lane for twenty-odd years and not know your way through a snow squall."

"Right. I noticed how your radar almost put you right through my house," I say, peering around him. "How close did you come? A foot?"

"More like three. Hey, I thought Ray was coming up this weekend." He reaches for a muffin on the table and pops the whole thing in his mouth.

"He is. Today."

Olive offers him some tea and he's soon settled into a kitchen chair, his coat open, his beard catching crumbs.

I reach over to whisk them away. "I wish you'd shave that thing off."

"Yes, mother."

He winks at Olive who giggles then snorts. Then he tells us he's on his way over to Sandra Birdshell's to help her with a stuck patio door. Apparently, the snow is blowing clean across her living room floor.

"So it's true that you provide house calls to damsels in distress." Olive gives me a knowing look.

"Now, where did you hear that?" Bear says.

Olive winks at me and says, "A little bird told me that you

practically delivered Gayl way back when."

"A little bird, you say?" he says, grinning at me.

I say, "It was Alana who told you that. Not me. And he didn't practically deliver Gayl either."

Bear laughs then. "That's true. Only in Trish's case it was Ray who stuck Gayl into her, so I figured he was responsible for helping to get her out. Unfortunately, I have to take full blame for installing those patio doors in Sandra's house."

I can't believe I'm blushing. Sometimes Bear comes out with the worst jokes, but that's not why I'm turning red. It's because of things we said about Bear a couple of weeks ago, the night when Olive and I were rug-hooking over with Alana at the Four Reasons.

Rug-hooking is something Alana and I have done since the Farm days. Our rugs hang on walls, are draped over the backs of chairs, and lie beside every bed. As soon as Olive saw them she wanted to hook rugs too. Mostly, I think she gets a kick out of telling everyone she's a "hooker." So she insisted we get together every two weeks at the store.

The last time we got together, Olive raised her bottle of fancy lager from Ontario that she'd brought for us and said, "Here's to you two women and your wonderful men. I don't know if Arthur and I would have lasted this long in Thunder Hill if it hadn't been for such civilized people."

"Don't forget Bear James," Alana said, as she clinked her bottle against Olive's. "If you're going to accuse us all of being civilized, then you have to include Bear."

"Yes. Mr. Bear," said Olive, laughing like she'd never heard his name before. "Bear, who believes it's a virtue to have not left the province in his entire life."

"He knows about a lot of things though," Alana said, stretching her rug onto her frame.

Olive said, "From what I can see, all he does is grow pot and make bad wine."

"I thought his last batch of wine was pretty good." I tugged at a strip of red wool with my hook. My design was of a maple tree in fall. At least that was my idea until the thing started to look more like a rooster than a tree, and if that wasn't annoying enough, Olive and Alana decided to list all the things they called "Bearisms."

"Toking while driving," Olive said, counting on her fingers.

"Showing up at mealtimes," Alana offered. She held out her work at arm's length and squinted at what she'd done so far. Her rug was a picture of the Four Reasons Gas n' Stop, but she was having trouble with the gas pumps in front of the store. So far, they looked like penguins. Meanwhile, the second rug Olive had ever hooked was so well done it could easily sell in Damrey's department store there in town. Alana told her that her lilies looked so realistic you could almost pick them off the rug.

Now Olive raised three fingers and said, "Bear tells really bad jokes."

Alana said, "And how about getting chased by the ladies."

"Oh?" Olive's eyes widened. "Bear gets chased?"

"You mean you haven't noticed? Trish, should we tell Olive about our Bear?"

"Huh?" Here I'd been thinking that Bear James really did know a lot about what really matters in life, like friendship and how to live in nature. I mean, the things about Bear that aren't easy to put into words.

"Tell me what?" said Olive.

In a last ditch effort to drop the topic, I said, "Let's just say that Bear doesn't have trouble finding women."

"Oh come on, Trish," said Alana. "Let's just say he has the biggest dick in the county."

While Olive almost choked on her beer, Alana nodding her head knowingly.

"It's not like that's all he has going for him," I said. It bugged me when Alana talked about Bear's penis like it's his finest quality. It's like saying Danny chose Alana for her tits. And even though Danny would be the first to agree and Alana would give him a swat for it, we'd all know it was a joke. "Anyway, I don't think it's fair to discuss Bear's penis behind his back."

"Uh, Trish," said Alana. "News for you. It ain't behind his back."

Olive snorted and said, "I can't stand it any longer. How big are we talking?"

"I don't know, maybe like this?" Alana said, biting on her hook so she could hold her hands apart about a foot. "Trish, remember when we went around naked back in the farm days?"

Of all the things that went on at the farm, the one day when we decided to go around nude is what Alana remembers most fondly. I said, "I think you're exaggerating."

Alana shook her head. "Bear is built like a horse. Everybody used to ask him how 'big guy' was making out. It made him all self-conscious so he tried to cover it up in a towel that looked more like a droopy diaper."

I frowned, remembering. "I thought it must have hurt, the way it flopped around."

"But more importantly girls, did either of you get to try out 'big guy' for yourselves?" Olive asked, her eyes growing wide.

"Good God, no," said Alana, waving her hand like it was the last thing to ever cross her mind, even though I know better. "Bear is more like a brother to Trish and me than anything. And he practically delivered Gayl, didn't he Trish?"

"Hardly. He drove me into town that night, that's all."

"And stayed with you at the hospital until Ray got there, don't forget."

"Oh really? Where was Ray?" Olive said.

And at this, I yawned, and said I had to get on home. It bothered me to know that Alana was itching to tell Olive the whole story about Ray in town drinking the night his baby was born, and how I had signalled to Bear that I needed help by flicking the porch light off and on, off and on. The contractions were coming about ten minutes apart when Bear slid down the path from his place up on Thunder Hill to ours.

"Yes, that was quite the night when little Gayl was born," Bear says with that sad voice he gets whenever anyone brings up the past. "I thought Ray would never get there, eh Trish?"

I nod and look out the window.

"And did he?" Olive asks.

"Oh yeah, we tracked him down at the Roll-a-Way Tavern. You never saw a drunk move anywhere so fast. I had to give him credit," Bear says, looking at me. "Somebody had to, remember Trish?"

"Not really," I lie. "I was too busy worrying about having a baby to bother with Ray."

Actually, I remember quite clearly, because I'd begged Bear to stay in the delivery room instead of Ray, that drunken father of my child.

Bear had stroked my forehead and said, "Ray's the daddy. He's the one who belongs with you. But I'll be waiting right outside that door when that baby comes."

I stare back at Bear, wondering if he remembers that. The expression on his face doesn't reveal a thing so I say, "What I remember most is that big rip in your pants from you sliding down the path to my rescue." I nod towards the window, and the path beyond.

"Look at it out there," Bear says, reaching over to tap his finger against the windowpane. "You can't even make out the stairway to heaven."

That's what Bear and Ray called the path leading up to Bear's cabin halfway up on Thunder Hill. They'd gotten a big kick out of building a door's frame right where the path starts. They even put in a screen door. In summer, the path is filled with raspberry bushes and Queen Anne's lace, but today it's choked with snow. The snow whips around the barn like angry bees and we can make out a drift halfway up the door. I'm starting to have my doubts about Ray making it home at all today.

My father was known for changing his mind according to his moods, so I still don't know if he decided to give Kyle House to Olive when I turned it down all those years ago, or if he'd had a change of heart near his death. When the lawyer read the will, everybody, including my mother, was surprised he'd left Kyle House to the daughter he refused to believe was his. Everything else went to my mother, and everything else was nothing to sneeze at, since my father had worked well over a million dollars out of blueberries. But still, the fact that he'd given his beloved house to Olive made for great gossip. Everyone knew his first marriage ended because Olive's mother had spent a week at some riding camp where there was a red-headed veterinarian and someone told my father there'd been talk of an affair. When my father confronted her, she admitted to it. And when she announced she was pregnant a month later, well, that was that, in my father's mind. Everyone in the county, except for the judge, agreed that the kid was likely the vet's. But the judge ruled in Olive's mother's favour, and Bernie ended up paying support for a red-headed kid he refused to accept as his own.

No wonder everyone was surprised that he left the house to Olive. I figured she'd sell the property right off and that the house would come down. That suited me fine, because by the time my father's will was read three years ago, the kitchen roof at Kyle House had caved in and the windows were rotting in their sills. In fact, I expected to hear any day that the house had gone up in flames. The local kids called it "the haunted house." I didn't blame them. Back when I spent my summers there, I thought it might be haunted too, the way the wind swept over the bluff and whistled through all those multi-paned windows causing paintings to fall from the walls and lamp chains to clink against their bases. I dealt with it by imagining that the ghost felt sorry for me stuck out there on the edge of a cliff with no one except my parents for company.

My mother didn't seem to mind that Olive got the house either. She was haunted by a different kind of ghost, in the form of Olive's mother. Phyllis had furnished the parlour with delicate furniture imported all the way from France and even had a bidet installed in the upstairs bathroom. When my mother moved in she had filled it with earth and turned it into a planter.

What haunted me in recent years was the thought of the local kids who liked to hang out in and around the house falling through a floor and suing our family. This so-called half sister could have Kyle House, along with all of its problems.

Olive didn't sell the house. Later, she told me that it was the vision of a Monet-inspired garden of perennials tumbling all the way down to Thunder Hill Road that moved her to keep the house. Then there was the path she tripped along through aspens and wild rose bushes to the edge of Kyle Point, whereupon she discovered that she was in possession of her very own ocean. That day she had an epiphany, a sea change she said, in the most literal sense. She was ready to leave the city to lead a cleaner, saner life where the children would thrive and Arthur could surely secure a position in the small but prestigious university, less than an hour's drive away.

I guess Arthur had put up quite a fight. Olive said she understood his reluctance as he had just received tenure at York University in Toronto and had no intention of giving that up to become a country bumpkin. But Olive persevered, because ultimately, she knew what was best for her family. She would take up painting, and writing, and best of all she would get to know her half sister, Patricia.

Lucky, lucky me, I remember thinking.

Now I watch Olive search through her pockets for her keys. A gust of wind snatches the hood of her cape clear away from her head and loose strands of hair whip at her face. She tries to rein in her cape from the wind tearing it off her body. Who but Olive would wear such a thing in a storm? I look around to see if she might have left her keys on the table. Upstairs, I can hear Gayl thumping around in her bedroom. Outside, I see that Olive has finally found her keys and is climbing into Billy. She waves to me and I wave back. As she drives up the lane I notice a corner of her cape sticking out of the door and it is almost white with snow. This snow is not about to let up. I wonder again if it's a good idea to let Gayl drive into town today.

As soon as I hear the toot of Billy's horn telling me that Olive has reached the highway, I start thinking it might be nice to go back to bed and wait for Ray there. That would be juicy, him finding me in bed. I could be all naked and ready for him to slide in between the sheets. But first I'd better go out there to the barn and secure that swinging door. I wouldn't want Ray to mistake sexiness for laziness. I start looking around the porch for my rubber boots, which I'd worn only yesterday. So where the hell could they have gone?

3. Instant Sister

THE DAY I'D BEEN dreading finally arrived. Six months after my father's will was read, Olive moved to Thunder Hill. My mother told me that inviting them over to supper was the right thing to do. That at least she could say we'd been hospitable.

On the very same day Alana called me to say that she'd spotted the moving truck pull up to Kyle House, I phoned over there to invite them for supper. "Fish chowder," I said. "Nothing special, but I don't imagine your kitchen's very set up over there."

"That is so kind of you," the voice on the phone practically screeched. "I can't wait to get to know my sister!"

They would come at six.

Suddenly, I had relatives where before there were none. Gayl was curious about having three new cousins, even if they weren't really related. While I chopped celery and onions into my red enamel pot for my famous fish chowder, Gayl made Rice Krispies squares for dessert. Ray had gone to town to pick up beer and fresh rolls at the bakery.

"Why are you so nervous?" Gayl said, after I'd asked her about fifteen times to wipe the crumbs off the table. "It's normal to have crumbs on the table."

I stuffed the dishrag in her hand. "It's not normal and I'm not nervous!"

"Well, they're not even our real relatives, since everybody knows Olive is a bastard."

"Wipe that word right out of your brain," I said. "And get out of your pajamas. It's time for supper already!"

Gayl said, "Well, isn't that the truth? I mean, does she even look like Grandpa? Or you?"

"We'll see soon enough," I said. "The point is to welcome Olive and her family to Thunder Hill, got that?"

"I still don't know why it's such a big deal," Gayl said, as she wiped the crumbs off the table onto the floor. "They might as well see what we're really like, right from the start."

"There's such a thing as being hospitable," I said, sounding exactly like my mother.

"You should shave your legs," Gayl said, "and paint your toenails red."

"Maybe you're right about the legs, but I wouldn't be caught dead in red toenails."

"Exactly," Gayl said. "So don't expect me to change out of my pajamas."

I sighed. Did anyone ever win with a fifteen-year-old?

The green Volvo soon pulled up to the side of the house. I expected us to be a little shy with each other, seeing as we'd never met, but this red-haired freckled woman who was supposed to be my half sister came marching right up to me, her long arms spread wide, screeching, "Patricia! Finally!"

"It's Trish," I said, as she pretty near knocked the breath right out of me with a hug. Later, Gayl told me that I'd looked like I wanted to dive for cover. But I stood there bravely and took the hug. Looking over her shoulder, I could see that when Gayl had mowed the lawn she'd left tufts of grass looking like a messy haircut, but still, the light of the late afternoon sun made our yard look golden and green. I stood there wondering when this hug would end and if Olive was getting some sort of sisterly sensation out of it. I sure wasn't.

When Olive finally loosened her grip, she went about introducing us to her husband Arthur and to their ten-year old twins, Kyla and Kira. Arthur looked like he'd rather be somewhere else. The twins had freckles too and when Olive nodded in my direction they both curtseyed and said in the same voice, "We're so happy to finally meet you!"

"They've been practicing their curtseys all day," said Olive, placing her hands on each girl's head.

Then we stood saying nothing until Gayl pointed to the back seat of the car and said, "Who's that?"

In all the excitement we, my family at least, hadn't noticed that someone was still sitting in the car.

Arthur said, "The boy who refuses to leave the car is our son, Byron, or Biz as he likes to be called. Biz is a bit of a loner I'm afraid."

"What Byron is, is rude," said Olive. "But we won't pay him any mind."

For someone who didn't want to pay her son any mind, she wouldn't let up about him. Even after we got ourselves settled in the kitchen and Gayl had taken the twins upstairs to show them her room, Olive kept looking out the porch window. "He is still so angry with us about leaving the city. Normally, he's so friendly."

"Maybe he's just shy," I offered.

"Who? Byron?" Olive laughed then, a cross between a shriek and a snort. "He's not shy at all, is he Arthur? *Arthur?*"

"Sorry, sorry... What was that?"

All this time, Arthur had been talking to Ray, who was loading beer into the bottom of the fridge. "Ray has just been telling me all about dog breeding. A most fascinating subject, I must say."

Olive said, "Oh yes, the real estate agent told us that you and Ray used to breed collies. I suppose that's country life for you; everybody knows everybody's business. We'd better get used to it, Arthur. We were thinking we'd like to get involved in some sort of small business venture, like truck farming, or ostrich ranching, isn't that right, Arthur?" Olive said. "Something for Arthur to do besides teach at the university. Something to help him integrate into country life."

I looked at Ray, but there was no way in hell he was about to meet my eyes. How many people move from the city to the country in search of a peaceful, and saner life? They learn pretty fast that country living is not necessarily peaceful or sane. With only a hint of a smile, he said, "There's always pigs."

"Pigs," Olive repeated. "But don't they smell?"

Ray raised his eyebrows and said with a perfectly straight face, "Pigs are known for being very clean animals."

"You know, I've heard that."

I kicked him then, a little sideways poke in the calf. Where was he going with this? Ray is not usually one to bullshit someone but here he was stringing these people along.

"The beauty of pigs," he continued. "is that you don't need a lot of land since they're not grazers. All you need is a barn."

"We have a barn!" Olive said.

"Don't listen to him," I finally said. "You wouldn't want pigs. There's no money in them nowadays and don't believe for a second that they don't smell."

"Oh," Olive chuckled, thrusting a finger at Ray's shoulder. "You were teasing us."

I frowned at Ray, who was still grinning like he'd just won something big at the annual Blueberry Fest carnival. I turned back to my chowder.

"Anybody want another beer?" he said.

While everyone squeezed around the dining room table, I stood in front of the stove ladling out the fish chowder, then handing the bowls to Ray. Gayl pulled the rolls out of the oven and we all sat down to eat.

"This is delicious, Patricia," said Olive.

"You can call me Trish. Everybody else does."

"Oh, but Patricia is such a beautiful name," Olive said, her eyebrows rising. "Now what kind of fish is this in the chowder?"

"Flounder."

"Mmm, I love fresh fish."

"Fresh out of the freezer," Ray said, as if he was proud of the fact. I narrowed my eyes at him.

"It's superb in any case," said Arthur.

"So, tell me, Raymond, why didn't you stay in the dog breeding business?" Olive said. "You don't mind me calling you Raymond, do you?"

"If you don't mind me calling you Ollie," Ray said, giving her a playful push on the shoulder when she actually gasped.

"Touché, Ray." Olive said, and turned to me. "Now tell me, Patricia, what happened with the dogs?"

"It got to be too much," I said. "With both of us working, I couldn't keep up."

Ray said, "You didn't want to keep up."

I said, "Excuse me, I forgot the napkins."

Olive said, "I'd like to have Weimaraners. They are the most beautiful dogs with their blue-grey coats."

"Can I get you more chowder, Arthur?" I said, carrying the pot in from the kitchen.

"Oh, no thank you. It's delicious, but I'd better save some room for the next course."

I stopped right in the middle of my step. "The chowder is the *only* course."

Everyone stopped eating, some in mid-slurp.

"Oh dear, I am so sorry!" Olive exclaimed. "This is my fault entirely. I told Arthur that we were coming for supper."

"This is what Trish calls 'supper' around here," Ray said.

"I thought it was what we *all* called 'supper' around here," I said, glaring at Ray who continued to attack his chowder like it might be his last meal on earth. "Please forgive me," said Arthur, whose face was about as red as the chowder pot. "For being ... so presumptuous."

Everyone got quiet after that and the only sound was the clinking of spoons against bowls. The twins kept looking at me and then at each other. Finally, I couldn't stand it any longer so I told Gayl to go show the twins the new kittens out in the barn.

"Remember not to touch them, Kyla," Olive said, and turned

to me. "By the way, Patricia, does Gayl have any allergies? I wondered if they might be hereditary. I have so many questions to ask you about our father, I don't even know where to begin!"

"The one about the allergies is simple enough," I said. "My father had none, Gayl has none, and neither do I, so that answers that."

"Oh," she said, suddenly looking down at her hands. There was that silence again. And Ray shot me his look that always makes me feel small. Later, he would ask me why I hadn't come right out and said Olive should ask the veterinarian, her real father, if he'd had any allergies. He also said straight out that I have a mean streak in me. I told him he was every bit as mean, the way he'd strung Olive along about the pigs.

Meanwhile, I couldn't sit a second longer so I went to put the kettle on and tried to calm myself down the way I always do, which is by looking out my kitchen window at what I figure counts as the real world, and not the one churning within my own walls. Did Olive really think she could move into Kyle House and claim my father as her own? Was she actually going to pretend that she was my blood sister?

The sky was growing dark over Thunder Hill. Sure enough, I heard a low rumble even though it was still sunny in my yard. I looked out the porch window and wondered out loud, "Now, what the hell is she doing?" There was my daughter, out there in the yard, running around Olive and Arthur's car. The boy inside was still trying to stare straight ahead, but that was obviously getting harder and harder to do as his eyes were clearly on Gayl. She ran around that car about eight times before he showed the first movement since they'd all arrived by giving her the finger. I could see the glee in Gayl's face as she shot her finger right back at him. Then, she grabbed each twin by the hand and pulled them to the barn.

4. Boiled Icing

"**D**ON'T YOU THINK IT'S time you outgrew that habit, Ma?"

I look up at my daughter who is leaning against the porch door, strands of hair tumbling down from where it is scrunched up in a loose bun.

"What habit would that be?"

"Sucking your thumb?"

"Don't be silly," I say, wiping my thumb on my jeans. It was sore from where I'd chewed off my thumbnail after Olive left my yard.

Still searching for my boots, I kick aside a bag filled with wool mitts and scarves and hats, that gets them spilling over the braided rug. So much for trying to be organized enough to put away winter gear. I might as well leave all the mitts and scarves and hats lying here since winter has decided to return to today. Whoever said that spring begins in April?

I find my rubber boots stuck halfway under the freezer.

"You're gonna tear your boots, pullin' at 'em so hard," Gayl says.

I blow a strand of hair out of my eyes and say, "It's 'going to' and it's 'pulling' and it's 'them.'"

"Huh?"

"Your words. You sound like a hick."

"So what? That's what I am," says Gayl, now in a thick hick accent.

"You are not! Your father and I aren't hicks, so you aren't one either."

"Sure you are. Isn't that why you moved out here in the first place? To learn how to be hicks?"

"No. That wasn't why at all."

"Oh right. Excuse me, not hicks, *hippies*. But I bet when you were running around naked in your little commune, you never dreamed you'd turn into hicks."

I suddenly feel tired. I rest my forehead on my arm against the doorframe and say more to myself than to Gayl, "We weren't hippies…"

We wanted to run a farm as a co-operative, and we did, for a good two years. A pretty successful run it was too, in spite of how it ended. Ray and I had Gayl during this time, while Danny and Alana were the parents of two little kids. There was this American couple, Sly and Sheena, who'd met up with Ray that year I stayed in Toronto and they were the ones who'd gotten him so inspired about co-op living and farming. They introduced him to organic gardening and yoga and the whole idea of a counterculture. When I returned from Toronto, Bear moved in with us too, and before long there were seven of us pooling our resources. Our door was open to every freak who needed a place to crash. Some stayed for days, others for months. They all left something behind. We got a goat named Gert that someone had brought all the way from BC in a school bus. They were headed for the States next and didn't want the extra hassle of bringing a goat across the border. So we had fresh goat's milk for the kids. Someone else stole into the electric company's yard and brought us back a wooden wire spool, so we had a coffee table. Somebody also left some of us the clap, which had some others, like Alana, really pissed off, and then there was the guy who pretended to be cool but ripped us off of some of our pot plants one night. We never saw him again. But that was cool too, we decided, all a part of karma. As long as we practiced good karma, nothing worse than that could ever happen to us.

We may have thought of ourselves as seventies freaks, but never hippies and certainly never hicks.

"I like being a hick," Gayl is saying, bringing me back to the present. "Nobody expects much out of you, so if and when you do something halfway decent, everybody thinks you're a genius."

I sigh into my sleeve. "I can't tell you how encouraging that sounds."

"How come you're so tired today?"

"I don't know," I say, my head feeling too heavy to lift. "I'm sure it has nothing to do with Olive coming by this morning and the table being a disgusting mess."

"I'm sure it doesn't either," Gayl answers cheerfully and turns back into the kitchen, "because that would be a stupid reason to be tired."

I watch my daughter slap some of Olive's homemade pear compote onto toast. Olive is forever charging over with her latest home-made stuff. Last fall it was the compote. Before that she had filled up some thin bottles with oil and herbs and garlic. The garlic floating around in the bottles reminded me of the floating pig fetuses in Gayl's biology classroom. But I told Olive how pretty they were and that I'd keep them on my pantry sideboard, which I did. They sit there still, coated with a layer of dust. Not only that, but the last time Gayl made muffins and used the mixer, bits of yellow batter had splattered onto the bottles. The splatters are still there, only now they're not quite so bright. Given time, dust dulls just about everything.

In three weeks it'll be Gayl's seventeenth birthday, which will make it a year since Ray first left. Last year, her sixteenth birthday had started out like all of her birthdays, with me in the kitchen wrestling with my mother's recipe for boiled icing. Tricky, boiled icing was. Especially when your mother's recipe does not even call for a double boiler. Everything had to be perfect: the purity of the egg whites, the exact consistency and measurement of brown sugar and water, and my mother says, the barometric pressure.

Even one's mood has much to do with the icing's success rate. I rarely get it right on the first try.

The only difference between the start of Gayl's birthday last year and her other birthdays was that ever since I'd gotten out of bed, I'd been crying. Not a solid cry with a damned good reason attached to it, but one of those cries that well up in the eyes without warning. "This is just silly," I said out loud. I tried to shake it off since I knew my period was at least two weeks away, but the tears kept coming and later Alana said I should have taken this as an omen about Ray leaving me that exact same day. Especially the part when some of my tears fell onto the stove and sizzled next to the pot of boiling brown sugar.

I ignored the tears as I beat the egg whites, checking that the hot syrup was stringy before pouring it into frothy peaks. Even still, before I'd poured half of the syrup into the egg whites, I knew the icing wouldn't work.

I wiped my eyes with my sleeve when I heard Gayl bounce down the stairs. There stood my daughter, hair wet from her shower, breasts popping out of her tube top.

I stared.

"Wha-at?" she said, her hands spread wide.

"A tube top?"

"What's wrong with a tube top?"

"It's only April?"

"April 29, which is almost May, you know."

"You know what I mean."

Perhaps my voice caught ever so slightly here, because Gayl said, "What's wrong?"

"Nothing. The onions, I guess."

She leaned around to look at my face. "No way is that onions."

"Yes way. I just chopped some for the hamburger."

"Those aren't onion tears."

"Okay, then, hemorrhoid tears. How's that?"

"Ugh," Gayl said. "Are those things hereditary?"

"I'm not sure," I said. "I didn't get them until after I got pregnant with you."

"Well, sorry for being born."

My daughter's face hadn't quite matched her tone, so I'd handed her one of the gooey beaters to lick.

"But I loved you so much I would have happily suffered a thousand hemorrhoids."

"Oh yeah, good try," Gayl huffed. Then she softened. "Do they hurt so bad they make you cry?"

"What, having children? You better believe it."

She laughed then and tossed the beater into the sink. Then she bounced back up the stairs and began to sing, "*It's my party and I'll cry if I want to, cry if I want to...* Oh, sorry Ma, that just popped out."

Out of the mouths of babes, I thought, as I called up after her, "If you really care about me you'll change into something else before everybody gets here. And wake your father up, will you?"

Later, when my mother's housekeeper, Karen's car pulled into the yard, I realized I should have warned her to hide my mother's rum. As soon as Karen opened the passenger door for my mother I could tell it was too late. My mother was wearing heels and one of the big hats my father used to wear in the blueberry fields. The only way she could see out from under it was to tilt her face upwards and that didn't help her balance on the gravel.

Olive and Arthur had already arrived, so they got to watch my mother make a total fool of herself, out there in the yard.

"What gorgeous shoes, Bette," Olive shrieked, reaching out to take my mother's arm as she came through the door.

Things went downhill after that. I got busy frying up the hamburgers and onions while Ray was supposed to keep all the guests happy in the living room. All the guests included Gayl's two best friends from town, her oldest friend from out here in Thunder Hill, Olive's family and Bear James of course. Alana and Danny hadn't yet arrived and I was just thinking I should call them to see where the hell they were because everybody was getting hungry. After I made myself a rum and coke, I went into the living room to look for the phone and just in time saw my mother reach behind the curtain for a glass.

As soon as she saw me, she tried to put the glass back on the windowsill, only it hit the edge of the sill and broke, so now I had sticky rum and coke all over my curtains and broken glass scattered all the way from the window to the middle of the living room, and of course Gayl and her friends were in stocking feet so I yelled, "Don't anybody move!" Then I shouted at Ray to get the vacuum cleaner and the broom and a cloth to clean up my mother's mess, but really what I meant was Ray's mess, because obviously he'd given her the drink. When he *knew, knew, knew* how I felt about my mother being drunk, especially in public, especially on our daughter's birthday. But that was Ray for you, everybody's friend, especially when he's been drinking himself. Meanwhile, Bear had run upstairs to get the vacuum cleaner and Olive fetched the broom and there she was cleaning off the windowsill, which she could likely tell hadn't been wiped in probably a year. And then there was Ray, helping my mother up from the chair and moving her over to the couch next to Gayl, who wore a look of pure disgust, and who could blame her since her friends and cousins had to witness all of this, but why she kept looking at me like it was all my fault was beyond me. To top it all off, there was my mother crying, and Gayl hushing her, telling her not to worry, that it was just a little accident and not worth getting all worked up about. And what was I doing in all this? Marching to the kitchen to mix myself another rum and coke thinking my own bloody family drives me to drink.

I cornered Ray in the pantry where he was way ahead of me by happily mixing up more drinks. "How could you give my mother a drink when you saw the kind of shape she was in?" I asked, arms folded, foot tapping.

"I didn't think she was all that bad," Ray said.

"How would you know?," I said. "You're already drunk!"

"So? So are you."

"Bullshit. I've only had one."

"Two. I saw you drinking two."

"One. You've had at least three."

"Oh, but who's counting?"

I wheeled around to see Olive standing in the pantry doorway. "Patricia, I have to apologize. I made Bette's drink."

I looked at her and I looked at Ray, who hadn't even bothered to deny his part in this. "You watched Olive get my mother a drink? When you knew I'd have to scrape her off the floor later?"

"Trish," Ray said, in that way he has of making me feel like I'm ten years old, "you're making too big a deal out of this."

"I swore Ray to secrecy," said Olive, as if that would change everything.

"Oh you did, did you?" I glared at Ray, who sighed loudly. I grabbed the kettle off the stove and filled it under the faucet. "Amazing. Even though he knows what one too many drinks can do to my mother, he can be sworn to secrecy." I wheeled around to drive this point home, just in time to catch Ray actually wink at Olive. I probably started foaming at the mouth right about then.

"What?" said Ray, hands outstretched, a guilty grin on his face.

Olive cleared her throat. "I think it's time for me to go and join the party."

Ray cleared his throat. "Me too."

Fat chance of that, I thought as I grabbed his arm and hissed, "Thanks a lot."

He pulled his arm away, and the change in his face was sudden and dangerous. "Lighten up Trish, I was just joking around. And can you try to remember it's our daughter's birthday?"

"Oh. I don't see how I could forget that seeing as how I'm the one who spent the morning vacuuming and putting away a week's worth of laundry. Plus making the cake for *our* daughter's birthday."

"It was a cake mix," he said with what looked a lot like a smirk.

"So what? I'm the one who made it."

"And I'm the one trying to keep things cheerful around here, which is pretty hard the way you're acting."

"That's fine," I said, tossing a tea towel. "But it seems to me that when you lost the school bus job, heaven help anyone who went around acting too cheerful then, right?"

"It's hardly the same thing."

"You're right mister, because when you're freaked out about something, I don't turn into your fucking enemy! No, when Ray's fucked up, everybody better be careful or he'll run off to town and get so stupid drunk he ends up in jail, or somehow finds his cock in Rena Dickson's mouth."

I knew I'd just trodden into dangerous territory by digging up something that happened almost two decades ago, but the picture I have in my brain of walking into a bathroom one night at a party and seeing Rena Dickson on her knees in front of my boyfriend has never quite left me.

Maybe it's not fair of me to dredge up something he claims he's been paying for our whole lives together, but still I wasn't prepared for him to grab me hard by the shoulders now and spin me around to face the mirror. "You know who your real enemy is? Look! You see how bitter she is?"

There was a freshly opened can of tomato juice on the table. That can was in my hands for only a second before it flew through the air and hit him squarely in the chest. The juice splashed upwards to his face before the can clattered to the floor, sending rivers of thick tomato pulp across the linoleum.

Isn't it amazing how life can change in an instant? Looking back, I could have apologized right there on the spot. For a second neither of us spoke, but, as I stooped to pick up the can from the floor, he threw up his hands and said, "That's it, I'm done."

I stood there with the can in my hand while he walked right out the porch door.

I could tell from the sudden silence in the living room that everyone had heard. I knew they'd be drifting in at any moment. I looked down at the pool of red liquid, which had already started to seep under the wainscoting. I pulled on my rubber boots and ran after him.

"Hey!" I shouted as I struggled up the lane through the mud. It felt like running in a dream when you use all this energy but don't get anywhere. "I'm sorry, okay?"

Ray wheeled around and held his hand straight in front of him. "You stay back, Trish! Just keep away from me."

I did what he said, halting right in my boot tracks. I called out, surprised at the plea in my own voice. "Don't do this today, okay, Ray? It's Gayl's birthday?"

Ray paused at Gayl's name but then kept walking. I shouted, "This is just stupid!" I watched him, hoping he'd turn around. When he disappeared behind the spruces at the top of the lane, I started back to the house and must have been in such a stunned state I didn't hear Alana's car until it was right behind me.

"Hey, we just saw Ray hitchhiking," Alana said, rolling down the window. "He was getting into Whitey Forbes' truck. Is everything okay?"

"Why, sure," I said. "Everything's a birthday party, right?"

Danny leaned towards me from the passenger side. "Hey, is that blood?"

I looked down at the tomato juice all over my shirt and it could have been blood the way I stared at it.

"Oo-kay," Alana said, raising her eyebrows at me. She put the car in park and opened the door. Without a word, Danny slid over to the driver's seat.

"Oh God," I said, when Alana and I were alone there in the lane. "I don't think I can go back in there right now."

"Tell me what happened."

I let her take my arm because my knees felt too weak to stand. I may not be psychic like Alana, but I knew a real bad thing had just happened to Ray and me.

5. Alana Who Knows Everything

ALANA HAS ALWAYS BEEN one step ahead of me. When I first met Ray she was already pregnant with Kim. By the time I got pregnant with Gayl, she was the mother of a four and five year old. She knew everything about babies and I knew nothing. So when Gayl had a high fever and then a convulsion, Alana happened to phone right then and she talked me through it. "She'll be okay," she said calmly. "Lay her down and rub her arms. Say soft things to her. Do it now, while we're on the phone." I did what she said, and Gayl came out of the convulsion looking rested and none the worse for wear. Alana's Kevin had had one when he was two so she knew exactly what I was going through.

"Maybe this explains why you were crying over your icing," she'd said there on the lane, after I told her about my fight with Ray. "Your own psyche knew something bad was going to happen."

When she called earlier to see if there was something she should bring to the party I'd told her about the silly tears over the boiled icing. Adolescence was also her specialty, so she had a theory about that. "Of course you were crying. You probably don't remember the hell I went through back when Kim turned nineteen."

Alana was wrong. How could I forget the day a few years ago that marked the end of what Alana still calls her "prime time?" And when hers ended, so did all of ours. We were driving along

Thunder Hill road towards town in the back of Bear's Rover one day in early September and I was noticing how everything we passed seemed to sparkle and not just the water out in the strait. I mean everything, like the leaves on the quaking aspens, the cornstalks or oats in the fields, even the spruces high up on Thunder Hill shone bright in the late afternoon sun. Up front in the Rover, the boys were yakking about music or boats, and suddenly I noticed that beside me, Alana was crying. I don't mean she was bawling her eyes out, but her eyes were glassy with tears and she was sniffling. When I pressed her about it she blurted out, "You know, it's not like I'm jealous because I've got this beautiful daughter whose function it is to replace me as a baby maker. Hell, I went through all that when she turned fifteen and men were staring at her and not at me." She'd paused here and shuddered. "No, I think what's getting to me is that as of today she's old enough to get into bars."

"That's why you're crying?"

"I don't know. Maybe it's just a premonition, but I just have this feeling that nothing is ever going to be the same after today."

Alana was right. I can even pinpoint the exact moment our lives changed because when it happened later at the Roll-a-Way Tavern, I was dancing with Danger Dave, who everyone knows is anything but, and we were goofing around to the music, slipping into old dance steps like the "Funky Chicken" and the "Frug."

The dance floor of the Roll-a-Way Tavern was bouncing so hard you could see it move. The Roll-a-Way used to be a bowling alley. The dance floor was laid right over the lanes, which made our footsteps all that much louder and springier too. Danger Dave and I were laughing and I suppose my eyes were closed, my elbows and knees flapping to the music. I was working up a buzz from the rum, as well as the vibrating floor, when I suddenly realized the floor had stopped moving under my feet. I opened my eyes and talk about embarrassed. I was the only one still dancing. Danger Dave was shouting in my ear. "Isn't that Alana and Danny's daughter?"

There stood Kim in the doorway, her black hair shimmering around a turquoise dress. I watched Alana rush to her daughter and link arms with her. She steered Kim to the bar to buy her first legal beer. When Kim touched the bottle to her lips, this big cheer came from the crowd and everyone toasted her on her birthday. Then things turned quite comical, when, instead of Danny dancing with the prettiest girls in the place, as he usually did, he spent the whole time with his arm fixed around his daughter's shoulders. We even spotted him trying to cover her up with his jacket.

But the real clincher came when it was time to slip outside for a toke with the gang. I gave Alana the signal to follow us, and she nodded. But after waiting and shivering in the alders surrounding Emily's Pond, Danger Dave went ahead and lit the joint without Alana. I kept an eye on the Roll-a-Way entrance but Alana never came. Maybe this was what Alana had meant about nothing ever being the same again. But when we went back in, there was Alana wheeling about the dance floor with her head tossed back and her arms out to her sides like always. I joined her up there on the dance floor and everything seemed normal enough until I noticed Kim and her friends smiling at us like we were the cutest little kids. I knew right then our days at the Roll-a-Way were coming to an end. We kids were being replaced by our kids.

Now, for the third time today, I'm watching someone drive up my lane and out of my sight. My own almost grown-up kid. Gayl has had her license for almost a year but I have never let her drive in real weather.

I watch the Toyota bounce up the lane. Gayl reaches her arm out the window to snap the ice off the windshield wipers. That snow has now turned to freezing rain. Earlier, I'd told her it was too messy for her to drive, but she'd held her ground and said,

"You've driven in way worse weather than this."

"But I've had almost twenty-five years of experience driving in this kind of weather," I said, knowing full well I was about to lose this one.

"And how am I supposed to get *my* experience? You want to tell me that?"

"Just be careful. Gayl, I mean it," I said finally. "And call me when you get to Gran's."

"Okay, Ma. I got it," she said, slamming the door on her way out.

Now that the fog has moved in, I can barely see the Toyota's taillights. I listen for the horn to toot before she turns onto Thunder Hill Road. It was Alana who started doing this tooting of the horn business but it has since become a custom and now just about everyone toots their horn as they leave my lane. Maybe everyone has a different reason for doing this but Alana told me it was to let me know that just because I was out of sight, I wasn't out of her mind.

When I finally hear Gayl's beep, I can't help but think she's sounding it more as a good riddance.

6. Flue Fire

THE BATHROOM IS SO cold, steam rises from the tub as I take off my clothes. The sight of me shivering in the mirror behind the door makes me think I'd like to get rid of it. The mirror I mean, not the body. That I still need. But does a barely forty-year-old woman always need to be reminded of how she looks? I pull my shoulders back and when I tilt my pelvis forward like I learned in that aerobics class I started in town last fall, I don't look quite so bad. Alana's right that I've lost lots of weight since Ray first left for Newville. I run my fingers up through my hair, holding it behind my head. I wonder how it might look cut really short. Maybe I'd look like those snooty university types Olive and Arthur have as guests over at Kyle House.

Normally, it is Gayl who stands in front of this mirror looking this way and that. It's my daughter's turn to be young and pretty, I remind myself when I see her posing. Just like it's my turn to be, what? A middle-aged woman? What's so good about that?

Then there's Olive who goes on about a woman's forties being the most productive time of her life. "Time to kick ass," she says.

No wonder Olive says that. The year she turned forty was when she took possession of my father's house and moved her own ass down here.

And I'm here looking at my ass in the mirror and wondering how far it will have dropped by the time I'm fifty. Fifty! Fuck.

I wince when I step into the bath water, water that feels slightly less than boiling. I wait until my feet get used to the temperature before I lower the rest of me into the tub. I'd rather feel like an ice-cube slowly melting than a lobster in a pot.

If it was summer, a bath would be a whole other story. On really hot days I often climb the path behind my house up Thunder Hill through raspberry brambles scratching at my legs and cobwebs draping my arms like silk. By the time I make it to Bear's cabin I've worked up quite a sweat, and then I have to scramble even higher to the enamel tub perched on a rocky ledge.

Bear has figured out a way to divert a spring so that it flows into the tub. As soon as the water fills the tub, he re-diverts the spring and the sun warms it up. Warms it up to just above heart stopping cold, that is. I'm the only person I know who'd work up a sweat just to cool off in that tub when everyone else is making for the beach. But that's because the tub is one of Bear's coolest creations and if I didn't use it he'd neglect it and it might fade into the landscape.

If Bear isn't home, I go straight to where I hang my towel and clothes on a branch and grab the bio-degradable shampoo Bear makes me use. The tub is long enough to float in so I do, staring through the trees to the clouds, feeling like there's nowhere else on earth I'd rather be. The spring water on my skin feels way softer than well water.

Sometimes, if Bear happens to be home, I'll first share a toke with him before confiscating his binoculars. I do this partly because he's a guy but mostly for the view to be had from the tub. Farms and fields stretch toward summer cottages strung along the red shoreline. I can't see my own house from here, but the Four Reasons is in plain sight and sometimes I can tell who has stopped there for gas. Further up the coast, where Thunder Hill Road turns sharply toward town, Kyle House stands nestled under two giant elms. I can practically scope out the county and if I look down to Bear's cabin and he happens to be working on his deck or yard, then I take a peek at him too. No beer belly yet on that boy.

Funny where the mind drifts, I'm thinking, home in my own bathtub, surrounded by the sight of blackened grout and cracked tiles. This bathroom needs fixing, but I've resisted my mother's offer to pay for it. Because then I'd need to get someone in to do the work and she'd start asking questions about why Ray can't do it on one of his weekends home and I don't want her to think he has left me again. And besides the bathroom's not so bad if I keep my eyes closed.

Lately, the idea of a hot bath is the only thing that keeps me going after a day of standing on the cold cement floor of the factory. No matter how many sweaters I wear, the chill stays even after I blast up the heat in the car on the drive home. But once I'm in my bath my mind can drift to the hottest places. For years, the big crush I had on Kelly, my boss, was enough to keep me warm. But then one day Kelly came really close to my ear and asked me to stay after work. I wondered if I'd finally get to act on the fantasies I'd had about him. Like the one where he looks over his glasses and asks me to lock his office door. Without another thought everything on his desk goes flying off, including the picture of his wife, Jilly, and his children, and then we're both crashing and banging away on his desk or else I'm bent over the same desk staring at the picture of Jilly and the children while he's busy filling me up from behind. I've often wondered about women who fuck their bosses. I suppose nothing ever works the same between them after that.

Alana didn't know about my fantasies, but she sure knew about the crush. She thought it was healthy. "Look," she said. "First, you invest enough into it to keep your imagination alive when you're having the same old, same old, with your real man. Second, when your man is being a real asshole, which, face it, they all are, it's nice to know someone's out there who thinks you're pretty cute. Fact is, it's much easier to get out of bed in the morning when there's someone to look forward to seeing at work."

So imagine where my head was at that day after work and I stepped into his office. I sat across from his desk, flipped back my hair, which was longer then, and certainly a lot less grey. Mind you I was fatter then too. But in my daydreams, he raves about my roundness.

"Been doing some thinking," he said, looking at me all earnest like. He tapped a pencil on the notepad in front of him. "It's nuts on my part really, that it's taken me this long to realize this. And on your part, well…"

"What?" I licked my lips then, and realized I was starting to shake like I had a fever. "On my part what?"

"Irresponsible. On your part, downright selfish for not coming forward with … your …" The phone rang then. By the way he was talking, I guessed it was Jilly on the phone. When I got up to leave, he raised a finger to keep me there. I could feel my heart race.

What was it Alana had said about actually seeing a fantasy through? Something about it usually not living up to the billing. I thought at the time to ask her how she had come to know this, but the subject had somehow changed before I'd had the chance.

"Earth to Trish, earth to Trish." Kelly was smiling and snapping his fingers at me. The phone was back on the cradle.

"I'm sorry," I said. "Did you say something?"

"I was saying that Jill sold a crib for a hundred dollars at the school bazaar."

"A hundred dollars is great."

He leaned back in his chair and put his hands behind his head. "Wherever you were a minute ago looked a lot more interesting."

I cleared my throat. "So Jilly's at the big bazaar right now?"

He nodded and stared straight into my eyes. "Uh huh."

So this was why he chose this day to invite me into his office. The question was, would I risk my marriage to make love to this sexy, but more than that, one of the most decent and fair men I have ever known? It crossed my mind that if he were to actually make a move, I might be forced to change my opinion of him. Meanwhile I couldn't help but think ahead to going home right after doing the desk thing with Kelly, and how I'd need a shower because Ray is sensitive to smell and he can always tell when I've snuck a cigarette or even eaten a piece of licorice.

"I want to ask you something," Kelly was saying. "And I don't want you to answer right away, okay?"

"Okay." I whispered.

He took his glasses off. "You know how we've been having problems with defects lately, especially with key-rings?"

He must have thought my silence meant I was interested instead of feeling confused because he went on about the time I discovered the tiny but sharp filament jutting out from the side of the mold. When the entire quality control team hadn't been able to figure out why there were so many complaints of pricked fingers! Would I consider becoming his Production Co-coordinator?

"I ... I ... you know, I pricked my finger while I was handling it and that's how I found it."

"Now stop being so damned humble, I've also noticed how much your co-workers like and respect you. How many people can claim that? Take me for example," he joked. "No-one around here has neither respect *nor* admiration for me. So let me tell you, I am always impressed when I discover those qualities in someone else."

"Don't be silly," I said, "Everybody loves you."

"You see? You even know how to butter up the boss!"

I laughed. "This may be true, but what does that have to do with production co-ordination?"

People skills, he told me. It always boiled down to that. Then he went on about getting workers to take pride in their productivity by appealing to their team spirit, their sense of community. I sat there wondering how I could have been so wrong about everything. I used to think I could read men's signals.

He winked. "And if that fails, then you offer them shares in the company. So how about it, Trish?"

"Well, can I think about it?" I said.

"Sure you can. Take all the time you need." He leaned back in his chair again and folded his hands in his lap. "Okay, time's up. Seriously Trish, this would be a great opportunity. So just say yes."

"Yes, okay," I almost looked around to see who could be so rash as to say yes without even talking this over with Ray.

"Great!" said Kelly, standing up to shake my hand. "Let's get you started next week."

I drove the whole way home in a total daze.

As soon as Olive heard about my promotion, she invited us to supper to celebrate. "It's not that big a deal." I told her over the phone.

"It's not every day one lands a big promotion! We'll expect you at seven."

A big promotion. All that it meant, I tried to convince myself in the middle of the night, was that my duties would shift a bit. *A bit?* I'd be responsible for products traveling as far away as California. England, even. And I might even have to go to these places too.

The next day everyone lifted their glasses to toast my success.

"England, you say?" said Arthur, in the British accent he and Olive seemed to acquire whenever they drank.

"How much of a raise will it be, Patricia?" Olive said, looking up from slicing a leg of organically grown lamb.

I stared at the knife. "I don't know, probably not that much. Actually, we didn't talk about that part."

"You mean you didn't discuss a raise?"

"No." I reached for the Swiss chard.

Olive was staring at me in disbelief. "How can he do that? I can't believe the nerve of people who come into depressed areas and take advantage of their workers."

Ray said, "Foghorn Pewter pays decent wages. Eight dollars an hour.

Olive waved the knife in the air. "Perhaps for unskilled labour, but Patricia is no longer unskilled. She has just been promoted to management, which carries far more responsibility than merely working on the line. In fact, the success or failure of the whole operation falls squarely upon her shoulders. Isn't there something like seventy families depending on their jobs? Seriously. And her boss doesn't bother to mention a raise?"

"Workers of the world unite!" Arthur said, standing suddenly, and almost losing his balance in the process. "Olive, I do believe you've found your true calling."

Olive gave Arthur a look that might as well have been a push, the way he fell back into his chair.

She continued, "Well, at least Patricia won't have to actually work with pewter now. I can't get over these companies who expose their workers to health hazards they wouldn't get away with in a more environmentally conscious area."

"What's wrong with pewter?" said Ray.

"Lead!" Olive practically shrieked. "Don't you know how much lead is used in pewter? Look at your wife's hands. Patricia, show Ray how rough your hands are."

I put my hands behind my back. "Ray has seen my hands for almost twenty years, so I don't know why I should have to show them to him now."

I didn't sleep at all that night. The next morning I knocked on Kelly's door and told him I couldn't accept the promotion, that all I needed was a change from pouring molds. Maybe I'd buff for a while, and then move on to picture frames. I hadn't yet poured picture frames.

He held up his hands. "Look, I thought you'd do well at it, but hey, you don't need to explain."

But explaining was all I seemed to do for the next while.

"When do you start the new job, Irish?" said just about everyone.

"I decided not to take it after all. Too much stress for one thing, and not enough pay for another."

Only to Ray did I confess I couldn't handle the responsibility of being in charge. I couldn't take the blame if things went wrong.

"You used to like being in charge." Ray said. "Think of all those times your father offered his accountant to do our income taxes. But you made us sweat over them every fucking year."

"You used to be so pissed off about that."

"But I'm not anymore because it turned out that you were right. That way we knew exactly where we stood. If his accountant had done it, then your father would have known more about us, than us." He reached his arm over in the darkness of the bedroom to stroke my back. "It's your decision not to take the job, but I'm surprised because you're so good at ordering people around."

"Thanks."

"No sweat. That's what I'm here for."

Gayl's reaction stung the most. "Chickened out, eh?" she said, spitting toothpaste into the sink. "Way to go, Ma. Great role model you turned out to be."

"I didn't chicken out," I said, as I smeared night cream over my face. "I just thought it would be too much with all my other responsibilities."

"Like what?"

"Like taking care of this place. And your father. And you."

"Oh yeah, as if you have to take care of me. Or Dad."

"And your Grandmother."

Gayl stopped worrying about a pimple on her nose long enough to look at me in the mirror. "You hardly ever see Gran. I bet Olive sees her more than you do."

"That's going to change. In fact, we'll invite Gran here for the weekend and you can play cribbage with her the whole entire time. What do you think of that?"

"I think you make it sound like some kind of a punishment."

The next day, I went back to work at the buffing bench and felt totally relieved. Who needed work that would follow you home at night? Olive was right. Feeling responsible for seventy families was a lot to handle. I could buff pewter pieces with my eyes closed. And then there was Paula with her funny stories about her idiot husband Larson and her insane mother-in-law.

One thing changed though. I stopped thinking about Kelly as anything other than a boss. And if I happen to take my mother to church and I run into Jilly, I make sure to ask about their kids.

Yep, funny where the mind drifts, I'm thinking, here in my tub. I reach for the hot water tap with my toes and slide my body down until only my knees and chin ruffle the surface. Olive had said she'd stop at Alana's to get gas before heading home. I picture her shaking the snow off her cape just as Alana's pulling on her garage parka to pump Billy full of gas. Inside the store, Olive will move past the canned goods and pickles to where the stove and couch and chairs are at the back of the store. She sits right down in Alana's rocking chair, the one that faces the window and has a long view of the road. It always amazes me how Alana doesn't shout at Olive, "Hey! Outta me chair!" like she does if anybody else takes her seat.

Olive looks around the store like she's sizing it up. She told me that if it were up to her, she'd have a garden center over by the window where the videos are kept. She might keep the sitting area, because of the country store quaintness about it. But she'd get rid of the nubby couch and chipped enamel table where Alana keeps her tea canister and cookie tin. The pinball machine would be out on its ear, replaced with bins of nuts and grains and assorted dried fruits. I told Alana about these plans and she found it funny that Olive wanted to turn her place into one of those fake country stores you see in resort areas.

Wouldn't the rats love all those open bins of nuts, I'm thinking, as my toes once more reach for the hot tap. Olive would be in for a rude awakening.

Only last week I found Alana smearing peanut butter onto a big old rat trap.

"Ugh, I hate these traps almost as much as I hate rats," she said, as she secured the spring. I watched her place the trap on the floor near the wall behind the cash. We both held our breaths as she released her hand because once Danny's finger got broke from a trap and he hasn't set one since.

"It's understandable to hate rats," I said. "But lately I've been wondering why do you think people hate people?"

"Hmm." Alana said. She had picked up a cloth and began wiping the counter but now she stopped wiping long enough to consider my question. I thought she might wonder why I asked but she said, "I think hate happens because of two things. At least that's what I've noticed."

"Who have you ever hated?" I said. "Except for Rena Dickson."

"I don't think I ever hated Rena Dickson."

"You hated her for screwing Danny that time."

"Yeah, well, who didn't she screw back then? Or blow, as you well know. I really never thought that much about Rena, you know, whether I hated her or not." Alana said, as if this might be something worth thinking about now. "Is it Rena you're talking about? I thought you'd gotten over all that long ago."

"Yeah, like you ever forgive a woman for doing your man," I said.

"Yeah, and just think if she'd been a lesbian. Then we'd all be in trouble, and not just the men!"

Before Alana had a chance to run further with this idea, I pressed on. "Now about those two reasons for hating someone."

"First just let me write a note to remind Danny about the rat trap."

Alana disappeared behind the counter to rummage through a shelf and then popped back up. "This is just a theory but I think that when you find yourself hating somebody it's because that person has something you'll never have or never will be."

I waited while she scribbled a note and taped it above the trap.

"Or?"

"Or ... that person reminds you too much of yourself." Alana stared down at the trap like she was daring a rat to appear.

"Well that's stupid. You might as well go around hating yourself."

Alana shrugged. "Sometimes it amounts to the same thing, don't you think? But what do I know?"

"You know everything!"

"Right," Alana said. "And you keep on thinking that, okay dearie? It's music to a psychic's ears."

The subject changed back to the rats. There's no use telling her to get a cat either. A big tabby has been making the rounds in the neighbourhood but every time Alana goes out to pump gas she wears Danny's work boots in case it rubs against her leg. If there's one thing Alana hates worse than rats, it's cats.

Why can't I just enjoy my nice hot bath without thinking bad thoughts? At times I feel like my head is filled with stations of worry, just like those on a radio. Like right now, I've just switched the Four Reasons station to the Gayl station. She should have arrived in town by now. Hadn't I told her to phone as soon as she got in? She'd likely go straight to my mother's and chances are good she'd forget to call. But what if she got hit by one of the salt trucks that bomb down the highways like they own them? Minnie Partridge's car got slammed by one last year when she slowed down to turn into her driveway. She ended up walking away from it, but by all accounts she must have had a guardian angel watching over her that day. Would Gayl be so lucky? She could be in a ditch somewhere with the car looking like an accordion on account of the culvert it hit.

Time to change stations back to the Four Reasons. It's much safer than thinking of Gayl in a ditch.

Where was I? Oh yeah, Olive is there in Alana's chair and Alana will come in from the pumps blowing on her hands.

"I sure don't like the looks of this weather."

Olive will get to the point. "I was just over to see Trish."

"Oh yeah, how's she doing?"

Olive sighs here. "Poor Trish. She's a wreck without Ray."

I picture Alana cocking her head, like she does when she senses trouble.

Olive prattles on, "I worry about her, you know. Let me ask you something, have you noticed how she's letting herself go lately?"

"Like how?"

"She has stopped wearing a bra, when *really* she shouldn't."

"Oh well, I hate bras more than anything," says Alana. "Maybe even more than cats. I whip mine off the second the last customer leaves the store."

"But I don't think she wears one all day either. Even when people like Bear James showed up like he did today."

Hearing Bear's name, Alana will stop to think. "So that's where he went when he left here. Sandra Birdshell called in a big flap because of her window or something."

Olive says, "And sometimes her house is so dirty I don't dare sit down. Today there was a slice of roast beef sitting on the table, with no plate under it, just a piece of meat! And guess what was lying right next to it?"

"Let me guess, a fly-swatter?" Alana says. "She's been known to leave those on the table too."

"Not quite, but close," says Olive. "It was a hair brush! And the hairs in it were touching the meat! I hate to say this about my own half sister, but I can understand why Ray got fed up. You should have seen the dust balls that attacked me from underneath her couch!"

Maybe the bath water is hotter than I realized because suddenly I'm melting out of my tub with all my bones slithering under the bathroom door, out through the kitchen and porch and spilling into the gravel outside my kitchen door. There I go, swallowed up by the red earth around my house. And no one, but no one, will notice me missing until Monday morning when I don't show up for work.

Don't be silly, I tell myself as I waver between waking and dozing. If a person was truly melting she'd slip through the drain to the septic tank and not out the kitchen door at all. I pop out the bath plug with my toes. My ears are still full when the water drains from the tub. It must be picking up speed now because the swishing noise is now a roar, a roar that gets louder until I realize I'm not dozing and that the noise isn't coming from my tub at all. My heart lurches, and I bolt upright for the second time this day. Only now I know exactly where I am because of the sound a flue fire makes when it rages through the center of a house. Scrambling out of the tub I make a rush for the kitchen.

The stovepipe glows red, and the shrieking noise coming from the chimney sends me straight out the front door. Except for the rubber boots and the blanket I grabbed from the couch, I'm totally naked. From the yard, I peer up at the roof. So far there aren't any flames shooting through the chimney. I run back inside to shut the stove drafts. I can see the fire through a hole in the rusted pipe. For six months now, Ray has been after me to replace that pipe.

I phone the Thunder Hill Volunteer Fire Department and speak to Maynard Fleming. He asks me if everyone is out of the house and says to throw a box of salt into the fire and try to relax because there's nothing more I can do. Either the creosote will burn itself off or the flames will escape through the rusted pipe and the house will burn to the ground. Like the Morsey house last year. They've been living in a trailer ever since. Diana Morsey says what she misses most are her photo albums.

I run up the back stairs to where the stovepipe rises through Gayl's bedroom. It's red too. I kick away the pile of clothes lying next to the pipe. And then I tear down the front stairs and out the back door to watch the sparks flying from the chimney.

Snow pellets bite at my cheeks.

"Oh shit. Oh man!" I say to Suzie who has followed me out and is barking at me like it's all my fault. I can't blame her because only a few minutes ago her life was normal.

This isn't my first flue fire and I know they usually burn out on their own. Panic will do me no good. Now where did I last see my photo albums?

Back in the kitchen, I'm staring at the fire in the pipe like it's something in a museum, and then, just like that, it's over. The roaring rumbles and fades. The fire truck should be turning down my lane anytime, now that the danger is over. Of course it'll be all over Thunder Hill before the day is out, especially the part about the deplorable condition of the stovepipe. I sure hope Danny got called out to the salt trucks, and isn't on fire call today. Those firemen might like a cup of tea after they've stomped through the house checking for flames hiding in the walls. I go to fill my kettle before I remember that my stove is totally useless. When I finally find my old electric kettle under the pantry cupboard, I notice how frayed the cord is. When did I become such a fire hazard? I pull the red blanket tighter because I've begun to shake. Look at me. I have no clothes on and the volunteer fire department will be here any minute.

PART II

7. Hog Holler

THE WIND SOUNDS LIKE the hurricane we had about seven years ago. It sounds even louder than it did an hour ago.

Bear and I are at Hog Holler and Perry Card is drinking the last of my rum. Perry says he's drowning his sorrows because now he'll have to cancel his fishing trip tomorrow down at Diligent Brook. And here he'd thought he'd get a jump on the season, before the black flies came. "Who'd'a known the weather could turn around so much in twenty-four hours?"

I don't bother telling him that Alana predicted this storm last night when Gayl and I stepped out of the Four Reasons. There was an orange ring circling the moon. Alana had said that meant trouble.

One of the lamps in Hog Holler is shaped like a pig's head. Its light bulb snout flickers every time the wind gusts around the building. Old stickers of Porky and Petunia Pig cling to the beer fridge door. Porky gives a bouquet of flowers to Petunia who bats her eyes.

Almost everything in Hog Holler goes along with the pig theme. There's a calendar of pig pin-ups; the teats on this month's sow are covered with tiny black brassieres. Perry tells anyone who bothers to ask that he was forced to open up Hog Holler because everybody was always giving him pig paraphernalia. And here he is a bootlegger, not a pig farmer. But his father was.

I hang up the phone. There was no answer at my mother's

house so I left a message saying that I'd taken Gayl's advice to leave and that I was safe and sound. What I forgot to mention was that I had ended up at Hog Holler.

Earlier, when Bear and I had brought in a swirl of snow, Perry turned his hooked nose towards me and proceeded to act far more shocked than he needed to: "Well, look who's slumming it tonight."

"Try not to get too excited," I told him. "I'm here because I had nowhere else to go."

Perry laughed. "Why do you think anyone ever comes here?"

It's true. I'd never dream of hanging around Hog Holler, except maybe to pick up rum or beer and then it's just in and out. Half the time I don't even bother to look around to see who's there. It's well known that Saturday night is "ladies" night, and that Perry lets what he calls "the pussies" drink for free. But some of them must drink too much, because right under the sign saying, "Saturday Night is Ladies Night" it says, "Except for Deenie Card and Mary-Lyn Carty."

"Hey," I say "Where's all the free booze that sign says I'm supposed to get for being a lady?"

"No free booze," Perry says, his hands behind his head. "Unless you can prove you have a pussy."

I say, "But that was my bottle we just finished!"

Perry wags his finger at me. "No way. Just because you're Trish Kyle doesn't mean you get out of spot checks. Right Bear?"

Bear is busy patting Suzie and acting like he hasn't heard Perry, which turns out to be the smart thing to do.

I'm not so smart, so I say to Perry, "What do you do, make all the women drop their drawers at the door?"

"Nothing like that," he says, leaning so close I can see all his blackheads. "It's a manual check I do." He raises his fingers to sniff them. "This is how I tell them apart."

I turn my head and say, "Okay, Perry, you win the award for the grossest human on earth."

Perry cackles and Bear shakes his head at me. "You asked for it."

I say, "I need a drink."

"You'd best be careful tonight, Bear," Perry smirks and points to the cupboard next to the fridge. "Pussies will do just about anything for a drink. Maybe even you!"

Bear winks at me. "Only in my dreams."

This shouldn't be making my face grow so hot.

Then Perry says, "Hear you had a little excitement over your way today with the flue fire. If there's one thing I know, it's that you got to keep on top of your stuff, you know. You should hear the stuff I hear about people who don't take care of their stuff. It's the same old story. Someone forgets the dog in the car on a hot day and it cooks. Somebody don't bother to take their socks off the electric heater and the whole house burns down. Careless people are with their stuff."

I stare at him, thinking I've reached a new low having to put up with a Perry Card rant. His yard is full of junked cars and leaking refrigerators, and the two beef cows he keeps in a shed next to the house live in manure up to their bellies. And here in Hog Holler, it looks like he's got about fifteen electrical cords all running out of two sockets. Hog Holler is the only bar between Thunder Hill and town and he gets away without a license because he doesn't charge for the booze. Not outright anyway. But everyone drops two bucks into the piggy bank by the fridge for every drink they take. So Perry never has to leave home to party, and everybody has to show him respect because he's always threatening to close the place.

"Hurry up over there, laddie," Perry shouts at Bear, who'd been rummaging through some cupboards. "You're keeping the lady waiting."

Bear returns with a bottle of rum. I watch the way he moves his lips as he's filling my glass and I think he really does look good without his beard. I think that just before I take a long sip. That rum sure does warm the throat. There's nothing like behaving like a yahoo at Hog Holler when you thought you were in for a quiet weekend with your husband. Oh well, I decide, as I clink glasses with Perry, I can always blame it on the rum, or the storm, or Ray.

Less than an hour after the flue fire, Ray phoned. I still felt pretty shaken up and was getting the guts up to tell him about it, because Ray is fanatical about insurance policies. He is always after me about things like car inspections and fire hazards. I was supposed to get someone over here to fix the stovepipe but I hadn't gotten around to it. Anyway, before I even had a chance to say anything, he said, "I don't think I should drive anywhere today, honey. It's storming pretty bad down here."

He never calls me "honey." I looked out the window and up the road. "It doesn't look all that bad out there to me, *honey*."

I heard him sigh. "Okay, Trish, if you want I'll jump in the truck right now and spend the next five hours on the road, that's if I'm lucky enough to stay on the road."

"I guess it's a question of what you want."

"You think I want to stay here and listen to the guys fart and tell dirty jokes all weekend?"

"The guys? That's not what I hear," I blurted out. "Olive said she heard all kinds of women when she spoke to you earlier."

"Women?"

"Yeah, women," I said. "You know, the other half of the human race?"

"Okay, okay. But I don't know what Olive's talking about. Unless..." He suddenly got right quiet on me.

"Unless? Unless what?"

"Unless..." he said, "unless there were women near the phone at the gym this morning."

"There's a gym in Newville?"

Hearing about this gym felt like something had just been spliced into the film clip of Newville that I carry around in my head. The one that shows Ray waking in the morning, walking to work, spending a long boring day on the Payloader, heading back to the boarding house where old Mrs. McCarthy fixes the men hot stew with dumplings. In the evenings he plays cards with the farting joke-tellers, or watches TV, and except for the past three weeks he usually phones me before going to bed. How did a gym suddenly get into this picture?

"Gym?" I said, clearing my throat. "You ... why would you join a gym?"

"Why does anybody?"

"I never thought you were interested in that stuff."

"Maybe I've changed. Do you think it's a bad thing?"

I guess my silence let on what I was thinking, because he said, "I only joined a while ago. I haven't been going for that long."

"Well, when did you start?"

"Oh, I guess about five weeks ago."

"But you've been home since then. We've talked on the phone at least a dozen times. Why didn't you tell me?"

"Because ... because I'm tired of being grilled all the time about what I do here in Newville. And I knew you'd have something to say about me joining a gym."

"You mean like I might ask how much it costs to watch a bunch of women sweating in tight clothing?"

"Something like that, yeah."

"So," I said. "I guess that explains why you're not in any big hurry to get home these days."

"Oh, Trish," he sighed. "Don't you see why we're not living together anymore?"

I couldn't answer because I felt like he'd just kicked me in the stomach, and it reminded me of how bad things had gotten between us before he moved to Newville in the first place. Since he'd come back that first weekend we'd both tried so hard that we'd convinced ourselves that we could be happy together. I guess we must have been thinking the same thing because for the longest time we stayed quiet, listening to the hum of two hundred kilometres of phone wire.

Finally, he broke the silence. "Gayl up yet?"

"She's gone into town."

"By herself?"

"She picked up Biz."

"How could you let her take the car out in this weather?"

"Because with me here and you there, someone has to make these decisions."

And that's pretty well where we left it. I still hadn't mentioned the flue fire. I stared at the hole in the stovepipe and all the bits of rusted metal that had fallen onto the stovetop. Ray had joined a gym, of all things, and he wasn't coming home this weekend.

I banged the phone down on the table and that's what sent me running straight for the rum.

"Goddamn spring storms. Every goddamned year I get screwed up because of some storm."

Perry has been staring out at the blowing snow for the past hour. Suddenly, he grabs his cap from his chair and goes out the door without even saying goodnight, without even reminding us to lock up when we leave.

For some reason Bear feels responsible for seeing that he makes it across the yard and into the house all right. In a nor'easter like this, a thirty-foot walk can turn into the last walk you'll ever take, if you're drunk enough. But we shouldn't have worried about Perry.

"He's on automatic pilot," Bear says.

We're standing at the window, our hands cupped around our eyes. The snow or sleet or freezing rain whipping around out there makes it so we can barely see Perry stumble up the stairs to his back porch. We watch him crash into both sides of the doorway before heaving himself into his house.

Bear laughs, "He always does that when he drinks."

"What?"

"Goes through the door like he's trying to thread a needle."

"Jeez, Bear, I didn't think you came here to the Holler all that often."

"I don't usually, Trish," he says, slipping into a cowboy voice at the same time as he hooks his thumbs into his belt loops. "But a man gets pretty lonely way up there on Thunder Hill. In the dead of winter his thoughts might start wanderin' over to the Hog Holler gals."

"You must get *real* lonesome, then," I say in the exact same cowboy voice but suddenly the fun fades from his eyes and is replaced by a look that really is lonesome. Seeing Bear looking so lonely is making me feel mighty lonesome too.

8. The Failed Hermit

FOR SOME TIME BEAR has been calling himself "a failed hermit." This after he used to call himself "a failed freak." Right after our farm got busted, he decided that trying to live with lots of people in harmony was impossible. Perhaps it would be better for everyone if he was to become a hermit. Yet, every year, he throws a huge gathering in August and calls it his "Failed Hermit Party."

Once, when we were helping him get ready for one of those parties, Alana asked him how he thought he had failed.

He turned away from the pot of venison and turnip stew he'd been stirring and said, "Look, I've been living here alone for all these years. I have my own water and heat source, I grow almost everything I need, but look at me!"

We looked. After all, there's a lot of Bear James to see, which is how he got his name; well, that and because of all the hair. Whenever he slips into hermit mode, Bear grows out his hair and beard. He says he does this to keep the ladies away so they won't distract him from serious hermit business.

Underneath all that hair is a handsome face. He has strong cheekbones and soft brown eyes like a deer's. Dark curls tumble over his forehead and around his ears.

Whenever he shaves off his beard, even Gayl's friends go on about how hot he is.

"We're still looking at you, Bear," Alana said, poking him because he seemed distracted by the stew.

"And we're still waiting to hear why you've failed as a hermit," I said.

He turned away from the stove and waved the wooden spurtle he'd been using to stir the broth. I quickly held out my hand to catch the dripping stew. Last Christmas, he gave every household in Thunder Hill one of his hand-carved stirring spurtles. No one, not even Olive, who has the weirdest gadgets in her pantry, had ever heard of a "spurtle."

"I am a failure as a hermit because of how much I need people, like you two, for example."

"Us?" Alana said.

"Me and Alana?" I said to make sure I heard that right.

"What's wrong with needing us?" Alana said, "We're your best friends."

"Hermits shouldn't need anybody," he growled. Then he pointed to the bag of corn out on the back steps. Would we girls mind shucking it?

Of course we wouldn't, we said; we were his willing slaves. He once joked that unless he found someone like Alana or me, he'd stay alone forever. Of course, we were flattered. And, he added, if it ever came to pass that Danny or Ray dumped us for younger, firmer women, he'd be there for either of us. Thanks a lot, we told him, adding that he probably should have shut up a line or two back.

There were times when he got so lonely that he took to advertising in the city paper. His ad read, "Wanted: Female cabin mate. No electricity/phone. Must like woods." If he thought they were nice, or hot, he'd invite them to "try it out," meaning the hermit life. Danny and Ray thought this was a great scam, but Alana and I said we hoped he'd find someone to share his life. We advised him not to make a big deal of the fact that the outhouse was a two-seater, although he seemed to think this was a selling point.

All sorts of women came to try out the hermit life with Bear back then, just because of this ad. Two were artists. One was there to oversee the installation of the gas pipeline over in North Harbour. A few were simply looking for an escape from something. He ended up living with about half of them for a couple of months until he began to miss that lonesome feeling and he'd ask them to leave so that he could continue his hermit work. This is what he would tell us.

These women adored him. They raved about what a great guy he was, how sensitive, how considerate. If they were lovers, they might add something about how generous he was in bed, how attentive, blah, blah, blah. Alana and I would offer them more tea, or beer, or whatever, and before long, it would come out.

"Say, do either of you guys have any idea just how *big* of a guy he is?"

"Big?" we'd say, innocently peering over our tea mugs. "How do you mean, *big*?"

"I mean, gigantic!" the pipeliner had said, illustrating with her hands.

Unfortunately, by the time this sort of talk came out, they were days or even moments away from parting company with Bear. When we ganged up on him for an explanation (we had particularly liked the pipeliner), he shook his head and said, "One thing I've learned is that two hermits are one too many."

Bear may love Alana and me equally, but I think he trusts me the most. We've always been able to talk about most everything, from the sense of spirituality he feels whenever he's in the woods to roadkill. Around here there's lots of roadkill, with everything from deer to porcupines wandering down off Thunder Hill onto the highway that runs between the hill and the strait. It's likely due to the cottages built between the road and the shore. The cottagers want to feel like they're spending their summers in the country, so almost every plywood shack has its own tidy vegetable garden. And that's why you can't drive down this stretch of road in the summer without passing a mound of mangled fur that used to house a hungry animal. One year, Bear brought this to the attention of the county and found himself in charge of cleaning up roadkill. He'd tell us about it, listing off the numbers of fawns and raccoons he'd had to pick up. Once, he'd even had to remove a moose.

"And there's no such thing as a car hitting a deer. What usually happens is the deer attacks the car."

I still can't drive at night without expecting an ambush from a light-crazed deer.

I'm even comfortable talking to him about his love life. I'm one of the first to know how lonely he gets. He just can't picture ever settling down with one woman is what he usually tells me. One night, we'd all been sitting out on his porch watching shooting stars. Everyone had gone inside because of the dew, but Bear and I hadn't gotten our fill of comet tails. So after a blue streak scratched the sky he suddenly blurted right out,

"Yeah, that Sharon was nice."

"She really liked you too. So what happened?"

"Can you keep a secret?"

"Of course I can."

"Good," he laughed. "So can I." Then he got all serious and said, "Okay, okay, if you must know, it's because of the size of my ... my size."

I laughed then because I figured he was still joking around. One would think a large penis might be an asset. But then I didn't know what to think when he said that women found sex with him painful. Everything else about their relationship might be great, but the whole thing was doomed because of his size.

"How do you know?" I said, "You're always the one to break up with them!"

He winced and said, "Because I see it coming. It's okay for a time, but then they start tensing up when, you know, *it's* coming at them and soon sex becomes painful or even impossible for us both."

We stood there awhile, listening to the dew dripping off the trees. I guess he thought I was uncomfortable with this information, and he was probably right, because he dropped the serious voice and started joking around again, asking me if I thought it would be a good idea if the next time he ran his ads to ask that only women with roomy vaginas need apply.

I laughed then, but was surprised to feel this tug happen all the way up to my womb at the thought of Bear pushing into me. I mumbled something about it being time to get home, and I hurried inside the cabin to find Ray.

And here I thought I'd gotten over these feelings for Bear. Back when we all lived on the farm, Bear had built a tree house in the big old maple by the barn. It was a very impressive tree house complete with a sleeping shelter and a cooking area. He had a rope ladder he could throw over for visitors but he and I were the only ones who could climb up the tree without it. One lazy summer day I went up for a visit and we'd gotten sleepy after smoking a joint and drinking the beer I'd brought up in a backpack. We crawled under the little tent he'd rigged up for a nap. It was that innocent, really. Somehow in our sleep we'd moved closer to each other and were now face to face and I fairly squirmed under his hand that was pressing me even closer to what felt like a big zucchini in his pants, I realized that I was not the only one pretending to be asleep through it all. I bet we could have fully done the deed and later woken up to yawn or stretch and look at each other as if nothing had ever taken place. That's if Ray's voice from below hadn't interrupted our dreams and made us jump apart like we were on fire. Which we were, but you'd never know it by how coolly we reacted.

"Hold on there buddy," Bear said. "Ladder coming down."

"Did you remember to pick that lettuce for the salad?" I called down to Ray.

I don't think Bear and I dared to look at each other for a whole week after that.

A flash of lightning causes Bear and me to crash back into the pool table.

"Whoa!" says Bear.

"That was freaky," I say. "Lightning in a snowstorm."

"Only it's more like freezing rain at this point," Bear says. We can hear it clicking on the window.

A low roll of thunder causes Suzie to tremble and she paces around our chairs. The lights start flickering, so that doesn't help matters much.

"Poor, poor Suzie," I say, smoothing my hand over her worried face. "Scared of thunder."

"Me too, me too," says Bear. So I reach out and pat him on the head too.

The cards lie scattered across the table where Perry had flung them. Clayton Card is passed out on the couch over by the fridge and everybody else left some time ago.

When Bear and I came through the door a few hours ago, the place had been far livelier. There was Mary-Lyn Carty and her sister and her sister's year-old baby taking up the couch. And there was Clayton Card lurching in front of them. He was rambling on, as he's known to do, about absolutely nothing that anyone can understand. When he's drunk, which is almost always, it's like a wire in his brain short circuits and he babbles about things he may or may not have done.

"...That time me and Bugger Larch took a taxi all the ways up to Moncton to hear Pink Floyd. Best concert I ever saw."

"You mean the best concert you *never* saw," Perry called over from where he was loading the fridge with beer. "Pink Floyd never played in Moncton."

Clayton froze for a minute, his hand high in the air, before saying to Perry, "You're just jealous because you missed that concert." Then, clenching up his face, he started playing air guitar for the girls on the couch. All this time they'd been twiddling their hair and not paying attention to anything. In fact, the baby was the only one who looked our way when Bear and I walked through the door.

I must say I didn't think Mary-Lyn Carty would go so far as to bring her sister and her baby to a place like this. It was obvious she'd been into the beer fridge a few times herself, because not long after we came in she stood up and started slow dancing with herself to Shania Twain and Clayton Card joined her, throwing his arms over her shoulders. Then she threw her own over his until their heads were touching and they were really just holding each other up. You'd think they'd discovered each other for the first time, instead of having known each other since kindergarten. Meanwhile, Mary-Lyn's top had ridden up over her leggings and, let me tell you, she has one serious butt. I wouldn't think that dancing with Clayton Card could be any great thrill either. He's one of those stubble-faced types who think all women want him.

Mary-Lyn hollered over to her sister, who was getting hit up on by Perry.

"You keepin' an eye on him over there?"

Perry had given the baby a case of empty beer bottles to play with, and so far he hadn't broken any. In fact, he seemed pretty happy to suck away at them. Ronnie tossed beer caps at the sister's chest. The sister blushed every time a cap landed down the front of her blouse, but then she'd make a big show of pulling it out from between her breasts. I got to watch all this, which was a thrill a minute. Eventually, Mary-Lyn came to her senses, or maybe sobered up enough to see who she was dancing with, because she pushed Clayton onto the couch, where he must have given up on any idea of romance or life, because so far, since then, he hasn't moved. Mary-Lyn wasn't about to let her sister get romanced by Perry Card either, because just as Perry was in the act of fetching his own bottle cap from down her sister's chest, Mary-Lyn yanked on her arm so hard that Perry almost got jerked right off his feet. They left after that, roaring down Perry's lane in Mary-Lyn's pick-up.

One of the windows out back began rattling even louder than before and the lights continued to flicker on and off. Just before Perry left, he'd tried to phone his buddy down in Diligent Brook, but then he slammed the receiver down. "Just my fucking luck! Now the phone lines are down too," he'd said, kicking the door open into the night.

His luck? Think of the mess *my* luck was in. The phone lines were down, Bear was in no shape to drive out there in the storm, and even if I did get home I had no kitchen stove to keep me warm, let alone a man. It looked like we'd be stuck in Hog Holler this Saturday night, with nothing to do except to ride out the storm.

9. Road to Hog Holler

SOON AFTER THE FLUE fire, and right after Ray had called earlier today to tell me he wasn't going to make it home, I phoned Alana to tell her we wouldn't be coming over for cards. She told me to come over anyway, and I said I'd probably just stay put since I didn't have the car.

"I heard about the flue fire," she said. What a surprise. Of course she would have heard the news by then. The Four Reasons Gas n' Stop is the gossip hot spot of the entire community. The biggest news of the day would be my flue fire and the storm. Unless, of course, someone had driven off the road somewhere.

Thinking about that reminded me again about Gayl. She still hadn't phoned. But then again, she often forgets. Knowing this has probably kept me from falling over the panic cliff on many occasions. It's a kind of insurance, thinking she probably forgot to call. Instead of lying broken in a ditch, she was likely rooting around in my mother's freezer hoping to find some frozen gingersnaps. I sure hoped so. I didn't want to call and worry my mother in case Gayl got sidetracked there in town.

"Want Danny to come get you on the snowmobile?" Alana was saying.

I looked out my kitchen window. The frozen buds on the maple tree by the barn looked like Christmas ornaments. It was still light at six o'clock. Normally, in April, we'd be hearing the frantic mating calls of songbirds, but it seemed as though they'd given up on the day as well. Tonight, the clocks would spring ahead.

I said, "No, I'll call you later."

Alana's voice had barely left my ear when the phone rang again and it was Gayl, calling from town. "Yeah, I don't think I should drive back today."

"You mean tonight," I said. "You were supposed to call hours ago." I pointed out the fact that if she'd picked up the dog food and groceries and phoned me like she was supposed to, I would have told her to head back then.

"You were right about the road. It was real bad."

"I knew I shouldn't have let you go in the first place."

"But I did it, Ma. I drove slow and I survived. Aren't you proud of me?"

"Sure, but now I'm stuck here alone with no car and a hungry dog." I stuck the phone under my chin and opened the fridge which was pretty much empty except for a bit of the roast beef

"Ma, tell me what you want me to do and I'll do it, okay?" Gayl was saying into my ear. "Like, I could leave now and go off the road, or Biz and I could stay here at Gran's tonight and come home first thing in the morning. It's up to you, Ma, because of course your judgment is always right."

"Okay, okay," I said. I scraped the leftovers into Suzie's dish and watched her savour it slowly in the way of old dogs. "I guess I should speak to your grandmother."

"Um, she's having a nap."

The clock over my sink read six-fifteen.

"What do you mean she's having a nap?"

"She was tired."

"You mean she was drunk."

"What am I supposed to do, Ma?" In her sigh I could hear her thoughts. She was trying to protect us both.

"Your Gran is lucky to have you there," I said as I reached behind the fridge for my bottle of rum. "I wish I had someone to tuck me into bed tonight."

"Where's Dad? Isn't he home yet?"

"Seems like the road's too bad for him to drive home too."

"Oh." Another sigh. "Well, I'm sure he would have come if he could."

Poor Gayl. Protecting her father too.

She said, "Why don't you go over to Alana and Danny's, and not worry about Dad or Gran or me. It's not like you can do anything about anything anyways."

"Maybe, I'll see."

She's got it right that there's nothing I can do about it, I thought, as I hung up. I poured some rum and coke and leaned against the doorway between the living room and dining room. What happened to that family who lived here just minutes ago? I wandered upstairs to my bedroom, and then to Gayl's disaster zone. From the doorways I searched each room for a clue as to how things could have all changed without me even noticing. The only thing I found was what looked like my mother's sad face in the hallway mirror. "Now how the hell did *you* get here?" I said out loud.

I used to think of my life as time divided by two. Time before Gayl and time after. That's why I remember our farm so clearly, because that's when Gayl came to life and a couple of years later was when the farm died. Danny and Alana went on to buy the store, Bear built his log cabin up on Thunder Hill, and then it was just Ray and me and Gayl. We took out a loan and the house we used to call the farm was ours. After that, all that mattered was Gayl. All those summers filled with respectable vegetable gardens, with not a single pot plant peeking above the corn. Then there were all those winters of Gayl hopping onto the school bus that her own Daddy drove. I'd go feed the dogs and do the dishes, all before starting up the Toyota so I could go to work at Foghorn Pewter. Winter night after winter night, Ray and I would lie under the weight of half a dozen quilts, our child safe in the next room, the dogs on the floor beside the bed. I must have felt pretty content back then because I thought those years would last forever. That life now seems like one big blur.

Suzie's fur was so full of ice it sounded like the beaded curtains we used to have hanging in every doorway of the farm. I hoped her arthritis wouldn't get any worse because of all this.

Ice pellets stung my face. It was the kind of storm that leaves some fields bare, but will pile a ten-foot drift right across a road, just like the one ahead of me at the top of the lane. It's because of the spruce trees we planted almost fifteen years ago. Ray and I argued about those trees. He wanted to cut them down to prevent these drifts, but I wanted privacy from everyone who drove along the highway.

Today, when I finally reached the drift I figured I'd either have to climb over, or go around it, which meant tramping through swampy ditches. So, over the top I went, and got soaked anyway because I sank up to my hips in the snow and ended up feeling like I was swimming through the thing. At one point I didn't think I'd be able to pull myself out, but after one good fortification of rum I managed to slip out.

From where I stood on the highway, the Four Reasons was less than half a mile away and normally I could have seen it from here. But the wind had picked up and the ice pellets had turned to a mix of snow and freezing rain. Add that to a bare highway, and you've got *slippery*. I was thinking I should have brought my toothbrush because I might end up spending the night on the couch at the Four Reasons. The next thing I knew, my foot had hit a patch of ice and I was sitting on the road with a wrenched ankle.

I could see the Four Reasons' yard light up ahead. It was so close, but from where I sat it could have been in the next county. I also noticed Billy parked in the lot, which meant that Olive and Arthur were there, along with the pot of mulled wine simmering on the stove. Olive would have whipped that up the very second Alana called to tell her that Ray and Trish couldn't make it for cards. Could Olive and Arthur come instead? Alana wasn't about to spend Saturday night with nothing to do.

I was thinking about how I should turn around and go back home when I almost got run over. I was sitting right where Thunder Hill Road meets the highway to town when the black of night turned to blinding light. Normally, because there's a bend in the road near the bottom of the hill, cars slow down well before the intersection. But they wouldn't expect to see a person sitting just left of the stop sign, or the wet hairy dog standing there licking that person's face. The car skidded to a stop but not before it spun out and the headlights were again in my eyes. More annoyed than scared, I lifted my arm to shield my eyes and waved the other at the driver to turn off the fucking lights. Then someone came walking towards me and I almost didn't recognize Bear because he'd gone and shaved off his beard since I'd seen him in my kitchen earlier this morning.

I grabbed the stop sign post and pulled myself up. Good old Bear was pretending to be more concerned about Suzie's welfare than mine. I thanked him for that as I wiped the snow and ice from the seat of my pants. Then he asked me what the hell I was doing out in the storm. I said I might ask him the same thing.

"Hog Holler." He pointed down the road.

"Doing it up tonight, are you Bear?"

"Didn't feel like being alone."

"Me neither."

"Ray didn't make it home?"

"Nope."

There was some foot shuffling. "Want a lift to the Four Reasons?"

"I don't know if that's where I want a lift to, but I guess I can't stay here either."

"At a crossroads, are we?" He laughed.

"Cute."

Bear helped me into the front seat of the Rover. Then he gave

Suzie a boost into the back seat.

"A couple of old cripples," I said.

"Suzie's not *that* old, is she?"

I said I'd go with him to Hog Holler, if only to keep him out of trouble. The wind was driving the snow so hard that we crawled along that stretch of Thunder Hill Road that runs close to the water. It was so wild out there a person wouldn't have been able to make out the string of summer cottages that sit right beside the road. I was thinking this but then I saw a sliver of light coming from where I knew the old Chase cottage to be. No one had occupied it for years.

"Did you see that?" I said to Bear. "It looked like there was a light on in the old Chase cottage."

"No shit," he said, but when he suggested we turn around to investigate I said it had likely been a reflection from our headlights on a piece of metal and we dropped it. This was no night to be frigging around. Bear turned on the radio to an "Oldies" station and we sang along at the tops of our voices all the way here to Hog Holler where Bear is now sorting his cards.

"Whose crib? Mine?" Then, "So where's Ray? I thought he was coming home today."

"Well, he's not."

"Ah, that explains it. Fifteen for two."

"Twenty-four. Explains what? My grouchiness?" I ask.

"Go. No, the reason why you were wandering around out there on the roads."

"Six for thirty. Is that a go? My being out on the road had absolutely nothing to do with Ray not coming home." I move my peg and count up my points.

"Sure," he says, nodding his head. "So, then, why didn't he come home? The storm?"

"That's what he said." I move my peg six holes. I watch his face as he counts up his points and moves his own peg seventeen holes.

"Sounds like you don't believe him."

"Of course I believe him. Why should he lie?"

Bear shrugs. He has just skunked me in the game, so he sniffs and says, "Something smells around here."

I ignore him and say, "It doesn't take much these days for Ray not to come home."

Bear raises his eyebrows. "I thought you bought his excuse."

"Would you?" I watch him closely, because if anyone knew if Ray has a hot one down in Newville, it would be Bear.

He shrugs. "I guess it's up to you to decide to believe him or not."

"Yeah, but if you knew, would you tell me?"

"Are you nuts?" He laughs, but then he sees how serious I am because he says just as seriously, "I haven't a clue what Ray is up to."

"Oh come on," I say, poking at his shoulder like this subject is all a big joke. "Don't give me that crap."

"Don't put me in this position, okay Trish? And don't say you don't know what I mean, because I know you do."

I don't say a thing, because he's on to me, and I'm scared my tears will bust right out of my eyes.

"Trish?"

"Okay, okay," I say and then I try laughing. "God, I sound so bitter, don't I? Sometimes Gayl calls me a bitter old woman. And the other day she called me an immature freak."

"Bitter old woman and immature freak," he says, shaking his head. "That Gayl sure has your number."

"Which do you think I am, Bear? Or is that also an unfair question?"

"Yes it is, but this is more fun, at least." He pretends to seriously mull this over. "Hmm, bitter old woman or immature freak. I'd have to say that, ah, I've seen you both ways. So it's a question of deciding which I've seen more often."

"Thanks, pal," I say, still fighting back the tears, which now sting my eyes. I must look awful when I cry because last year, when Ray was packing to leave for Newville, I was crying my eyes out and he kept emptying his sock drawer and all I could think of was how he once would have held me tightly and not let go until every single sob had stopped.

If Bear has noticed the tears he isn't letting on. He folds up the cribbage board and says, "It makes sense at our age to fit somewhere between bitter old and immature. Hey, I know, maybe they should call it middle age."

I smile at this. "You want to know what pisses me off about getting older, Bear?"

He shakes his head and mouths the word, "no," so I plunge ahead. "Maybe this is silly of me, but I thought I'd have everything figured out by the time I turned forty."

"Silly you."

"Didn't you think that too?"

"I've always avoided thinking about the future," Bear says. "But then again I never got much done in life. There's always a trade-off, don't you think?"

I nod, but I'm distracted because he has suddenly reached down to lift my injured foot into his lap. Now he's rubbing my ankle and now he's unlacing my boot, so when he says, "No, I didn't care much about what was ahead either, except for what was about to happen in the next hour," I realize I have forgotten what we were talking about. He grips my boot and tugs.

"I used to live that way too, remember?" I say, wincing as the boot gives way.

"Didn't we all?"

"You still do. You've got the perfect life. You don't have to deal with anyone if you don't want to." I reach down to pat Suzie who has rested her snout on my knee. Before he left Perry had even found a can of dog food that was who knows how old but Suzie didn't seem to mind. I say to her, "What are you so worried about? You have the perfect life too!"

That had been obvious, from the moment we arrived at Hog Holler hours earlier and Bear fetched a towel from the bathroom and proceeded to rub Suzie dry.

"You spoil her," I'd said.

He smiled, "Don't be jealous. If you let me, I'll dry you off next."

10. Waxing

NOT FIVE MINUTES AGO the lights in Hog Holler flickered twice before going right out. Bear poked through drawers and cupboards until he found a candle shaped like a wild boar's head.

"Where does Perry find this stuff?"

He struck a match and we've been staring at the candle ever since. Not talking, just staring.

Now the wax drips around the wild boar's tusks and pools over the table. I fiddle with it, pinching and rolling it, while Bear rolls and pinches joints out of his super home-grown. This is the stuff Alana calls his "wheelchair weed," because after she smokes it, she really can't move. Never stops her from smoking it though.

Sometimes Alana falls off the booze wagon. Everyone can see it coming when she starts drinking in the daytime and staggers out to the pumps wearing her blue corduroy bathrobe tied so loosely her boobs swing in and out of sight. When it gets to that point, Danny runs her into town to the detox center. A week or so in there is usually all it takes to get her to swear off drinking forever.

At least she tries, but around here it's real hard to stay on the wagon. People tell her they're proud of her, but secretly they hope it won't last too long. The problem with Alana is that she's never satisfied with quitting drinking herself, and it becomes her mission to rescue everybody from the bottle. Everybody agrees that the world might be a better place if booze didn't exist, but like I tried to tell her once, nobody likes to be told they're all fucked up when all they want is a good time.

"You think your mother's just looking for a good time when she drinks?" she asked.

Normally, Alana would never mention my mother's drinking to me, but get her sober and look out. She's not afraid to cross any lines, and that one she really shouldn't. It's not like I haven't tried to get my mother to quit drinking. It's just that we have an agreement. I don't complain to my mother about Olive busting into my life if she promises not to complain about how lonely she is. She has lots of friends in town, but no, she'd rather drink and miss my father. I've told her she has to move on. Once she painted a portrait of him holding a pint of blueberries. It's a pretty good likeness but I think she painted his long nose a bit *too* long.

Sometimes my mother spends the whole day in bed staring at him there on the wall. A few times, I've even heard her muttering to him.

When it comes to Olive, my mother's take is that since she's here and might very well be my actual half sister, I should try to be friendly.

This always gets my back up. "First of all, I do make an effort. And second, she's not my actual half sister and you know it."

"I don't know it for a fact," she said. "But I do know why you're so stubborn about it. Because you are definitely your father's daughter."

"That's right. And he wasn't fooled."

"He did leave her Kyle House, remember?"

"Yeah, but more to punish me than anything."

"You know," she said, and reached over to tap my hand. "Your father and I talked about Olive near the end and I think he realized he could have been wrong."

"He probably wasn't in his right mind at the end." I'd said, fiddling with the braiding along the edge of my placemat.

My mother looked at me over her glasses. "Sometimes I wonder how you got to this age without learning a few important lessons about life."

I knew whatever I might say would sound mean, so I went to the window and pretended to be interested in the back yard. I heard my mother's stick clicking along the floor until her hand was on my shoulder.

"Why not think of Olive as a work in progress rather than a festering thorn?"

"Festering thorn," I laughed. "Thank you. That's the perfect word to describe how I feel about Olive."

"And that's really too bad, because years from now, you'll wonder how you ever let these feelings get the better of you."

"That doesn't help me much now, though does it?"

"No, it doesn't. Not one bit."

"Then what's the point of saying it?" I asked and almost laughed. Now my mother considers herself a fortune teller too?

"Look at those starlings out there," she said, pointing to the bird feeder hanging from the juniper tree. "If your father was still around he'd be out there with a BB gun. He hated starlings."

"I remember that. But I can't remember why."

"He thought they were greedy birds. Dirty too. Your father was particular about certain things."

"But starlings are greedy. And they're dirty too," I said. "My father was right."

Out of the corner of my eye I could tell she was nodding her head up and down, but I wasn't about to show that I noticed.

When Alana is on the wagon I'm not apt to see her on an evening like I normally would simply because I like to have a drink or two. Instead we'll spend an afternoon together. We do lots of back-road driving. We track down water springs along the road or find abandoned farmhouses to poke around in. Alana walks from room to room in a total daze, feeling the energy of those souls who lived and died within their walls.

It's Olive who spends time with Alana when everybody else is busy celebrating the weekend by drinking. It's Olive who makes her some fancy espresso coffee while they sit and hook rugs. Alana gets all wired from the coffee and rocks to the rhythm of her hook while Olive sits upright in a straight chair, her head bent over her work. I bet they spend the whole time gossiping about who all's drinking.

Alana probably starts it off, telling the story of Clayton Card, the guy who's now sleeping it off over there on Hog Holler's couch. "Now there's someone with a big problem. Clayton starts every day of his life with a beer."

Olive will nod and say, "Probably doesn't know any better."

Alana will shake her head. "I knew Clayton when he was little and he was the sweetest kid you ever saw. Totally the opposite of Perry. When Danny and I first bought the store he hung around every day doing any odd job we could think of. He was about thirteen, I guess, not quite at the drinking age. But by fifteen he was drinking with his father. The both of them are the sweetest souls on earth when they're sober but they're some stupid when they're drunk."

"It's a shame," Olive will say.

Alana will add, "It's scary, how much people change."

Olive will say, "Look at Patricia's mother."

"Poor Bette."

"Would you say Bette is an alcoholic?"

"Oh, definitely. Has been for a long time."

"Patricia certainly gets testy about it."

I can almost see Alana heading right into this one. She'll say something like, "Well, look at what happened to her and Ray and that big fight they had over her mother's drinking. I'm telling you, it ruins lives."

"I'm beginning to wonder if there isn't more to the story about Ray being in Newville."

Alana won't catch this at first; she'll be too busy going on about me. "Not that Trish is one to talk about drinking. Just because she doesn't go on benders like Ray doesn't mean she doesn't have a drinking problem. Half the time you'd never know she's had a drink."

Right about now she'll wave out the window into the darkness. Cars passing by at night toot their horns when they see her sitting in the window. She'll say, "Trish would have a real hard time quitting herself."

"I've noticed how much she drinks," Olive will add, as if she doesn't drink her own self stupid with all her fancy wines. "I wonder if it's her drinking that sent Ray off to Newville."

"Maybe, but it wouldn't surprise me if it's his own drinking that sent Ray off to Newville," Alana will say, and that'll put an end to this pretended conversation with me thinking that even if she has it wrong, at least Alana's heart is in the right place.

On such a night, when my head goes in these directions, there's often an easterly wind blowing up off the strait. It whips around from behind the house so all I can hear are whistles and moans and the doors creaking in their frames. Suzie gets all restless and spooked on nights like this. So do I.

Funny how tonight at Hog Holler, Suzie hasn't moved an inch from where she lies between Bear's chair and mine even though the metal roof is cracking and banging so much it sounds like it might fly off at any second. Bear has this calming effect on people, so I guess this extends to dogs too.

The baseboard heaters are crackling as they cool down. I'm noticing the cold now, except for my injured foot, which is all toasty from the rubbing it's getting. The other foot has managed to find its way onto Bear's lap too and now that boot is off too and he's pushing his thumbs into both soles. Now what's he doing? Tugging on each of my toes, that's what.

"Where the hell did you learn how to do that?" I whisper.

"Olive loaned me a book on reflexology."

I can feel my eyebrows rising like Suzie's hackles do. Bear laughs and tells me he was over there the other day to sweep her chimney and to see about setting up some beehives in her garden. She was telling him about her sore back and how Arthur was so good at back rubs, and he told her he liked to rub feet. Ordering him not to move from the spot, she ran out of the room and up the stairs.

"Here I was, not knowing what the hell she was up to because I could hear her thumping and banging around so much. But then she comes down with this book, and makes me swear I'll read it."

I shake my head. "Who makes someone swear to read a goddamn book?"

"I thought she was going to ask me to rub her feet, but no, she just handed me the book."

"Close call," I say. "I hope you ran as fast as you could."

"Oh, I would have rubbed her feet too. And knowing Olive she would have cooked me up a lemon pie in two seconds flat. You know she makes them from real lemons. Oh man, I wouldn't mind one of those now."

He must have noticed the look on my face because he quickly changed the subject. "Anyway, I enjoy feet. I think they're so expressive." he says, pressing on the pad of my big toe, which makes my back arch. "They really appreciate a good rub."

"Sounds good to me," I gasp, as his fist pushes into my arch. His face seems entirely focused on my feet now, the way his eyebrows furrow and his teeth press against his lower lip. I give myself up to his magic fingers. Outside, the storm keeps raging and for the first time all day, I couldn't care less.

It feels like a ton of time has passed since Olive showed up in my yard. Could it have only been this morning? And it was only yesterday that she phoned to tell me her daffodils were popping up through the mulch.

"How I would have loved to have painted the scene outside my window this morning," she'd said. "I was bursting to share it with someone!" She went on about the contrast between the fresh green grass and last year's worm-infested leaves, and how it might inspire an interesting oil experiment in colour and texture.

"And the little Glories in the Snow!" she went on. "Those little pokes of blue are sure signs of spring."

"So, why don't you paint them?" I asked, trying to think of what the hell Glories in the Snow are. I know better than Olive about what flowers come up in spring, but I don't always know the name for them.

I'd been out raking the yard when I heard the phone and had to dash into the house to answer it. In the mirror above the sink I'd noticed flecks of rotted leaves stuck to my hair.

She said, "Well, I can't paint it today because it's Kyla and Kira's ballet recital tonight and I'm making cloud costumes for their class. We were hoping you all could come to see them. There'll be about forty little ballerinas."

I closed my eyes and said, "Uh, well, I'm not sure what time Ray is getting home tonight. It could be late."

"But you and Gayl could come for 7:00, couldn't you? Your mother is coming and it would be so nice for the girls to have their auntie and favourite cousin there too."

I waved frantically at Gayl, who was waxing her legs. On the stove sat a small pot of wax from which she was dipping and now smearing up her thigh.

"Oh, I'm sorry, we can't. Um, Gayl already asked me if she could borrow my car. She's going over to the Four Reasons because Alana's doing a reading for her tonight at seven. Right, Gayl?"

Gayl tossed me a "don't get me involved" look.

Olive was saying, "Gayl could still borrow your car and you could come with us into town to the recital."

"Actually, I'm getting a reading done too," I said, pulling the phone away from my ear.

"You are?" Olive screamed.

"You are?" Gayl shrieked, at the same time as she stripped

away the wax.

My face grew hot as I told Olive, "Everybody says I should try it some time."

Olive said, "But you told me you thought Alana was a quack!"

"What?" I practically yelled. "I never said that. I would *never* say that." But knowing Olive she could have twisted something I *had* said like she always does. Like maybe I rolled my eyes one time when we were talking about how Alana was getting regular customers, but I never once called her a "quack." In fact, I'd be the first to say Alana had a special talent for guessing the sex of a baby or predicting bad weather. But ever since a customer from further down the shore pulled away from the pumps and she'd had a bad feeling about him and then learned he was killed in a car accident two days later, she thought she should take this predicting stuff more seriously. So she visited that psychic who lives in a lighthouse over on the other side of Thunder Hill. The psychic said that she had a gift and that she should share it. But not for free. It had something to do with people more apt to have faith in her if they had to pay. So Alana drove down to Halifax twice a week for a year until she earned her Psychic's Certificate. Now she's got people, mostly women, coming from all over to learn if they'll meet the man of their dreams. She even admitted to me that half the time she's making stuff up that she knows people want to hear. But then she stopped talking to me about it at all, so I stopped asking. Customers keep rolling in to have their fortunes told, so I figure she must be making them happy.

"You said you'd never go to one of Alana's readings," Olive was saying now.

I frowned at the phone. "I meant I doubted if Alana could do a reading on me, seeing as she knows me too well."

"I see," Olive sniffed. "Well, you must tell me how it goes."

As soon as I hung up, Gayl said, "I didn't know you were getting a reading done too."

"Oh, I'm not really going to ask Alana to do a reading," I said. I glanced over at Gayl whose jaw was dropping way further than was necessary.

I said, "I wanted to be home when your Dad gets home tonight, that's all. But in order to do that I have to come up with a story. A person shouldn't have to do that just because they don't frigging feel like going to a recital. And pick up your hairy strips off the floor!"

"So what do you suppose this teaches me? That it's okay to lie?"

"No, it's not okay to lie," I said, pointing to a strip she'd missed under her chair. "But sometimes a person has to bend the truth so nobody's feelings get hurt."

"So how come you gave me shit that time Olive asked me to baby-sit and I told her I was grounded?"

"Probably because she asked me what you were grounded for and I had to come up with a lie to protect your lie."

"But this lie is okay, right? Because if she asks me how your reading went I'll have to lie too!"

I sure don't remember doing this to my mother. But then again, I don't recall paying that much attention to the way my mother handled things, period. In fact, when I was Gayl's age, I tried to avoid both my parents as much as possible. But kids today? They're in your face holding you accountable for every frigging thing you say and do.

"I don't know what to tell you, Gayl," I said. "Except don't look at me as your role model, okay?"

"Pfff, don't worry," she said, as she flounced out of the room. "I stopped doing that when I was ten and I saw you smoking dope up at Bear's."

"You did?"

And here we'd tried to be so careful.

I am so relaxed right now I could go to sleep. I am slouched down in the chair with my legs resting along Bear's thighs. I never knew how much a person's feet could enjoy this sort of thing. When I hear this low moan, I figure it's coming from Clayton over there on the couch, but it doesn't look like he's moved an inch since he passed out. That means the moan must have come from me. This makes me feel panicky. I know all too well what that kind of moan means. Does Bear know what it means? Ray would. *Ray.* I try prying my feet away from Bear's grip, but he decides to tickle my toes. I don't know which is more embarrassing, the shriek or the moan. At least the shrieking gets him to stop. All I need is for Ray to hear some story about Bear making me squeal like a pig over at Hog Holler.

If Bear has a sense of how I'm feeling, he's not letting on. In fact, he's humming a tune and stroking my feet like he's thinking about something else entirely, so I find myself relaxing once more. What's a foot rub between friends? It's only a foot rub.

Alana didn't seem the least bit surprised when I showed up with Gayl on Friday night. Sometimes I really do think she's psychic. But then she said Olive had dropped by on their way to the ballet recital and mentioned I was coming over for a reading.

"Don't worry. I pretended I knew all about it."

"Oh great," I said. "Now she's checking up on me."

"You should have heard Ma, Alana. She lied!" Gayl said.

Alana gasped and slapped her hand over her mouth.

I shook my head at the two of them. "Give me a break. It was a very small lie."

They decided the only way we could all live with clear consciences was if Alana actually did a reading for me. I had my doubts, but they told me to stop being so negative. We tossed a coin to see who'd go first and I won. So, I pushed aside the red curtain leading to Alana's little closet behind the cash register. She lit a candle and we sat down on the two tiny wooden benches. The walls were draped in orange fabric so I felt like I was sitting in a pumpkin shell.

I said, "There's nothing you don't already know about me."

"Don't be so sure," she said, handing me a crystal and telling me to hold it close to my heart. Then she swished my tea leaves and held my hands. I felt more than a little silly. Alana was my best friend in the world, but we have never held hands.

"Well?" I said when she didn't answer and I wondered if I was about to die. Or worse, that something bad would happen to Gayl or Ray. What a price to pay for not going to the ballet recital.

She pressed her lips together and said, "I'm thinking of how to put this."

"What is it?" I laughed. "Are you about to tell me that Ray really does have a hot one down in Newville?"

"What I see is a warning," she said. "Strange things happen to women in their forties."

"They do?"

"They sure did for me. Don't you remember? The way I was drinking?"

"Alana, you still drink."

"Yes, but remember the night I climbed on top of the gas pumps in the pouring rain?"

"It hadn't rained in twenty-five days and all the wells were going dry. We were all celebrating."

"Naked?"

"Why get your clothes wet?" I reasoned.

"Nobody else took their clothes off."

"But we thought you were just being brave."

"You're right," she said, letting go of my hands. "I can't do this with you!"

"No, please," I said. "Tell me what crazy thing I'm about to do. So I can at least shave my armpits before it happens."

Alana peered into my cup again. "It's not the future you need to worry about. It's the past that's staring you straight in the face."

As if I'm surrounded by anything *but* the past, I thought, as

Gayl and I drove home last night. Through my rearview mirror I caught glimpses of the streetlight at the foot of the lane to Kyle House where I spent all my childhood summers. Further ahead on Thunder Hill Road was the home where Ray and I have lived our entire lives together. This means that each and every day I'm staring at the past as well as the present. Is that what Alana was talking about?

"So what did Alana have to say in your reading?" I asked Gayl, who was fiddling with the radio dial.

"The usual stuff, I guess."

"What's the usual stuff?"

"Ma, it's not the kind of thing you talk about."

"Why not? I don't mind telling you what she said about me."

I beeped my horn and waved at Courtney Small who was standing by the road waiting for us to pass.

"She's getting her mail awfully late in the day," I said.

Gayl said, "Boy, she's due any minute, isn't she?"

"Alana told her to be ready to go in next Tuesday."

"Then she probably will."

"You have a lot of faith in what Alana says, don't you?" I said, glancing at Gayl. "Do you really think she can read your future?"

"I think Alana reads people the way they want her to read them. Like I know she told Karen Hastings that she used to be a handmaid for one of Henry the Eighth's wives. Karen just laps that stuff right up. But that sort of bullshit doesn't interest me."

"Then what does interest you?"

"Oh, just talking about stuff."

"About what stuff? Your family? Do you tell Alana things about your father and me?"

"This may come as a shock but we actually talk about me."

"Still, we're a big part of you."

She seemed to think for a moment before she said, "Seriously, Ma? It's none of your business what Alana and I talk about."

My hands gripped the wheel as we took a curve. Last year's

dead grass along the shoulder of the road glowed a sickly yellow in the headlights.

"There are things about your family that are none of Alana's business, either."

"Like what?" Gayl picked at a loose thread on the seat. "She knows everything about us."

"No, she doesn't know everything. There are lots of things she doesn't need to hear."

"You mean like the time Dad locked the bedroom door to get away from all your nagging and you went at the door with the axe?"

I sighed. Gayl had been about eight and it had only happened that one time, but to her it must have looked like I might murder her father. So I can see where it might stand out in her memory, especially since there's still a gash in the door. I considered it a battle scar of marriage.

I said, "Alana knows about that time."

"Yeah, that's what I mean. She knows everything about us."

"No, she doesn't. There are things that are none of her business, or anybody's business."

"You mean like you and Dad breaking up?"

I looked at her so sharply that one of my front wheels hit the shoulder and I jerked the car back onto the road.

"Whoa, Ma," said Gayl.

"Where in hell did you get such an idea?" I shouted. "Did Alana say something to you?"

"Why don't you give me some credit for knowing what's going on?"

"Nothing's going on. Your Dad and I are fine. In fact, things are really good between us right now."

"Pfff, yeah, right. He hasn't been home in three weeks. Is that what you mean by 'good?'"

"Well, he's coming home tonight. And even if what you say is true, it sure isn't Alana's business."

"Why not?" Gayl said. "I thought Alana was your best

friend."

"Stop picking at that seat," I shouted, knocking Gayl's hand away from the growing mess of unravelled threads. "This whole 'reading' thing is getting way out of hand. Next thing you know she'll be calling herself a qualified psychic therapist."

"Psychotherapist."

"Same thing."

"Um, not quite, but I bet she's better at it than the real ones," Gayl said, propping her feet up on the dashboard. "A lot cheaper too. You should think about seeing her, regularly I mean."

"Me? Why me?"

"Maybe she could help. You know, to deal with how you feel about Dad and everything."

"Once and for all, I ... don't ... need ... help ... dealing with your father."

"Ma," she said, in that mothering tone I can't stand, as if *I'm* in denial.

"Put your feet down," I said. "Remember how Kenny Briggs got his pelvis smashed in an accident?" That's the thing about Gayl and me. One minute I'm thinking we can talk to each other, and then the next she acts like she's about two years old.

That's how it is with Ray and me too. One day I think we'll make it and the next I'm sure we won't. When we turned down our lane last night I saw right away that Ray's truck hadn't arrived, meaning he hadn't driven home from Newville like he said he would. I wondered if he'd changed his mind about coming home after all. But then I saw that he'd left a message on the phone saying he'd really had some overtime work and he'd be heading out in the morning. So everything felt safe again until this morning's dream about that toothless slut going down on him got me going all over again.

So here I am on Saturday night shivering in Hog Holler with a certain Bear James, who has abandoned my feet and is now dealing out cards. Had Ray even planned to come home this weekend at all? What if the storm was just another excuse? He hadn't sounded all that sad about it. When he moved to Newville last year, and I thought we were through, I'd gone nuts trying to keep track of him. I'd phone the rooming house only to be told he was out. I'd call the salt mine, but he wasn't at work. When I started asking him questions, like where were you on Tuesday night around ten, he told me point blank, "Look Trish, let's face facts. We don't live together any more and since I don't ask you what you do all week, you can't expect me to report back to you."

"You don't need to ask *me* what *I* do all week," I protested. "You could ask anyone in Thunder Hill and they'd be only too happy to tell you where I was on Monday night, and Tuesday, and..."

"But I don't want to ask," said Ray. "And you know why? Because it's none of my business what you do."

"I see," I said. I remember thinking that he really had left me. In his heart, I mean.

I found myself craving him like I never had before. How different this feeling was from how I felt years ago when one night I'd woken up to his penis bumping against my lips. The nerve of this guy, I thought. The light from a full moon poured through the window into our bedroom. Even when I turned my face away, it kept following my mouth like there was some chance I'd change my mind.

"You gotta be kidding," I probably said, before turning on my side and drifting back to sleep. I remember not caring if he went back to sleep or jerked off. But last year, after he left, I found myself yearning for his dick more than the cigarettes after I quit smoking. I would have sucked that thing the whole night and the next day too.

Somehow it's different this time around. Maybe I'm feeling just as fed up with Trish and Ray as he is, but suddenly I find myself wondering if I should even care if he ever shows up again.

11. Road to Toronto

BEAR JAMES WAS RAY'S best man at our wedding. I remember the mouse-chewed tuxedo that he'd found at the dump a week before the wedding. He looked more like a groom than Ray, who just wore jeans and no shirt and a tie around his neck. I'd put on a purple dress that Alana had worn during her pregnancies. That's why it was so faded at the belly. I felt honoured to wear it to my wedding.

If my father had had his way we'd have been married at church with the reception in the back of his house. He had already spoken to us about renting a giant tent, about hiring a jazz band from Moncton, about serving baked Alaska to the guests. It was my mother who whispered to me that we should go ahead with our plan of a beach wedding with just our friends. How naïve we are in youth. Here I'd thought she was being cool when really she was just sick and tired of my father's spectacular parties, and she looked at my wedding as just another huge event she'd have to help organize.

Not long after my father died, we got to drinking together one night, which was weird since I can't stand seeing her drunk. But she confessed that, unlike my father's first wife, she hated parties. Mostly she hated the small talk. She just didn't know how to go about doing it and would start drinking about two hours before the event just so she could cope. Then she put on this far away look and said something about that was how the drinking started. I bit my tongue from saying something like, funny how you can find a way to blame my father for just about everything, even after he was dead.

I haven't had a drink with her since.

But she convinced my father that Ray and I should be allowed to have the sort of wedding we wanted and that he should back off. He put on that half mad, half sad look of his, before he threw up his hands and walked out of the room. When I stop to think about it, I wonder if that was the moment when he decided to leave Kyle House to Olive instead of to me.

Ray and I got married that summer without our families there. Everyone, except for the minister and me, had dropped acid. We were just stoned on hash. He was Ray's cousin and everybody thought he was so cool. I'd refused the acid because I was pregnant, but not the hash. Back then we trusted in the wholesomeness of cannabis.

It was a bright hot day so we waded out into the water up to our waists and when we were pronounced, "Husband and wife," we all splashed each other. The sparkle in the water spraying around that day looked like thousands of crystals. It was all the wedding I needed.

Hard to believe that a year before the wedding, I was the one who left Ray for what I thought was for good. My cousin Nancy and her boyfriend Ricky were driving up to Toronto and said they'd take me along. I thought of this as my big chance.

My mother was happy I was leaving. She'd said this was an opportunity she'd never had. One of her biggest fears was that I'd end up stuck in town, working out there at the Zellers. I wonder now if her biggest fear was that I might stick around and cause her more grief. Here all of her friends' children were away at school or were married and settled while I went around like some sort of a free spirit.

At that time, Ray and I lived in a one-room apartment over a burger joint where we worked just enough hours to pay the rent. The rest of our time was devoted to just having fun and partying. That was before Ray started drinking pretty much full time and that was before I caught him at the receiving end of that blow job care of one Rena Dickson. After that, life in town didn't seem like any fun.

My mother may have felt that I should head out into the world, but my father was another story. He didn't want me to leave, period. Oh, he wanted me to leave Ray alright, but he thought I should just move back home with them. My father had turned sixty and the day after his gigantic surprise birthday party, complete with his favourite, baked Alaska, he'd begun to worry about the future of his business. My mother wasn't the least bit interested in blueberries, and in fact, was pressuring him to retire. He told me he'd always hoped I might join him. I told him that capitalism, even in the blueberry business, went against everything my generation believed in. Back then we thought we had a valid mission, which meant staying stoned on weed as a way to stay free from society's hold.

We had gone for a drive, something my father liked to do when he had something to say. As we drove to the blueberry fields, he told me about all the things he'd hoped I'd do with my life. I said to him, "You really don't have any idea what I'm about, do you?"

"You believe in natural foods, don't you?" he reasoned. We stopped in front of the first field he had bought. "What's more natural than blueberries?" He asked me then if I had any idea how he got started in the business, how it had nothing to do with the frozen food plants, or the freighters hauling crates to Europe, or the wheeling and dealing that allowed him to reach the million dollar mark close to ten years after he scraped up enough money to buy his first field. "How? I'll tell you. I was bouncing in back of the pick-up truck with all the other scoopers, and I thought, Bernie, you belong in the cab of that truck, not the back. So I saved half of every dollar I made until I could buy this very field."

I'd been hearing this story since I was five years old.

He went on. Okay, so maybe his daughter wasn't cut out for

business. But shouldn't she at least consider going to university before it was too late? I had already told him I never cared to see a school again, that I only cared about today or maybe next week when my cousin Nancy and her boyfriend Ricky were driving to Toronto.

"But what will you do in Toronto?"

"I'll find something."

"What's something?" He was getting angry. "You need some sort of plan."

"The only plan I have is to get away from here. The rest will take care of itself."

"That's what I'm worried about."

The blueberry hill we'd been admiring had already turned crimson following the first real frost of that year. The same field in which there's this old home movie of me, running, then tripping, then falling just before reaching the bottom. Whenever he played the movie, my father would say, "Wait, here's the best part. Look at her, it's like she didn't even notice that she fell." True, the girl on the screen rose up from the shrubs and continued to run to the camera as if nothing whatsoever had happened. I'm sure that fall had hurt, but mostly I remember hoping he hadn't caught it on film. Every time my father watched that film he'd laugh so hard he'd have a coughing fit, and I'd find myself hoping he'd choke.

I wanted to prove that I could find my own way in Toronto, but when an old friend of my father's offered me a job as a receptionist at his advertising agency, I agreed to check it out. I left after only two days, glad to have escaped with my life. How could anyone expect me to work in a place where women wore pantyhose and men choked themselves in ties, all in pursuit of cigarette and booze jingles?

Besides, I had just met this cool guy named Slip, who lived in a much cooler building than the rooming house I'd been staying in. Slip paid his rent by selling hits of mescaline. Most of the people who lived in his building were serious political activists whose causes we supported by joining their protests against practically anything.

During the entire drive to Toronto I had watched the pavement whiz by through a hole in the floor of the car and couldn't believe how much I missed Ray in spite of him getting blown by Rena Dickson. But that wasn't the only thing about Ray that I was escaping. He had these little habits that bugged the shit out of me and it wasn't just his obsession with sweeping floors, walls, and ceilings. I hated how he'd do this little tongue flicking thing just to get a laugh. It was one thing to use his tongue on me that way in private, but quite another when he did it in public. I tried to tell him how it made me feel, like he was exposing the secrets of our sex life to the whole world. How often had someone embarrassed me by giving me a nudge and saying, "You're a lucky girl, Trish." He thought I was making a big deal out of something harmless. I thought he was repulsive. So when people asked me why I was going to Toronto, I said it was to find work. But now I think it was to find a better man than Ray. Someone who showed some respect for his girlfriend.

Ray is not a whole lot taller than me, and I am only five foot three. Short men make up for it by learning how to charm. Drop Ray into any crowd and he'll make friends with everyone. Except for thinking that the stupid tongue flicking thing was funny, he doesn't usually resort to cheap shots and dumb jokes, the way Danny does. And he feels just as at home with people like Olive and Arthur, as he does, with say, me. He has a low strong voice, especially over the phone, and he's always been able to get this woman's pants pretty wet just by talking into her ear.

Like that time in Toronto. There I was, lying on Slip's king-sized bed, where we seemed to spend most of our time. We were coming down from acid and had just finished fucking for what seemed like hours, and while it had been good while stoned, I now felt like throwing up. Slip's phone rang. It was Ray. The timing was perfect.

"Trish?"

"Ray? Ray!" I sat up in the bed. "How did you find me?"

His voice seemed so far away, like the acid was acting as a filter. But I remember him saying, "I will always be able to find you, Trish."

"That is a beautiful thing to say, man," I said, forgetting that I had given my parents this phone number and that he had likely gotten it from them. "So fucking beautiful."

Ray said, "So how are you making out there in the big T.O.?"

Slip was next to me in the bed, but it was Ray's voice that stroked every cell in my being. A final wisp of LSD let me slide right into the receiver and along six hundred and fifty miles of telephone wire so I could wrap myself around my Ray. Talk about cosmic connections.

That day in Toronto, after Ray hung up, I tried to keep his voice in my ear for as long as I could. When Slip pulled gently on my arm, I turned to him, thinking he might say something comforting. But when he went to suck on my nipple, I knew what had to be done. The next day I was on a train heading home. Stupid tongue flick or not, I was going home to the only man for me.

The second I stepped off the train, Ray whisked me out to Thunder Hill to show me the coolest farmhouse for rent. We would start a co-operative farm and fill it with good people like Alana and Danny and Bear, people who would share the cost along with the good vibes, and together we would show the world how a free and natural life should be lived. That day we walked around the property, deciding where we would plant our organic garden. There was a small barn so maybe we could have goats and a horse. And yes, we'd have lots of dogs.

Still, the next time he pulled the tongue flicking thing in public, I told him we needed to be clear on something. As much as I loved him, I could not live with the tongue thing. "What tongue thing is that," he said, pulling it right there on the spot. He must have seen the disgust wash over my face and I guess he didn't want to risk me running away to Toronto again because for the longest time, I thought the tongue thing was good and gone.

Bear deals out two hands in the candlelight. It seems we're storm stuck. I must be pretty drunk because I hadn't even thought about where the hell we're supposed to sleep tonight until I yawn and look around the room. Clayton seems set for the night over there on the couch even though he doesn't even have a blanket covering him. I'm growing colder just looking at him.

Bear must see me shaking, because he says, "You could always go over to Perry's house. He won't even notice if you curl up on his kitchen couch. And it's probably warmer there than it is in here."

"Bad idea," I tell him. What woman would take the chance of Perry Card finding her asleep on his couch? Knowing Perry, he would consider her a gift from Heaven.

Bear deals out another hand.

"How about Rummy 500 then? Think you could handle that?"

"Rummy 500 I can handle."

12. I Seen

I WONDER IF IT'S normal, the way men hold back on those things you can't stand about them until they've got you saddled with kids. It sure seemed that way to me because it wasn't that long after the farm dissolved and things had settled down that Ray started the tongue flicking thing again. He had played the wrong card in 45s, which cost his partner points, and his partner, being Alana, had chewed him out like he was eight years old. He leaned towards her and flicked his tongue, which got everybody laughing, with Alana saying that she'd forgotten all about that tongue thing he did. Would he do it again? She was drunk enough to say, "Would you do it to me where it counts?"

The next morning, I asked him what the hell he'd been trying to prove the night before. At first he acted as though he didn't know what I was talking about, and then he slapped the palm of his hand against his forehead and said, "Oh, you mean the tongue thing that you hate so much. I totally forgot that that's one of the things on the list that I'm not allowed to do."

"I thought I should tell you so you won't start making a fool of yourself again."

Ray came over to where I was sitting in the rocking chair with Gayl. She was busy sniffling on my shoulder because she had a bad cold and had woken up three times in the night. And since the card game had ended so late, none of us had had much sleep. Which is a great way to begin a fight.

"You mean this tongue thing?" he said.

"Fuck off."

"No," he said, taking my chin in his hand and forcing me to look. "It's time you took a good look at the look, cause this is who I am."

Not six inches from my face stood this asshole, doing the only thing I'd ever asked him not to do.

I hit him in the nose.

I didn't mean to make his nose bleed, but I learned that no matter how lightly it's delivered, a tap on the nose can hurt pretty bad, at least judging by how he reeled around the kitchen holding both hands up to his face. Gayl started to cry.

"Jesus, Trish."

"I'm sorry," I said, reaching for a box of cookies and giving one to Gayl. "I'm sorry, okay?"

"There's stuff about you that I don't like either," he muttered into his hands. "But I keep it to myself."

"What stuff?"

"Never mind. I try to avoid hurting people's feelings. Especially people who I love."

"What things, Ray? I'd like to know." I put Gayl down and then hauled myself up from the chair. I hadn't lost as much weight as I'd wanted after Gayl was born, and I still had to wear these special stockings because of all the wonderful varicose veins I had picked up during my pregnancy.

"Never mind, it was nothing. You were perfect in my eyes."

"And now I'm not perfect. So spell it out."

He seemed to think for a minute before he finally said, "Naw. I got used to your little habits."

He was trying to lighten everything up.

"Tell me! Quit playing with my head."

"Trish, oh shit, I'm sorry." He tried to put his arms around me and Gayl, who was still pretty upset from the shouting, and here I was crying about everything in life, and suddenly Ray began to cry too, which had the effect of making my tears dry up quicker than a shut kitchen tap. Then I bundled Gayl up and drove into town.

If my parents thought it odd, me showing up at their door at nine o'clock on a Sunday morning, they didn't show it. In fact, my mother popped Gayl into the stroller they kept for her visits and my father said I looked like I could use a nap, and that it was a perfect day for them to show Gayl off to the world.

Ray called me at my parent's house later that day. I told him I'd only come home if he told me what the big ugly secret was. He promised, and after we got home and got Gayl off to bed, and we got ourselves hunkered down on the couch in front of our favourite cop show, I realized I was scared to learn what it was. What if it was something I couldn't change, or worse, something I wouldn't want to?

As soon as the show was over I said, "Okay, Ray, spit it out."

"Come on, Trish, it feels so nice and cozy to be here with you. Can't we just relax instead of getting all intense?"

"Nope," I said as I turned off the TV. I sat on the arm of the couch and stared at him. "You tell me now."

Ray looked down at his hands. "Okay." He spread out his fingers and examined them carefully. "You do this thing that used to really bother me, and ... we both do really annoying things, and we shouldn't make such a big deal of them. They're what makes us who we are, right?"

"Ray," I said, with what probably looked like murder in my eyes. "What is it?"

"Why do I feel like I'm suddenly about to shoot myself in the head?" He sighed. "You know, you were a lot braver than I was when you clued me in about the tongue thing. Maybe it stung like hell, but now I realize why I was having trouble attracting girls. I mean, look at how they flock to me now!" He actually had the nerve to laugh, hoping, I guess, for a glimmer of amusement on my part. "And ... and," he continued, his eyes wildly searching the room. "Before we go any further, I just want to say that I wish I hadn't been such a coward about telling you this before. You were right to tell me about the tongue thing. You know, I think you're really smart, Trish."

Now he had me really scared. I'm smart enough to know that I'm no genius, but I've always felt just as smart as Ray. So where the hell was he going with this?

"Trish," Ray said, in the patient voice he uses with Gayl, "when you're talking, you have a habit of saying ... 'I seen' instead of 'I saw'."

I'm sure I gawked at him for a full minute before shaking my head. "I do not."

"Yes you do, Trish. Last night when you were telling Bear about the eagle you saw circling over his cabin, you said, 'I seen an eagle over your place yesterday'." He quickly added, "It's not like you say other things wrong. You never say, 'I done it' or 'they was'."

I cleared my throat. "People say 'I seen' all the time."

"It's a common mistake."

"Well, excuse me for being so ignorant." I folded my arms across my chest and turned away from him.

"You see," he said, as if I hadn't spoken. "You have to put in the 've' after 'I' when you're talking about something you've seen more than once. Like, 'I've seen eagles up on Thunder Hill many times.' But when you're talking about what you saw only once in the past, then it's, 'I saw an eagle yesterday'."

"But I *have* seen more than one eagle in the past!"

"See? That's it exactly! Now shorten the 'have' to ''ve' and you've got it. 'I've seen more than one eagle in the past.' Now say it!"

"But I was talking about the one I seen yesterday!" I cried.

"The one you saw yesterday."

"Did you ever stop to think you might be wrong about this?"

Ray shook his head. "I'm positive about this. Your father says 'I seen' too. That's likely who you picked it up from."

"And my mother?"

"No. She says it right."

"My mother would have told me if I was saying something wrong."

"She probably didn't notice it. I don't even notice it half the time, I'm so used to it."

"But you noticed me using it last night."

"Yes. Like you noticed the tongue thing."

"That's because you haven't done that in so long."

"You see, that's where you're wrong, Trish. I never stopped doing it. You just stopped being bothered by it."

We sat there for a while, listening to the east wind whistling through the house. I thought about my father and how he had made his fortune in blueberries. How he knew every politician in the province and even a lobbyist in Ottawa too, and how he had landed a major exporting contract with Germany only the year before. The fact that he used "seen" instead of "saw" hadn't hurt him any. I wondered what he would say if someone ever pointed out the big mistake that he'd made all his life, the big mistake that he had passed onto his daughter. He'd likely say, "All part of my charm." My father was that sure of himself.

Then I remembered that receptionist job at the advertising agency in Toronto. And how, after only two days, my father's friend approached my desk to tell me that his former receptionist decided to return to work. Not for one second did I consider that my father's friend might have been lying just to get rid of me. But now, after hearing about my great grammatical sin, I wondered if it had been 'I seen' that had really put me out of that job. I looked at Ray sitting there on the edge of the couch with his elbows on his knees and his hands drooping between his knees and suddenly I hated him. Not for telling me about "I seen," but more because he hadn't told me about it sooner.

I forgave him, though, that very night. He was a very grateful boy, I could tell, just by how skillfully he used the same tongue that got him into so much trouble. But that's not why I forgave him. It had to do with the fact that it dawned on me that he was the only person to ever tell me about "I seen." Since then I've said it right. But now I have to stop myself from correcting anyone who says, "I seen."

13. Pool Table Bed

NOW BEAR IS SHOWING me some simple card tricks. They are easy to see through and I tell him so. He looks quite hurt, so I ask him to show me another. I also tell him he is sweet to try and entertain me.

"Entertain you? I'm just trying to keep myself awake. And warm. It's freezing in here."

"Maybe *you* should go sleep in Perry's kitchen," I suggest, just as my teeth start clacking and a great big shiver almost knocks me off my chair.

Bear laughs. "That wasn't just someone stepping on your grave, it was more like they fell right in on top of you."

"That's a fun thing to think about," I say between chatters.

"Look at you," Bear says. "We have to figure out a way to get warm."

We look around the room. Other than the couch that Clayton occupies, there are only a few chairs, the cement floor, and the pool table. We look at each other, and then back at the pool table.

He smiles.

"You're joking."

"We'll be off the floor, at least." He pulls off his sheepskin vest, rolls it up and hands it to me.

"Your pillow, Madam?"

"Oh, I couldn't possibly," I say, before grabbing it. "What'll you use?"

He tiptoes over to the couch where Clayton is snoring, and slowly slides a cushion out from under his head. He holds his finger up to his lips when I begin to snicker. Then he takes a stack of old newspapers and carefully spreads them over Clayton.

"Very thoughtful of you," I whisper when he returns.

He whispers back, "I thought so too. Besides, we wouldn't want him crawling into bed with us during the night."

"Bed?"

"That's right. Here's your side." He takes my "pillow" and sets it down on the table. Then he places the stolen cushion next to mine. "And this, is my side. So see that you stay on your own side."

"That goes for you too."

Bear spreads open a crumpled piece of tinfoil onto the pool table's bumper. "I've been saving this for special occasions. Like a nightcap."

We smoke. I never could resist a toke of hash, let alone that of the finest quality. This will surely take the edge off the nasty headache that's creeping up on me. Sure it will, I repeat to myself, deciding to forget that it will lead to an even worse hangover. For now, at least, the sharp edges of the headache are growing fuzzy. And that candlelight gives off such a warm glow to Hog Holler. That pool table looks pretty welcoming, so here I go, crawling over the side. It's so nice to be off that cement floor. I think I'll curl up on my side.

Bear has just now draped his parka over me. It smells like him and feels heavy and soft at the same time.

"What'll you use for a blanket?" I mumble, because he has crawled onto the pool table beside me.

"We'll share," he says, slipping his arm over mine and snuggling up to my back. "Ah, finally, after all these years, here's my big chance to sleep with Trish Kyle."

"Whoa!" I say, struggling to sit up on the table.

"Just kidding," he laughs, and eases me back down to the felt. "We're freezing, right?"

He hugs me once and then all is quiet until we hear Suzie whining as she circles around the table. I catch glimpses of her nose reaching up and over the edge.

"Poor Suzie," I say. "Even a year ago she could have jumped right up here with us."

Bear sighs and pulls away, swinging his legs over the side of the table. "Come on Suzie girl, we'll keep you warm too."

He picks up all fifty pounds of Suzie and plunks her down beside me and she settles in, her tail tickling my face, her long snout resting across my leg. It's getting pretty crowded here on the table, but with her on one side and Bear on the other, I'm finally feeling warm.

Outside Hog Holler, the ice still pelts at the windows but now it sounds gentle and soothing. Behind me, Bear's breathing has slowed down. I try to match my own breathing to his, something I always used to do when Ray was sleeping and I wasn't able to.

"Can't sleep?" Bear whispers.

"Not yet."

"What are you thinking about?"

"Nothing."

Bear says, "You want to know what I'm thinking? About how funny it is that the two of us are lying here on a pool table, but how it feels like we've been doing this forever."

"We have in a way. Remember that day in the tree house when we ... we went to sleep?"

He gives me a hug in response, and for a second I think I might actually fall asleep.

But then Bear starts rubbing my shoulder and I jar myself awake. What the hell is going on here? This is Bear James spooning with you tonight. Not almost twenty years ago, but now. This is Ray's best friend. Hell, this is one of your best friends! Okay, calm down, it's not like he's humping you or anything. Bear is lying so close because tonight is an emergency, and emergencies call for drastic measures. And obviously, this snowstorm is a big emergency, because isn't that why Ray didn't make it home to you this weekend? Or the last three weekends either for that matter?

Into the darkness I whisper to Bear, "You know what I hate?"

Bear stops rubbing my shoulder like he's seriously considering the question. He clears his throat and whispers back, "I'd rather hear about what you love."

I am suddenly filled with so much desire it makes me want to cry. Desire also makes me want to squirm, but I resist that too.

He says, "You're not going to tell me?"

"What I love? It's warmth. That's what I was thinking. I want to feel warm."

He holds me even closer and in a flash I feel an ache surge up the core of my body. So I press back at him, but ever so slightly, as if I'm not even aware. And then I wait. Twenty years of sleeping beside a man has taught me that it doesn't take much encouragement. I'm still waiting ... and waiting. I press against him with more encouragement. Where the hell is it? There would be no missing it on a man like Bear. Back at our high school dances he used to press up against us girls so hard that we'd laugh later about getting zipper imprints up to our bellies. Yeah, I know, there's a big difference between a teenaged boy and a middle-aged man, but we're talking about Bear who continues to stroke my arm like it's something precious.

I have to know. Now. So I twist around in his arms until our noses are touching. His face feels cool and soft against my own. I kiss his mouth and run my tongue between his teeth and when he kisses me back I am greatly relieved. So this is not some big brother thing. Bear still wants me as badly as I want him. I press against him harder, already thinking about how wide my legs will have to part, how he'll probe and tug, how we'll have to work at it until ... I am already wet knowing it's about to begin. And there escapes another low moan. I press against him, again. It's hard evidence I am after, but for some strange reason it's not there. Suddenly I'm aware of how pathetic this is, and how desperate, and wrong, but still some nagging force tells me to keep working at it anyway, until ... without warning he pulls his body away from mine.

"Trish?" he says, his voice sounding lusty and low.

"Oh, hi, Bear," I say, wishing my face wasn't pressed so firmly against his.

"I don't think..."

I cut him off before he finishes the sentence. "Hey, don't mind me, okay? I just felt like kissing someone tonight, and you were here, right?"

"I'm glad you kissed me," he says, murmuring into my hair.

"Me too. Sometimes you just have to kiss somebody, right?"

"I'm a great believer in kisses," he whispers. "Good night, Trish."

PART III

14. Kyle House

IT'S SUNDAY MORNING AND here I am lying in this old claw-foot tub, remembering when I was ten and how the tips of my toes barely reached the other end. Now, adult knees rise out of the water like scaly sea monsters.

It's true what my mother says about long-term memory growing sharper with age. I can barely recall what happened last night at Hog Holler, yet I remember how my child body looked in this tub. Sharp little pelvic bones stuck up from the sides of a belly that sunk so low I'd have to arch my back to see the bead of water sparkling in my navel.

Now I open my eyes, fully expecting to see the stretch marks and dimpled fleshiness of my forty-plus body, but somehow, today, in this old tub, my body doesn't look so changed. Maybe it's the light through the stained glass window over the head of the tub. I'm glad Olive decided to leave that window when she renovated this old house. I'd always liked how the small squares of colour danced over the bathwater.

"We are so fortunate to have this great stove at a time like this!" Olive had said, when we walked through the back door into the warmth of Kyle kitchen. For once I had to agree with her as my body dove for the kitchen couch and my head sought the relief of a real cushion, and not some rolled-up coat. Just like the tub and stained glass window, at least Olive had the good sense to keep a couch in her kitchen.

I watched her lift the lid of the water reservoir. Steam billowed up to the ceiling.

"We have plenty of hot water for a bath. Who needs a nice hot bath?"

The twins shouted, "I do! I do!"

"Girls, girls, remember we said we would be storm rescuers today? And since we rescued your Aunt Patricia, we'll do everything possible to make her feel at home. So, who would like to carry buckets of water to the bathtub?"

"I will! I will!"

"Great. You'll take turns, okay? And Patricia, we want you to let us take care of you. After your bath, we'll have some nice hot curry, and then later you can rest in your old bedroom. How does that sound?"

"Sounds great, but don't bother," I said, wondering how the hell she manages to get those girls to do chores.

"Oh, let us, just for today. The girls and I want to, don't we girls? And besides," she lowered her voice. "You look like you could use a bath, Patricia."

"I do?" I said, knowing full well that I did. Hung-over and unwashed, I likely stunk of rum and smoke. A hot bath, good meal, and a night in my old room above the kitchen sounded good.

I've been at Kyle House many times since Olive and Arthur moved in, but I haven't felt as connected to it as I do in this tub at this moment. In the past, whenever Olive had led her guests on a tour of the house, she insisted I come along as well. She'd march her guests through the great upstairs hall like we were in some museum and then through the passage to the back of the house and we'd stop in front of what used to be my old bedroom. As if it had some historical significance, she'd say, "This is where Patricia slept as a child. We even kept some of her old books and things! And don't you love the dormer window? If you've ever been to the *Anne of Green Gables* house over in PEI, you'll notice we've decorated this room in much the same fashion. Muslin curtains were very fashionable then, as were quilts, of course."

I commented once that all that was missing was the rope barrier in front of the door to keep the tourists out. Olive didn't find that so funny, but her Toronto friends did.

She always ended the tour in the kitchen. If the bathroom off the kitchen and my bedroom have stayed pretty much the same as when I lived here, the kitchen sure hasn't. Olive had the ceiling exposed to the beams and boards and she replaced the old linoleum with battered looking softwood floors. Choosing the right look had seemed important to her, and before renovating she asked me over to look through countless magazines. My input was critical, she'd said, as no one had a stronger feeling for the place than I did. A Kyle kitchen called for a Kyle opinion. I said I liked natural wood. But instead she ended up finishing the cupboards in what she called distressed paint.

I couldn't care less about what Olive did with the kitchen. My feelings haven't changed from the day my family turned the key and our backs on Kyle House. As far as I was concerned, all we were leaving behind were ghosts. Friendly ghosts, my father would say and he'd tease me about the noises I heard at night, the pencils and things that fell off my bureau, and the cold drafts that seemed to follow me from room to room.

"You must get that from your mother," he'd say about Bette, who often complained about another kind of ghost, the spirit of Bernie's first wife. Once she actually shivered after crossing the threshold into the front parlour. She put her hand to her chest and said, "I feel like Phyllis Kyle just walked over my grave."

My father laughed and reminded my mother that his first wife was still alive and enjoying his hard-earned alimony money up in Toronto.

On my last visit to the palliative care unit, I fluffed my father's pillows and got him to sip at peach juice. Twice he tried to get his cracked lips to close around the straw. I wet his lips with

with little drops of juice at the end of the straw. When he'd had enough, he said, "Ahh. Now that was to die for." He opened one eye. "I hope you'll tell everybody I was still making jokes on my deathbed." He said his back was sore. I offered to rub it, but he wanted to wait until Bette returned from smoking in the visitor's lounge.

"Do you want the nurse to give you something for the pain?"

He looked worse than the week before. I hated seeing his spindly arms that used to be so strong. When I was little he'd toss me up so high in the sky that my breath would catch before falling back to the safety of his arms.

Now my father struggled say, "I used to worry about all the drugs you were taking. Funny, huh? Now I'm the one who is as high as a kite. Help me to the window, would you?"

We shuffled from the bed over to the window where he had his cigarettes hidden behind the blind. While he blew smoke out through the screen, he told me to watch the door in case a nurse came by.

"Sometimes they forget who helped pay for this wing," he said, slipping into a coughing fit that lasted until Bette returned to the room.

"I still don't understand," Bette said, picking up the same conversation that had sent her out of the room in the first place. "Why you would want to be buried in a place that your first wife loved so much?"

"Who says *I* didn't love Kyle House?"

"You never said you loved it. You didn't, Bernie, not once."

"Did you ever stop to think that maybe it was because I loved *you* that much more?" he said, with a voice so tender I turned to see who was speaking.

Bette wasn't buying the tone, because she cried out, "Ha! So now you're saying you're prepared to love me *less*."

"You see? I can't win." My father winked at me, his laugh shifting to a choking cough that sent Bette to the window to stare at the parking lot below. "You watch," he whispered. "She won't let up, even after I'm dead and gone."

The next day, just before he died, he patted Bette's hand and told her to do whatever she wanted with his mortal remains, that he was heading for a whole new beginning somewhere new.

She let him have his way, though, and had him buried in Thunder Hill Cemetery, right next to Kyle House. It was a breezy summer day filled with the sound of quaking aspens and scolding crows. Dappled sunlight lit our faces and behind us the ocean sparkled. There was something about all that sun and sea that made my father's burial seem less final than I expected. But I still feel sad that my father died believing my mother wouldn't bury him in Thunder Hill Cemetery.

"When you're ready we'll have some nice hot curry!" Olive says from the other side of the bathroom door. "And I even have that home-made bread you like so much."

I'm still soaking in the tub at Kyle House. Feeling a whole lot cleaner than when Olive rescued me this morning from Hog Holler.

I'd been in such a deep sleep there on the pool table that I might not have heard that soft knock on the door if Suzie hadn't woofed. Before she had time to break into a full bark though, I had my hand around her muzzle.

"Shh. Listen," I'd said, waiting for another knock. I was laying there trying to put together the pieces of last night. Card games. Too much rum. The foot rub. That hashish nightcap! Bear was still asleep behind me, his arm draped over my shoulder, and a glance over at the couch told me Clayton was still there. I had no idea what time it was, or what I was supposed to do now. I knew I shouldn't be found curled up in Bear James' arms on Hog Holler's pool table.

I relaxed my grip on Suzie's muzzle, which made her sneeze. Behind me, Bear breathed in deeply, and already I wondered what I'd say if he opened his eyes right then. Something like, hi, old friend, fancy meeting you here. His breathing went back to normal though and I relaxed against his warmth. Maybe I imagined a knock at the door? Maybe it was only something banging around in the yard. Besides, who would be knocking on Hog Holler's door at ... at ... shit! There it was again.

It was louder this time and I held Suzie's snout whispering, "Shush," into her ear. This was just fucking great. I lifted Bear's arm high enough to pull myself away. My head was pounding and my legs felt stiff when I swung them off the pool table. When my feet touched the cold cement floor, I remembered my sore ankle. Sunlight poked through the grimy window.

I gave a hand signal to Suzie that she should stay on the pool table, but then my heart jumped when a dark outline filled the window. I didn't recognize who it was until I spotted a tassel bobbing on the top of the head. Only Olive had a hat like that. Suzie whined then and I lifted her off the table but when I set her down my knees cracked so loud I wondered if Olive might have heard. She wasn't at the window when I looked up so I was hoping she'd gone away. Even so, as I crouched there beside the pool table, I wondered what I'd do next. I couldn't walk all the way home with this foot. And I wasn't sure I was up to facing Bear today.

As I lie here in the cooling water of Olive's tub there's a knock on the bathroom door and Olive says, "Patricia, are you alright in there?"

"I'll be out in a minute."

"The curry's ready whenever you are."

The woman does not let up, just like this morning when I realized she wasn't about to leave Hog Holler without me. When after a few minutes it had gotten too uncomfortable to stay crouched by the pool table, I went over to the door and opened it a crack. A crack was the most I could open it anyway, since snow and ice had drifted up against the door. When I looked out, the sun hit my eyes and that just about killed my head. Through my squinting I could see how the ice covered everything in sight. Even the old pieces of metal in Perry's yard looked like ice sculptures at the winter carnival. Then there was the silence. I had to listen real hard to catch the rumble of surf way out in the strait, or the whispering sound the wind makes as it rushes through the spruce trees up on Thunder Hill. Then I heard the crunch of footsteps as Olive rounded the corner carrying the shovel she keeps in Billy's trunk. It was too late to duck back. She'd spotted me.

"Hi Olive," I croaked.

"Patricia! What happened to you?"

"Just help me get out of here, okay?"

"Bear James must be in there too, is he?" Olive tried to peer around me.

"What makes you think that?" I answered, and then remembered that Bear's Rover was parked right outside.

Olive didn't seem to hear me. She was already hacking away at the drift as if her life depended upon it.

Olive does everything as if her life depended on it. Like the time she and Arthur came to a dance at the Thunder Hill Community Hall, and her eyes popped open at the sight of the older farmers clogging away. She screamed, "Why, this is a form of Gaelic step dancing! And of course it makes perfect sense since practically everyone around here has their roots in the British Isles." Then she went on about how traditional dances were her passion. It seemed she gathered them in her travels like some people collect thimbles. It didn't matter if she was in Argentina, Egypt, or Iceland, she said that when she dances she flies free of earthly restraints. So that's what she did that night at the hall. Got right up there and started stomping her heart out. She clogged and clogged, adding spins and twirls and didn't notice when people stopped dancing out of fear of being knocked over. I could feel their eyes on me as the one who'd brought Olive along.

Then there was the video show a week later. She invited some of the "farmers" over to Kyle House to see footage of her favourite traditional dance, that of the Chewa people of Central Malawi. As the video played, she also stretched her arms wide, thrust her pelvis forward and leapt and spun to the drums.

Later, she said she'd assumed people would be curious to know about cultures in places they'd never travelled to. But she'd been disappointed by the comments after the video.

"Don't go much below freezing over there, I don't imagine," someone had said.

"These pictures remind me of those *National Geographic* magazines I looked at as a kid. Closest I ever came to watching porno."

Jean Bradley said, "Coffee is served."

They stayed on a while, longer as Olive helped serve up the cakes and squares the women had brought. I was glad she'd had the good sense not to demonstrate the mating dance she'd shown me that afternoon.

Then the talk moved on to Maynard Fleming's young fellow who was building houses and barns out of bales of straw.

Someone said to Maynard, "Didn't you teach your boy about the three little pigs?" Everyone got a kick out of that.

Olive and I climbed into Billy and started down Perry Card's lane. The questions began. How in the world had I ended up at Hog Holler? What had I done all night that made me look so damaged? That was the word she used, "damaged." She kept looking over at me when she wasn't busy steering Billy in and out of the tracks she'd made earlier driving up the lane to Hog Holler. To avoid her questions, I made a point of turning around to ask the twins how their ballet recital had gone. Then I asked her how she'd found me anyway.

I got the whole story. How she'd awoken this morning to a cold house and the sight of a quarter inch of ice coating everything outside her window. How she'd lit a fire in her big old Enterprise stove and gone out to the summer kitchen to the old hand pump and wasn't it fortunate that she hadn't gotten rid of that old thing because with the electric pump out, there was no running water to be had! She'd filled up the reservoir on the stove and then bundled up the twins, saying there would be lots of cold and hungry people out there who'd need rescuing this morning.

I nodded and settled in for the blow-by-blow of how she came to rescue me.

She said that next she had driven, no, slipped and slid all the way to the Four Reasons. Through slush and snow and ice, they charged, "Because, Patricia, you know how Billy loves a challenge."

Inside the store, Alana and Danny were at the freezers pulling out food and stuffing it into burlap bags. Alana told the twins to help themselves to the ice cream since it was all going to melt anyway and while they were insured for most power outages, they weren't sure they were covered for ice storms. So they were hauling it across the road to the Bradley Farm, which, and did I know this, had a generator large enough to serve the house as well as the dairy barn. The power lines were down all over the county and no one knew when they'd be back up.

"But I still don't get how you knew I was at Hog Holler."

"That's what I'm getting at. Just as Alana was saying that at least her phone wasn't out, Gayl phoned, looking for you."

"And Alana knew I was at Hog Holler?"

"No, Alana thought you were still at your house. In fact, she told Gayl you were likely sitting in front of your stove reading a book with your feet up on the oven door. That's when she remembered the flue fire, which came as a total surprise to me since I'd just been over to your place yesterday."

I shrugged. "It only takes a minute for it to happen."

"Well, I decided you might need rescuing and I was just about to head out in Billy when Gayl phoned back saying she'd *69'd your call to her last night, did it sound familiar? Alana knew right off it was Hog Holler's number."

Olive took her eyes off the road to stare at me.

I pretended to concentrate on the road ahead of us. The sun had disappeared and now it was snowing again, sleet really, and ahead of us the tracks that Billy had made on the way to Hog Holler were barely visible.

We'd almost reached the curve in the road just before my lane. I said, "You can just drop me off here, thanks."

"I can't do that. You have no heat at your house, remember?"

"I'll manage," I said, trying to sound firm.

"Quite frankly, Patricia, you don't look like you're in any condition to be alone."

I must have looked pretty green at this point because the next thing I knew we were pulling into the Four Reasons and I was opening the door and puking my guts right in front of the gas tanks. The rest of me just about followed it to the ground, but Olive was suddenly there, catching me under the armpits. I caught a glimpse of the twin faces staring at me from the window as Olive half dragged me towards the store.

Then I was lying under an afghan on the couch at the back of the store and Alana was passing a wet cloth over my face. I could hear Danny muttering that someone was going to have to go out there to clean up the mess I'd made.

I jumped suddenly when I saw something slink around the cooler. When I realized it was a cat, I looked up at Alana expecting her to react like it was a rat. But she didn't and *that* more than anything almost had me jumping out of my skin. Had I landed in some sort of parallel universe? A person disappears for one night and suddenly their whole world changes?

Danny said, "Alana had a change of heart when the cat left a dead rat at the door. She actually opened the door for the cat."

Alana said, "Go figure. Cats. The lesser of two evils."

"Admit it," Danny said. "You like the cat."

Alana muttered something about it not being so bad. Then the bunch of them followed the cat up to the front of the store.

For a second there, I even fell asleep. Then I heard Danny say, "Don't even think about driving Trish into town. The road's closed anyway."

Olive said, "But what if she has food poisoning?"

Alana said, "Looks more like rum poisoning."

One of the twins piped up. "Is Aunt Patricia drunk?"

"No dear, she's just a little off her oats today," Alana said, her voice unnecessarily loud. "Who wouldn't be, spending a night at Hog Holler?"

"With Bear James, no less," Olive said.

"Bear? Bear was there?" This piece of information had Alana rattled. I could tell by the way her voice kind of cracked on "there." Everybody knows Bear James goes to Hog Holler when he's feeling lonely. She lowered her voice. "Are you sure he was there?"

"Well, his Rover certainly was."

Alana marched over and stood in front of me with her hands-on-hips pose. "Bear was there? You spent the night together?"

"Guilty as charged. We even slept on the pool table." I added a laugh here and rubbed the back of my neck. "But I wish I hadn't, because now I have an awful crick in my neck."

"Hmm," said Alana, her foot tapping the floor. "Must have been crowded on that table."

"It was. Especially with Suzie sleeping on it too."

"Hmm."

"A pool table?" Kira asked. "Wasn't it uncomfortable lying on top of all those balls?"

Alana suddenly snorted, and said to Kira, "It all depends on whether or not the balls stayed in their pockets, my dear."

"Ha, ha, ha," I said, wondering where the hell Alana got off suggesting such a thing, even as a joke. But I answer, "No it didn't hurt at all, dear, because all the balls stayed in their pockets. But I can tell you this ... Kira," I had had to search for the mole on Kira's earlobe as this was one way to tell the twins apart, "sleeping on a pool table is no fun at all."

No fun sleeping on a pool table, indeed, I was thinking, even if you are lying in the arms of a man who's rubbing you like you're someone pretty special. And you're rubbing against him like a cat in heat. That thought must have crept into my face, in the form of a silly smile no doubt, because Alana cast me this I think you're hiding something from me look.

I chose that moment to say that I should probably call my mother and Gayl.

According to Gayl, everything in town was operating as usual, with just the regular problems a snowstorm brings. Places were closed, shovels and scrapers were out, getting around was difficult, but not impossible. At least they had power.

"How was your night, Mom?"

"Lovely, dear, it was just lovely. Gayl had a friend over and I watched them play Scrabble. Did you know that Gayl has an excellent vocabulary?"

I could tell that my mother was trying to keep me from asking about her. She needn't have worried. I didn't have the energy to get angry about her drinking, because to do so would be calling the kettle black, now wouldn't it?

"What friend of Gayl's?"

"Dixie. Lovely girl."

Dixie. I didn't know any Dixie. I used to know all her friends.

"Dixie who?"

"Now, I'm not sure about that. Why don't I pass you over to Gayl?"

"Wait, I haven't..."

"Hi Ma," Gayl was cheery.

"Who is this Dixie person?" I ask.

"A friend of mine," Gayl said. "What were you doing at Hog Holler last night?"

"I ... I ..." I began.

"And thanks for lying to me about it too. You're busted."

"Busted? Why?"

"Because you told me you were going to the Four Reasons."

"No," I said, in the firmest voice I could muster. "I said I *might* go."

"I'll be sure to remember that line myself, cause I'd be in big trouble if I ever told you I was going somewhere and ended up somewhere totally else."

"It's not the same thing at all," I said. "The circumstances were unusual, I didn't want you to worry."

"Worry? We all thought you were dead in a drift somewhere. But instead you were tying one on at Hog Holler."

Take control of this conversation, I told myself. Know when to admit you were wrong. "I'm sorry. I should have let you know where I was."

"Hey, no problem, Ma. Just remember this the next time you freak because I'm a little late getting home."

"Whoa. That's where you're dead wrong, kid," I said, and seizing the moment, added, "I am an adult who is responsible for my own actions. You, meanwhile, are still my responsibility and therefore you have to answer to me." I said all of this in a calm voice too.

"Pretty hard for me to answer to you when you're out drinking with a bunch of dirt bags."

"I was with your godfather, for Pete's sake. And we just happened to be there when the power went out, and you might as well know, because I'm sure it will be all over Thunder Hill by tomorrow, we had to sleep on the pool table because Clayton Card was already on the couch, and the floor was cold, and I hurt my ankle, and we couldn't drive home."

"Wow, so now you slept with Bear James. Dad know yet?"

"Don't be silly, it was no big deal. By the way, your grandmother doesn't know I was at Hog Holler last night, does she?"

"No."

"Good. Let's leave it like that. You know how much she worries about silly things."

Gayl laughed. "Yeah, okay, responsible adult, but you owe me big time."

Okay, I told myself, maintain the calm that's supposed to come with maturity. Resist the urge to blurt out, I owe you? Why, you owe me so much that you'll never know how much you owe until you have kids of your own. And believe me, I hoped to be around to see that day because revenge was surely the greatest reward for any parent. Instead, I said something like, "And how are you doing, dear? You think you can handle your grandmother alright? You could make her some tea. She likes that when she's ... off her oats."

"Way ahead of you, Ma. You know, I was thinking. Maybe I should move here into town. That way I could look after Gran, and then you wouldn't worry about her so much." Typical Gayl. Picks the worst time to throw something huge into the arena.

Before I can answer, she adds, "So can I? I already talked to Dad and he said it was okay."

He did, did he? Typical fucking Ray. Telling Gayl whatever it was she wanted to hear just so he wouldn't have to deal with her nagging him about it. Let me be the bad guy.

"Look, could we talk about this later?"

"Like when?"

"Like when we get the power back and the road gets cleared and you can bring my car home. How's that?"

"Think about it, okay Ma? You know how lonely Gran gets."

I got off the phone thinking that Gayl was like a bulldog, the way she grabbed onto something and hung there until she got exactly what she wanted. Sometimes I admire that quality in her and I tell her so. That sort of persistence, I told her, is how her grandfather did so well in the blueberry business. Now, if only we could get her to channel it into something besides bullying her mother.

I remind myself it was the promise of a hot bath that put me here at Olive's house. I'm sitting at her big oak table in the kitchen listening to her go on about the wood stove that my parents hauled out of this kitchen forty years ago in order to install the avocado-coloured electric range, and about how Olive had happened upon its rusty cast-iron self in the back of the barn, and had it restored and reinstated into the kitchen, and to think how fortunate we are to have it at this moment.

Maybe she's right but what I remember is feeling sad when I spotted the avocado stove at the dump. It hadn't even been placed by the side of the road for someone to adopt. Like most of the stuff left in my parents' house, Olive had tossed the stove out on its ear.

"I'm just so amazed at how it practically heats the entire house," she says.

I'm wishing I'd stayed on Alana's couch at the Four Reasons so I wouldn't have to hear anymore about the stove. The twins clear the dishes off the table and Olive spreads out some newspapers. Looks like she has an after-lunch activity planned.

"I'm sorry, Patricia," Olive says as she sets a large bowl of water in front of me. "Given your present predicament, that must have sounded terribly insensitive."

"What predicament?" I say, trying to remember what she'd been saying.

"We don't have to talk about it if you don't want to."

"What's to talk about?" I say, trying not to shift my eyes away from hers. "It was cold at Hog Holler, the pool table was the only place to lie on and ... that's what happened."

Olive looks over her glasses. "I meant the predicament of not having a stove."

"That can be fixed," I say, my face flushing. I stare down at Olive's new Weimaraner pups who are finally dozing around our feet. Ever since we arrived they've been pestering poor old Suzie to the point where she'd snarled and nipped at them both.

"Of course the stove can be fixed," Olive says. "But can the other?"

I say, "There is no other predicament."

She leans close and whispers, "You know you can always talk to me, Patricia. It must be hard for you these past few weekends with Ray not making it home. I mean, you must wonder what he's up to down there in Newville."

Wonder? Now there's a key word. I've only been *wondering* about Ray this entire past year, *wondering* if he's eating okay, *wondering* if his back is bothering him. I doubt he thinks about me a fraction of the amount of time I think about him.

Sometimes I picture him working in the mine. I was so surprised the time he took me to see it how big and bright it was, kind of like a giant snow fort. The walls were the colour of dirty snow, yet they shone like blocks of ice under all the lights. There was lots of heavy machinery moving around. Ray had proudly showed me the Payloader he was learning to operate. His job was to pick up blocks of salt and move them outside to awaiting trucks.

This is what he does all day. It's at night that I start to *wonder* if he's working some other woman's mine.

Not today though. Today, Ray has hardly crossed my mind. So I say, "No, I don't wonder that much about Ray. He'll get home when he can. By the way, I thought Arthur was supposed to get back from Toronto yesterday."

"His flight was cancelled because of the storm."

I can't resist saying, "Don't you ever *wonder* about Arthur when he's away?"

On her way to the pantry Olive laughs like that's the most ridiculous question she's ever been asked. She returns with a large bag of flour that she plunks onto the table. Apparently, we'll be spending this stormy afternoon making papier-mâché masks.

15. The Big Red Monstrosity

S OON AFTER OLIVE MOVED to Thunder Hill, she invited my mother and me over to Kyle House for what she called "a family meeting." She wouldn't tell me what it was about over the phone, only that it had to do with "our" father. I gritted my teeth and said we'd be there.

Once we were seated in the parlour, a room my mother hadn't entered since the day we moved out, Olive brought in a tray of tea and homemade biscuits along with a drawing of what looked like a large red penis. This drawing was pasted to cardboard, and she had propped it up on a straight-backed chair. I looked at my mother who seemed to be more interested in looking around the room that had once belonged to her. Since Olive wasn't saying anything about the drawing, I decided I wouldn't either. So we munched and sipped like it wasn't sitting there and Olive told my mother she should pursue her painting talents more seriously. My mother said, "Thank you for saying that, Olive but I haven't done much painting since Bernie died. And besides, you are the one who is so talented. What's this you've been working on?"

"Oh this," said Olive, as if she'd never noticed it before. "I drew it myself."

"Why?" I asked. "I mean, why is it on the chair?"

"I, um, called you both here to ask you about an idea I had." She laid her hand on mine. "It has to do with our father, Patricia."

I felt like making a joke, like, "No! Don't tell me he's dead!" But I held my tongue while she ranted about how a man of

Bernie Kyle's stature should have a more impressive monument than what he now lay under. That this is what the drawing represented. She felt this would be a way to feel closer to a father she'd never met. Then she added that she and Arthur would handle the arrangements.

"Well, we would certainly want to share the cost of the stone," said my mother, as if this was all okay.

"Whoa! Wait a minute," I said, wondering if Olive had managed to spike my mother's tea when I wasn't looking. "Don't I have a say in this?"

"Of course, Patricia," Olive had said cheerfully. "After all, he was your father too."

Was she actually serious? I said, "Thank you, Olive, for pointing that out. But the stone my mother chose for my father will stay exactly where it is."

Had that sounded so harsh that my mother was forced to draw her breath in sharply? Olive, I noticed, had cast her eyes down to her folded hands.

I tried to explain. "It's just that my mother and I actually knew my father and we were the ones who watched him die. And maybe that's why I feel we have a right to the headstone we chose for him."

"Of course you do, of course," said Olive, looking thoughtful. "Believe me, I worried that I might be stepping on toes here. And if you feel so strongly about this, we'll forget I ever brought it up."

"Okay, great," I said. I started to get up from my chair but my mother's hand on my arm brought me back down.

Olive said, "I have to confess something to you, Patricia. I spoke to your mother about this beforehand."

"Oh, really," I said. The sun had chosen that moment to come streaming in through the small paned windows. I felt a buzzing in my head. My mother continued to look at Olive as if I wasn't even in the room.

"Yes," Olive said. "You know I've tried to talk to you several times about our father. So I just felt ... that this would help me to connect with him somehow. You see, I know you spent a lifetime with him, but all I have are a few snapshots."

"Well, why didn't you say so?" Maybe I sounded kind of shrill here. "We have a whole slew of home movies. I'll lend them to you so you can feel closer to my fath ... Bernie."

My mother jumped in then. "What a good idea, Trish. What do you say we go home now and think about the headstone, and then we'll get together next week to watch the movies."

"Excellent!" said Olive.

"You're forgetting I work all week?" I said.

My mother smiled at me the same way she used to smile at my father when he was being difficult. "You're forgetting you don't work on Saturdays?"

So Olive got her headstone. All I had to do was imagine giving up a Saturday to sit in a dark room with Olive watching my private family life. I got my way with one thing though. Olive's fancy headstone would sit next to ours rather than replace it. That was fine with Olive. The headstone was a symbolic gesture. That's all she really wanted.

"Sure, purely symbolic," I muttered to Ray, a week after the thing was installed and we had all gathered for the unveiling of said gesture. Looming huge over our simple stone was a massive red marble obelisk inscribed with the words: "O death, where is thy sting? O grave, where is thy victory?" There would be no missing Bernie Kyle's grave now. In the winter you can actually see it all the way from Thunder Hill Road.

It turned out that Olive had more in store for us. Apparently it would be *truly* symbolic, as well as healing, if Bernie Kyle's progeny held hands in a united circle around his grave. So there we were, Olive and me, the twins, and Gayl and Biz, with our heads bowed, observing a long moment of silence.

"Father," Olive spoke, addressing the ground. "We are joining you today to show you the fruits of your life. Standing before you are all three granddaughters, along with your only grandson, each of them special, each of them a part of you."

She bowed her head again. Above our heads the aspen leaves shimmered and sighed.

Beside me, Gayl tapped her shoe against mine. "Can we go now?" she whispered.

"Probably not," I whispered back.

Olive continued to address the headstone. "Your two daughters are also present, father. It is because of your generosity that we are able to stand united here, each of us filled with the shared honour of being your children. We hope in our hearts that you can, in some way, be a witness to this moment, and that you find yourself as pleased as we are, to have found each other."

As Olive squeezed my hand, I couldn't help but picture my father reeling in his grave. Here was Olive, making us all go along with the story of her being his child and leaving Kyle House to her out of love, when everyone knew it was an act of revenge for me turning it down all those years ago.

On the other side of me I could feel Gayl squeezing my hand too, like she knew exactly what I was thinking. I squeezed hers back and there we all stood, holding hands in the dappled sunlight filtering through the aspens for as long as Olive seemed to feel we should.

From where I now sit, at Olive's window, I can almost make out that big red monstrosity through the aspens. It's the only thing out there in the gloom that has any colour. The snow has been switching from sleet to rain this entire afternoon. A dirty day, my father would have said.

After lunch, Olive hauled out flour and bowls and newspaper and paints. The four of us sat down and got to work. So now, three hours later, four very ugly papier-mâché masks sit on the table. Three of them wear cheerful smiles, while one wears a mouth in the shape of an O and looks like it's terrified.

I guess I'll be staying here, at least for tonight. I'm feeling hungry so I offer to make some scrambled eggs for supper. Olive won't hear of it and when I tell her I don't want to be a mooch, she says I can take care of the clean-up. In the meantime, perhaps I could entertain the twins?

I take them up the front stairs to introduce them to my old banister horse. I get a pillow from the linen closet and drape it over the railing like a saddle just as I had as a kid. I ask them if they have a skipping rope, and when they fetch one, I slip it around the newel post to use as reins. They stare at me as I mount the old banister I used to call, "Thunder." I pick up the reins and pretend to break into a trot. Kira asks if my parents allowed me to play on something so high off the ground. It's only a three-stair drop to the landing, I tell her, but they keep looking at me like I'm batty, especially when I dismount and pat Thunder's head, which is, of course, the newel post. Then they run off to play with the cut-out dolls Olive made from cereal boxes.

Back in the kitchen, Olive had whipped up some oriental noodle dish. It's loaded with peas and the skinniest mushrooms I've ever seen. She even made what she calls miso soup, which feels pretty great on my stomach. When I ask where she ever found this, she says she always has it on hand, that the twins practically live on miso soup. I think I remember this soup from way back in Toronto, but this is the first time I've had it since.

It's time to clean up, and what a chore this turns out to be. The water has to be pumped from the summer kitchen, brought into the kitchen, and poured into the water reservoir on the stove, where it gets heated and hauled in here to the bathtub. Why the bathtub and not the kitchen sink? She tells me the sink is blocked because her fancy garburator can't function without power. So, as soon as the water gets hot enough, I take the dishpan into the bathroom and get to work. The twins help by bringing me all the dishes and pots, plus all the little sauce dishes and chopsticks, and here I am, on my knees, scrubbing and rinsing while out there in the kitchen Olive is setting up a chess set on the table for the twins. It's almost nine o'clock at night and I have a mountain of dishes to get through before I can collapse up in my old bedroom. Looks as though I'm Olive's new cleaning lady. I wonder what my father would think if only he could see me now.

16. The Blueberry King

EVERY SUNDAY MORNING MY father drove his Oldsmobile across the county to view his blueberry fields. Sometimes my mother made him take me with him. If there happened to be a fog sitting on top of Thunder Hill and if he was in the mood, we'd stop and watch thin blades of sunlight slice through the trees and the fog. The scene reminded me of the pictures of heaven hanging on the walls in Sunday school. And if my father remembered to bring along some empty jugs, we'd fill them with spring water gurgling from a pipe at the top of the hill. I loved going on these drives.

The other side of Thunder Hill is a whole different world from our side. Where we have red sand and loamy soil and fields full of clover or crops, this land is hilly and rocky and perfect for blueberries. While we drove, my father would say things like, "In the spring you can't drive by this hill without seeing a deer," or, "There's the first field I ever bought. It was nothing but alders then, but it sure has shaped up since."

In that part of the county there were many villages. They all had churches on Main Street and a cenotaph at the busiest intersection. Best of all, they had diners. We'd stop for lunch and sit at the counter, and I'd order a grilled cheese sandwich with chocolate milk. My father would joke around with the waitresses who called me sweetheart.

The last time I went on one of these trips I would have been about ten. We were having our lunch when my father suddenly

rose from his counter stool to go outside to speak to some woman
he had noticed walking by the window. Through the window I
watched the top of his hat as it bobbed and nodded at the woman
who seemed to be all upset about something. But then she must
have said something funny because I saw him laugh before they
moved out of sight.

The waitress who my father had been joking with just before
he went outside was busy talking to another customer at the
other end of the counter, but I noticed she kept looking out the
window too. I didn't like the way her lipstick made her mouth
look like it was only pretending to be a mouth. My father still
hadn't come back by the time I finished my crusts and I wondered
if he'd forgotten about me. Then I got bored, so I started spinning around on my stool. Faster and faster, I spun, like I was on
a carnival ride. How fun seeing the flash of green walls, shiny
counter, hat through the window, and glasses lined in front of
the mirror; then green wall, shiny counter, hat, glasses; and green
wall, counter, hat, glasses.... The waitress's voice sounded like
a slowed-down record when I heard her say, "Catch that little
girl, will you Carl? Before she hits the floor?"

He must have been too late, because the next thing I knew I
was looking up at the waitress and smelling her coffee breath
as she fanned my face with a place mat.

"Can you hear me sweetheart?"

When I remembered spinning on the stool, I started to gag.
I looked up to see my father rushing through the doorway. As
soon as he reached me, I threw up on his shoes.

"One minute she was sitting there and the next thing she was
on the floor," the waitress said, handing him some paper towels.
"I'm not a baby-sitter, you know."

My father squatted down and wiped my mouth with his hand-
kerchief. Then he started on his own shoes.

The waitress stood there with her arms folded, impatiently
tapping her toe.

On the way out of town, I pressed my cheek against the window and watched the houses flick by. My arm was still sore from my father squeezing it as we left the restaurant. The closer we got to the car the harder he'd squeezed and he'd practically thrown me into the car. I said I was sorry for throwing up on his shoes. He said I should be sorry for making a nuisance out of myself while he was discussing business with someone. He should have known better than to bring me along. For the rest of the trip home he didn't say a word to me, but I still felt sick to my stomach. I saw someone washing a car and I saw a dog tied up in a yard, but mostly I remembered my father forgetting all about me while he talked with the woman outside the diner.

Well, I have just collapsed onto my old bed in my old bedroom. It took me over an hour to clean up all those dishes. And just as I had almost scrubbed the crud out of the frying pan, Olive said from the doorway, "That's the problem with cast iron. They stick. But they also provide us with traces of iron."

"Does that make it ironic?" Kyla said from the kitchen.

Olive laughed and laughed. "That's very clever, Kyla. But what's really ironic is that we live in a house full of modern appliances and with one little storm, Mother Nature throws us back to an age as old as this house. I know I keep saying this but let's be thankful that we also have that wood stove." She had picked up a tea towel and had begun to dry and stack the dishes on top of the bureau beside the tub.

"Yeah, but too bad we don't have a kitchen sink," I reminded her, as I straightened up.

"Poor you," she said. "Let me rub your back."

"No, it's okay. Really."

That's when I lit a candle and headed up the back stairway to the little room over the kitchen that I used to call my own. Before I blew out the candle I took a good look around. I have to say that seeing my old furniture and the dormer window creeps me right out. It's as if the girl who used to live here is dead, and I have no right to be here in her place. Although I don't know

who else deserves to be here more than I do. At least I have
Suzie under the bed. I wait for sleep to take me somewhere far
away from here.

Bear used to sit beside me on the couch and lay his hand on
my belly. The first time the baby moved for him, he jerked his
hand away. "What was that? Jeez, that's weird."

I told him it was likely a knee or an elbow, and yes, it felt
funny to me too, to have someone living in my body like that.
Then I'd taken his hand and waited with it there until he could
feel it again.

"It's like there's a little alien living in there."

Another time he asked me if he could hear the heartbeat, so I
let him nestle his head in my lap and listen. I remember looking
down at his face, at how hard he seemed to be concentrating.

"Wow, you heard the heartbeat yet, man?" he said to Ray, who
was trying to fix the sound system. Ray had just brought down
his reel to reel from our bedroom to the living room because
people had been giving him a hard time about not sharing his
things. But now that it was communal property, it was always
conking out.

"Yeah, sure," Ray said, totally involved in the repair job.
"Cool, eh?"

That was Ray for you. It wasn't like he wasn't interested in
the baby, he just wanted the whole process to hurry up so he
could see and hold his own child. Plus, I think because it was in
my body, he felt it belonged more to me, which was true maybe,
but still…. I tried to involve him in every little sensation I was
feeling, like the time she seemed to be knocking on my cervix
to get out, or when she had the hiccups, that sort of thing. "Far
out," he'd say. So it was fun to have Bear pay so much attention to my pregnancy. Ray seemed to be happy about that too.
Maybe he was hoping I'd complain to Bear instead of him about
the heartburn and having to pee every ten minutes and all the
crying I was doing for no good reason.

On the very day that I had turned down the deed to Kyle House, Ray ran off to town to get drunk. The others had smoked some weed before heading down the road to a farm auction, but Bear said he felt it was his moral responsibility to stay beside a pregnant woman who had just been abandoned by her mate. I thanked him for putting it that way and told him if he really wanted to help he could help make a better world to bring a baby into. In other words, he could do some chores. So he did. He poly-filled some cracks in the kitchen windowsill and hauled wood up from the basement. I had him take all the rugs in the house out to the clothesline and give them a good beating. That evening he sat beside me on the couch as usual. I said, "Quick Bear, the baby's moving! Give me your hand."

He'd smiled. "Active little guy, isn't he?"

"Put your hand right here."

"Um..." he said, looking down at his hands. "They're pretty grubby from cleaning the rugs."

"So wash them."

"I don't think I should."

"You don't think you should wash your hands?"

"No. I will after."

Why wouldn't he touch me? I thought it had something to do with me, so I said, "Bear, do you think I've grown uglier since I got pregnant?"

"No way. Pregnant women are beautiful!"

"You're just saying that to make me feel better for looking so fat."

"You're not fat, you're sexy round, sort of like spaghetti squash." I guess he could tell this wasn't cheering me up, because he added, "Put it this way, if I was Ray I wouldn't dare leave you alone for a second."

I burst into tears, and Bear got up to go into the kitchen. Before he left the room though, he stood in the doorway and with his back to me said, "Good thing for Ray that he has me for a friend."

Somehow, that made me feel better. It was nice to know there'd always be Bear.

But after what happened last night on the pool table, only I guess it's safe to say, what didn't happen, I'm thinking of Bear in a totally different way. I want to think of him like he's mine. Remembering all that stuff going on there on the pool table, makes me replay it with the help of a few fingers. But just when I'm almost there, I remember him pulling away from me, and that cools me down quicker than a dip in the strait in January. Was it all about Bear's loyalty to Ray? It hits me now, like a snowplow, that maybe I'd always been wrong about Bear's secret desire for me. I'd always been so sure of that, kind of like I'd always been so sure of Ray's love for me.

17. My Father's Voice

MY EYES POP OPEN like I'd never even been asleep, although the taste of sleep in my mouth tells me I have been. I may have just been thinking about Bear and Ray but theirs aren't the voices that have just rattled me awake in my old bedroom. It's none other than my father who spoke my name. I swallow hard. His voice is still fresh in my ears. My father who art in heaven. And here I thought I'd gotten used to him being dead.

There's a hot air register in the middle of the floor. Directly below it is the kitchen. When I was a kid, I'd lie on the floor in front of it and listen to everything I wasn't supposed to hear. Usually it was boring talk about the blueberry business or gossip about people in town who I didn't even know, and sometimes I'd fall asleep there on the floor. When I woke up, I'd have an imprint of the iron grid stuck on my cheek. I'd rub at it until it smoothed away because I couldn't let my parents in on my secret spying place. It's through the register when I was about eleven that I first heard about Olive.

At first, I wondered what my mother was doing down there in the kitchen waving around a piece of paper. She was saying, "Now she's getting her kid to send you drawings."

"What are you getting mad at me about?" I heard my father say. "I didn't ask her to send me a drawing. But it's a pretty good drawing. She must know I like schooners."

"You mean Phyllis knows you like schooners. And this is how

she's trying to get at you."

My father said, "If you recall, Phyllis got to me long before you got to me. She's *still* got me if you hadn't noticed the cheques going out to her."

It got so quiet down there I twisted my head so I could try to see this drawing. In the meantime, my mother had rolled it up and looked as though she was trying to squeeze it to death.

"What I want to know is what you're going to do about it."

"I guess I should thank her for it when I send the cheque."

"You want to know what I think?"

I heard my father sigh. "No, Bette, what do you think?"

I heard my mother's voice rise, and I could hear the boozy edge to it. "I think she's getting her kid to send these drawings so she'll worm her way back into your life."

"So what if she is? We have a settlement and I'm not about to add to it," I could hear my father's voice growing cold. "So you can relax."

My mother's voice got shrill. "How am I supposed to relax when she's pulling stunts like this?"

"Here we go. Wind her up and let her go."

"I don't think you should be writing to Olive. It'll just get her hopes up and that's not fair to do to a child especially if she isn't yours."

Olive. That was the first time I heard her name. The only Olive I knew was Popeye's Olive Oyl. But here was this Olive who could somehow make my parents as angry as I could.

My father was laughing now. "As if you're concerned about Olive's feelings! Don't bullshit a bullshitter, Bette. But if you're so worried that I'll get involved with Phyllis's kid, then how about if *you* write a thank you note to her."

I must have moved and made a floorboard squeak because the next thing I knew, the talk in the kitchen had stopped and my father was standing right under the register. His voice switched to the jokey one he used with me.

"I think there must be a little mouse up there, Bette."

My mother must not have caught on because she said, "What are you talking about?"

My father's balding head had moved directly under me and he was peering up.

I opened my mouth to say, "Very funny," but instead, a gob of drool fell through the register onto his forehead. I didn't even get a chance to squeak out that I was sorry, that it was an accident, that I had thought the mouse joke was funny. The next thing I knew he was pounding up the back stairs.

I never knew what to expect at times like this. He might still be in a joking mood, which would mean torture by tickling, which would made me shriek and squirm with helpless laughter. Or, he might be mad enough to grab me by the arms and shake the living daylights out of me. My mother might call up the stairs, "Don't go crazy up there, Bernie." All I could do was to wait for this monster to leave my father. When it left, almost as quickly as it appeared, he'd sit beside me on my bed and read poems from a book by William Blake. And sometimes, if he felt really bad, there'd be talk about hunting, and how he might take me along with him next deer season.

This time though, as his footsteps came pounding up the back stairs, I slipped behind my door. He charged into my room like a mad bull, swinging his head looking around for me. When he saw me I stood up straight and folded my arms across my chest the way my mother did and glared at him. "Who the heck is Olive?"

I expected him to really lose it, but instead I saw a pained look. When he turned away to look out the window, I knew I had discovered a new power. After that day, I'd just have to mention Olive's name and he'd turn away. It was like magic.

My mother was another story. I asked her about Olive that afternoon. She was getting potatoes ready for baking and she started stabbing them so hard the pulp flew around the kitchen. Finally, she put down her paring knife and said, "Come with me. It's time you knew about Olive."

We went to the front parlour to a small cherrywood desk in the corner. I stood beside my mother while I watched her write a letter to this Olive girl who, my mother explained, mistakenly thought that she was my father's child. I had heard about my father's ex-wife Phyllis many times, but this was the first mention of Olive. "Another man was her father but he disappeared so Olive's mother wants her to think of your father as hers too."

"How old is she?" I asked.

"I guess she'd be thirteen or fourteen by now."

The letter, my mother explained, was supposed to be coming from my father, since he was the recipient of the drawing, but it was important that we keep it short. She wrote something on a plain piece of notepaper and read it to me: "Thank you very much, Olive, for the lovely drawing of the boat. My wife and I think you draw very well."

My mother's pen hovered over the next line for a time before she signed it, "Best regards, Bernie Kyle."

The envelopes were addressed to Olive's mother, as each month for eighteen years my father would cough up a cheque for this child he didn't believe was his. For a few more years a drawing would come addressed to my father near his birthday, and each time my mother would pop in the same note to Olive with the cheque to Phyllis. This was a strange time for me, to not only be learning about this false half sister, but to be in cahoots with my mother in this way. I thought all this pretending was very strange, especially because my father never mentioned Olive or her drawings again. All I knew is that he expected my mother to take care of this obligation, knowing full well how she felt about his former life and former wife. I guessed that Olive or her mother must have finally gotten the message because the drawings stopped as soon as the cheques had.

As for the possibility that Olive really was my half sister? Obviously, the letters hadn't rocked her faith entirely, seeing how, from the moment she arrived in Thunder Hill, she was hell-bent on making a sister out of me.

Like the time she phoned when Ray and I were hunkered down in front of the TV, not long after Ray had begun to come home from Newville on weekends. We were spending so much time bouncing on our bed that one night the mattress broke through the frame and we found ourselves on the floor. Thank goodness Suzie had always had the good sense to crawl out from her spot under the bed whenever she detected the slightest hint of activity. We could picture her rolling her eyes whenever she sighed and moved to the mat in front of my dresser. After the mattress fell through the frame, she stopped going under the bed at all.

On this particular night when Olive phoned, we'd been lying on the couch, just waiting for one of us to make the first move. Our legs were entwined, and I had been in the process of inching my foot up his leg when the phone rang and there was Olive screaming that we had to come over to Kyle House as soon as possible. There was no getting anything more out of her. We ran across our muddy yard, our jackets thrown over our heads against the rain. I imagined the worst as we drove the entire stretch along Thunder Hill Road — a fall, a serious cut, a heart attack. It's a good thing Ray knew the road so well, because the driving rain made it almost invisible. Finally, we parked the truck at Kyle House, next to two unfamiliar cars. We jumped over puddles and dashed through the rain to the house.

"Thank goodness you got here on time!" Olive said breathlessly as she greeted us at the door. Before we even had a chance to take off our jackets, she had pressed a wine glass into my hand. "I could not envision drinking this wine without my official sommelier present!"

Olive stores her wine in the cellar. Whenever she holds one of her famous dinner parties, like the one Ray and I had just been thrust into, she clumps down the stairs in her house clogs and returns with a dusty bottle. She passes it to Arthur like it's an infant to cradle and hold forth to be admired by the guests. The first time we came for dinner, Olive had pronounced me her official "sommelier," a word which, until that night, I had never heard. Now, as we stood dripping in the doorway of Kyle House, and the glass of wine was in my hand, several pairs of eyes peered at us, and I realized the reason Ray and I had been summoned.

"Well," said Olive in that shrill voice she gets when excited, "Taste the wine, Patricia. We've been waiting for your approval."

I did what she said, although I felt like screaming at her for being such a fucking maniac for scaring us like that, let alone dragging us from our comfy couch. I sniffed the wine and sipped. Then sipped again. I was introduced to the guests during all of this, Doctor Mirrin and his wife, Dora, who had recently moved to town. And I supposed the large man in the tweed jacket to be one of Arthur's colleagues from Toronto. How could I have forgotten? Olive had mentioned to me that very day that she was having a dinner party in honour of Arthur's colleague, whose name I forgot right away. Funny, though, I couldn't help thinking, she hadn't said anything about Ray and me coming then.

"What better way for you to meet my long-lost sister, Patricia Kyle, and my wonderful brother-in-law, Ray, than over a fine bottle of Coteaux du Languedoc?" Olive said to her guests, who looked happy to be finally allowed to drink their wine. "Patricia, what do you think?"

"About what?" I said. I had just noticed the doctor's wife glancing down at my nubby sweatshirt. "My dirty shirt?"

"No, silly," said Olive, in her tinkly social laugh. "The wine, of course."

As I stood there, searching for a word other than embarrassed, Ray clapped one hand onto my shoulder and almost shouted, "Robust!"

"That's the spirit, old man," said Arthur, who was obviously full of spirit himself, as he introduced Ray to his colleague as "a man's man."

The colleague, who had a big red face, acted as though Ray was really interesting, and Ray fell into the role happily enough, launching into his talk about road salt. He rattled off the numbers of metric tons used on the county's highways every winter and how a recipe of salt and calcium was spread on the roads in summer to keep the dust down. He scratched his forearm with his free hand. "But, like everything, how much we use depends on how dry the summers are."

"Fascinating," said the Doctor "And how long have you been in the salt business, Ray?"

"Only for about two months. Before that I was the school janitor."

"And a school bus driver," Olive added, passing around a plate of hors d'oeuvres. I could have sworn I saw her wink at the colleague. Why was it that only I could see how this whole thing was a set up to show off her quaint, yet inferior, relatives.

"Yes, and a school bus driver," Ray said, with genuine pride in his voice.

I have always been amazed by Ray's sense of self-esteem.

While Olive was showing off her summer kitchen, soon-to-be potter's studio, to her guests, I sipped my wine in the doorway of Olive's dining room and wondered how the hell I'd found myself in this situation. Each one of the seven settings on the table boasted silver napkin holders. Glasses and silverware sparkled under the antique chandelier she'd hauled down from Toronto. An arrangement of fall leaves and dried flowers sat in the centre of the table. It looked like Olive had been working on it the entire day. Wait a second, I thought. Seven table settings? That could mean that two guests had cancelled at the last moment. Ah, so that could also explain the last minute invitation.

And maybe that explains what I said later over supper.

It started off innocently enough, with Olive informing her guests that I had spent all of my childhood summers in the house.

The Doctor's wife asked me if I missed calling Kyle House my home.

"Not at all," I said, as I rushed down another gulp of wine. "My mother hated it here and truth be known, I didn't care much for it either."

"Oh no? But it's such a charming house! What could you possibly find wrong with it?"

"What was wrong with it?" I said. "You mean, what was right? First there were the earwigs. We used to find them crawling through our toothbrushes." I think I shuddered here just before I held out my glass for Arthur to refill. "But they weren't nearly as bad as the rats! You could hear them running through the walls. The only way to get rid of them was with poison and then they'd stink up the place for weeks. I bet there's hundreds of rat skeletons in these walls."

I felt a tap against my leg. I looked at Ray who was sitting across from me.

"I'm only telling you how it was when I lived here," I said, lowering my voice when I felt, rather than saw, Olive's stare.

"But we think Olive has done a fabulous job of fixing it up, don't we, Trish?" Ray said, kicking my shin again.

"Oh, for sure," I said, and even added, "she's done an amazing job with the place."

"And we appreciate it so much!" Olive said, waving her hand around the dining room. "I can't understand how anyone could not absolutely love this house!"

"I can't either!" gushed Dora, the doctor's wife, while the others murmured their agreement.

"Of course, everyone has his or her own taste," Olive said, as she passed along a bowl of chutney. "I must confess I've often thought it would be nice to have a smaller place, like Patricia and Ray's. It's as cute as a button with much less upkeep."

"Are you ever wrong there," Ray said, and then proceeded to cheerfully rattle off some of the many problems with our own home, beginning with the mildew in the bathroom. He moved through the draftiness of the windows and how each winter we tacked them up with plastic.

I resisted the urge to kick him back because I knew he'd come right out and ask me why I was kicking him.

"Eh, Trish? And the clutter! There's where you're wrong about living in a smaller place, Olive. Just look around this house and you can see there's a spot for everything." He shook his head and sighed. "I can't tell you how much I admire that in a house."

"Oh, come now," said a glowing Olive, who now passed him candied sweet potatoes and leaned forward in her chair to address her guests. "I've been to Patricia and Ray's place on numerous occasions and I assure you their home is very ... homey."

"Homey." I'd heard her use that word before when talking about the Four Reasons, and she used it sometimes to refer to people from around here, especially if they were overweight.

"Excuse me," I said, and left the table. I wandered down the hall to the front parlour.

My mother had called this room the red parlour because of the velour love seat and chairs that Olive's mother had bought. Three decades of renting the house out to summer vacationers had left them tattered and stained, but Olive had had them re-upholstered in green velvet. It felt like forever since I'd been in the room. The writing desk where my mother had penned the letters to Olive was gone, but I noticed the door of my parents' old hi-fi was open. I'd forgotten about this thing, and I was surprised it hadn't been tossed out on its ear as well. I reached in and pulled out an old record. Nancy Sinatra.

"Did your parents dance together in here too?"

Olive's voice almost made me drop it. She swept into the room in her long corduroy dress and took the record from my hands. I watched her pop it onto my parents' old turntable. Nancy Sinatra's "These Boots Are Made For Walkin" suddenly filled the room. Olive turned to look at me, her hands gripping the edge of the hi-fi. "My mother told me she and my father danced at every ball and dance in the province. Not to this fluff, of course.

They danced to the big band sound. She said that everyone in the room stopped what they were doing, just so they could watch my parents dance."

Maybe it was her look of satisfaction that ticked me off.

I said, "You know, I can't say I ever saw my parents dancing in here. But they used to play some of these old records at suppertime. And sometimes my father would jump up from the table and get my mother dancing with him in the kitchen. And sometimes..." I looked her straight in the eye. "I danced with him too."

Olive's mouth twisted, like she'd just bitten into a lemon. Then she sniffed and said, "Byron informs me they're now called vinyls. Naturally, he thinks these things were invented by his generation. Do you find that with Gayl? That absolutely nothing existed before she was born?"

I had to smile at this, because in spite of the crap between Olive and me, there's nothing like the subject of kids to bring two mothers around to the same page. I said, "Absolutely nothing. Including us."

Then I followed her back to the dining room where the others sat admiring a large bowl of trifle topped with freshly whipped cream.

18. Day Three

I'M AWAKE. AND IT must be morning. That's all I can tell.
Because except for that dormer window, the one that has
clumps of little lacy flowers on the sheers, I can see that I'm
not home. *Home?* Maybe I'm in one of those dreams where
I'm in a place that only *seems* familiar. Oh, now I hear a slurping noise that can only come from a certain dog named Suzie,
who's probably licking her privates under this bed. Okay, it's
coming back to me now. My old bedroom in Kyle House, me
at forty-some years of age, not a child at all, which explains
why there aren't horses on the curtains like there used to be.
There was a bad storm and now I'm Olive's pet refugee.

"Time to face the day, Suzie," I say, as my feet hit the floor.
A very cold floor, in spite of the warm kitchen below. No
sounds are wafting up from the kitchen, but the smell of porridge sure is.

I throw on the sweater Olive loaned me yesterday, and with
Suzie at my heels, I squeak my way down the dark back stairway
to the kitchen. I wonder if I'll be greeted with another mountain
of dishes in the tub to wash. Here it is Monday and for once I
wouldn't mind going to work at Foghorn. No question of that,
I see as I look out the kitchen window at the snow that's still
coming down. I feel like shaking my fist at the sky out there
and shouting, don't you know what month it is?

There's no sign of Olive or the twins. The table, I notice, is set
with bowl and spoon and a teacup with a note tucked inside.

*Have gone for provisions with the girls. I'll phone your
mother and Gayl and Ray to tell them you are staying
with us. Porridge is on stove. Make some tea and be cozy.
We'll be back before you know it, Olive*

Wonderful. I bet she'll tell Ray all about the flue fire. And
then she'll tell him all about my night on a pool table with Bear
James.

At the thought of Bear James, my stomach lurches like a teen-
age girl thinking about her first kiss. Ever since the other night,
the man I've valued as nothing more than a friend for twenty
years, suddenly has this whole new role in my life. I remember
way back to a night at the Roll-a-Way Tavern when I sat in the
booth between Bear and Ray. Bear's thumb was wrestling with
mine, and Ray's fingers were braiding the fringes on my vest, and
judging by the way neither of them were about to give up their
game I figured a choice had to be made. Someone had put on a
reggae tune, which was a new and interesting sound. We got to
dancing and swaying to "No Woman, No Cry." Bear had his arms
across my shoulders and I could feel Ray move behind me and
it must have been the way he held my hips that made my head
tip back and he kissed my hair and the choice was made. We all
seemed to know it too. Bear just sort of backed up and started
dancing with Angie Dove and when I caught his eye he winked
at me. He left the building then, with Angie hanging on to his
sleeve. After that, Ray and I found ourselves bumping around in
the girl's bathroom stall, all elbows and knees. It was a magical
night, I remember thinking, because it seemed like Ray and I
were meant to be. I used to think that that meant forever.

Here I am now, looking out Olive's window at the clouds
regrouping over Thunder Hill and I'm thinking that maybe the
time has come to play things out in a different way. Now, is this
wisdom talking here, or simple foolish fantasy? Maybe Alana
is right when she says that all wisdom amounts to is a bag of
marbles if you can't apply it to your own life. Is it wisdom that

screams out that life is short and I should have a go at Bear? Or
is this simply a case of hormones gone wild?

Out the window I see Billy chugging up the lane looking like
a tank trying to pull through mud instead of snow. The engine
roars past the summer kitchen kicking up all the fresh snow
that has fallen and pulls up beside the barn. The twins tumble
out of the back while Olive and a fourth person grab groceries
out of the back.

Now, who the hell is that woman? Is it a woman? By the way
the figure is hunched under the weight of a parka that looks two
sizes too big, it's hard to tell. Olive is pointing in the direction
of the cemetery. The way she's waving with her hand suggests
she's talking about my father being buried there and how she
had created this amazing monument in his honour. The figure
shields its eyes with one hand even though there's no sun. Now,
they're turning towards the house. There's something familiar
about the way this person carries one arm in front of its body,
like it's in a cast. It's a she, I'm pretty sure of it, and she reminds
me of Rena Dickson whose arm got mangled in a wood shredder
when she was a kid. Everyone felt sorry for her, that her father
would have taken her to his work like that. Funny how public
opinion changed when she grew up and started going through
all the boys in town like a deck of cards. Back then, the boys
just thought it was cool that this girl would get high with them
and politely ask them to pull out their dicks. I heard that if they
resisted she'd talk so dirty they had no choice but to obey. Hey,
free love and all, the boys would say, looking all sheepish and
confused if anyone found out. And really, what could we girls
say at the time? After all, we were trying to be cool about our
sisters. Sisterhood was powerful, right? Until we sisters started
getting pregnant, that is, and suddenly we weren't so generous
in our thinking. We began to watch Rena Dickson like a flock
of wary hens.

Whoever she is out there, she seems to be asking Olive a lot
of questions. There they go, to the barn, their boots breaking

through the crusty snow. And here come the twins towards the house. Into the summer kitchen they stomp, their arms loaded with grocery bags. I go out to help and ask, "Who is that?"

They shrug. "A woman was standing by the road."

"Where? Near the Four Reasons? Near the bridge?" I unravel Kira's scarf and hang Kyla's jacket up for her.

"Near that old cottage down from the store."

It comes back to me then; the cracks of light coming from the boarded up Chase place, and me not wanting Bear to turn around in the storm. So it *was* Rena Dickson in the Chase cottage. And now Rena Dickson is here at Kyle House.

Back in the day, Rena didn't limit herself just to the boys. We'd sometimes see a car idling out there by the industrial park, some business guy sitting straight up in his seat, his eyes staring straight ahead.

When Rena gave all that up to move in with Ricky Chase, who was my cousin Nancy's boyfriend before she left for good, it would have been fair to say a collective sigh of relief ran through the town. And not just from the women. I wouldn't be surprised if the men may have been the most terrified. After all, getting caught in a romp with Rena could have cost them their entire families.

"Rena, this is..." Olive begins, as they enter the house

"Nurse Trish. I know," says Rena with a smile that says she knows me only too well.

"Nurse Trish?" Olive repeats, looking confused.

Just hearing her call me that name causes my bowels to churn and believe me it has nothing to do with her blowing the boys way back then.

"Oh, that." I force myself to chuckle because that's the only thing that keeps me from choking. No one has called me that since the night the farm fell apart. So I say, "Oh, 'Nurse' was a little nickname I picked up because I was so good at removing splinters. Everybody was always getting splinters back then from handling barn boards, right Rena? I don't know about up there in the city, Olive, but down here everybody was nailing up old barn wood in their kitchens. You know, for that rustic look. But the problem was, besides it being full of bugs, there were all those splinters we got from handling the wood. Splinter removal has always been my specialty."

Olive looks at me like she's never heard me put so many words together at once. I've been staring at the walls all this time and don't dare look at Rena. I can feel Rena looking at me too, and just as I turn to meet her eyes there's a knock at the door. We hadn't even heard a truck pull into the yard.

19. The Linemen

OLIVE OPENS THE DOOR. Standing there in storm gear is a lineman from the power company. Could he trouble us for some hot water for his thermos? He and his buddies have run out of coffee and they're working on the transformer at the end of Olive's lane.

Ten minutes later, all three men are in the kitchen, boots warming in front of the stove, gloves propped up in the bread warmer along with Rena's. The drying pole hanging above the stove is bright with wet, yellow snowmobile suits. The room suddenly smells like men. I had been thinking that it was time to make a trip to the Four Reasons myself, but now I'm thinking I might wait a bit.

When they first came in the door they'd all looked like heroes to our rescue in their yellow gear and hard hats. Now that their suits and hats are off they look like three regular guys standing in a kitchen. The oldest guy has a pouchy face. The taller one looks like Billy Bob Thornton. The younger one with the tousled brown hair has eyes the colour of blueberries and the way his eyes are looking at me right now is making me squirm in my chair.

They're all standing there like they don't know what to do with their hands. A moment later and Olive has hustled them to the table. So now they're wearing the biggest smiles you'd ever see on three men. For a moment I forget I'm in my forties and think those smiles are about finding themselves in a the company of young women, but now I'm realizing the smiles might be more about the good fortune of stumbling into a warm kitchen belonging to a cook named Olive. Olive, who is, today, dressed in a soft flannel skirt and capable looking apron.

Today's soup contains eggplant and potato and zucchini with a sprinkle of grated Parmesan and fresh parsley. Who has stuff like that kicking around their kitchen in Thunder Hill at the best of times, but, especially, at the end of winter during a snowstorm?

Blueberry Eyes says, "This is the best soup I've ever tasted, and I'm not kidding."

The others seem to agree as they reach for more bread. We ask them questions about the storm. How widespread is the power outage? Sporadic, they say. One county might be down and the one next to it up. The roads are bad everywhere. In fact, they'd had to get here by way of Newville.

"The road is open through to Newville?" I say.

One of the men nods. "Oh it's open, and not nearly as drifted over as some are. But some slippery! A salt truck must have passed a few minutes ahead of us, but the freezing rain covered the salt right over." They tell us that with any luck we should get the power back within a day or two.

We eat in silence for a bit. Well, hardly silence, since Rena is slurping up her soup like she hasn't eaten in days. Then she licks her spoon and points to the cracked and blackened bowl holding the bread. "How'd that bowl get so burnt?"

Olive's eyes brighten. "It's an ancient Japanese method of firing pottery. It's called raku."

"You mean they made it that way on purpose?" Rena says.

Olive laughs. "Actually, I made it that way on purpose. Shall I tell you how it's done?"

"I'm way more interested in knowing why it's done."

"Why it's done?" asks Olive.

"Yeah. Why would anyone want a perfectly good bowl to look all burnt?"

I try not to smirk. Olive is always going on about her bloody raku pieces.

"Excellent question!" says Olive. "But I warn you, don't get me going on the aesthetics of raku."

Time for me to jump in. I lean over to Blueberry Eyes, the one the others have called John, and I say, "I hear the storm is especially bad down Newville way."

He pulls his gaze away from Olive's bowl. "It's pretty bad all over. This is the worst sucker I've ever seen in April."

"No kidding," I say. "My husband is stuck down in Newville."

He grins. "No shit! My wife is stuck in the city."

"Hey, it's like God created this storm just for you two!" the pouchy-faced guy nudges Billy Bob.

I can't believe I'm blushing. I'm quite used to getting teased by Danny and Bear, but having Blueberry Eyes, I mean, John, acting like he's checking me out is making me resist the urge to run my fingers through my hair, which Alana once told me was a blatant sexual signal. Stop it, I tell myself. I likely remind him of his mother or something. But when I sneak a peek at him his eyes squarely meet my own.

"You make a lot of these bowls on purpose?" Rena is asking.

Olive suddenly pushes her chair back causing the sleeping dogs to raise their heads from where they are sprawled all over the kitchen floor. "Come with me, all of you. I'll show you my pottery room. Come!"

"I'll wait here," I say, and quickly add, "and clean up."

"I think I'll stay here too," says John. "Where it's warm."

Olive's shoes are already clumping up the back stairs, leaving Rena and the two linemen no choice but to pad up after her in their stocking feet. They are followed by the twins and the pups. As usual, Suzie stays right where I am.

"Watch your heads," Olive calls back as the men duck their heads under the doorway. "Men are a lot taller today than they were a hundred years ago."

This means I am left alone, alone with what I've decided is a fine specimen of a man indeed. Barely thirty I'd say, and looking hard as rock. Did I just run my tongue over my lips? What the hell is going on with you, Irish? It's like you're in frigging heat.

"It's the dampness out there that gets to you," he says, rubbing his hands over the stovetop.

"I know what you mean," I say, sitting up taller in my chair. "I hate feeling chilled."

He looks up at the ceiling. "Noisy bunch up there."

I roll my eyes and nod. I can tell exactly where the tour is by where the footsteps are over our heads. They have passed my room and the bathroom next to it and are lingering long enough to admire the clawfoot bathtub that Olive had placed right in the middle of the floor.

I know this tour well. A marble statue of a nude couple locked in an embrace — a gift to Olive from Arthur — stands in one corner of their bedroom. Engraved upon a bronze plate are the words of some poet named Robert Herrick: *"Thou art my life, my love, my heart, / the very eyes of me: / And hast command of every part, / To live and die for thee."* Olive will say something like, "My husband had this inscribed for me. His is the most romantic soul."

I bet those linemen are starting to wonder what they're in for with this tour.

"Do you all live here in this house?" John asks me.

"No, I got stranded here because of the storm," I say. "I'm staying in the room right at the top of these stairs."

"Oh." He nods.

"Yes," I say this firmly, pointedly. I decide to clear the dishes and in the process manage to knock a soup spoon off the table. We reach down at the same time and bump shoulders. Then I manage to spill some leftover milk onto one of his feet. "Sorry."

"Not nearly as sorry as I am." He laughs and takes off his sock.

"You would have been safer taking the tour," I say, slinging his sock over the drying pole. "You'll want to wash this when you get home. Otherwise it will stink like, like..."

I watch him knead his bare foot, especially the way his thumbs press into the flesh of a smooth arch.

"Like sour milk?"

"Exactly." I rub my hands up and down the sides of my jeans because I'm imagining how his hands might feel on my body, and that song "*if you can't be with the one you love...*" starts playing in my head because here I am, stuck in a storm, with no mate for a hundred miles and who knew if I had any mate left at all? Right now, right before my eyes is this very cute stranger who seems to like my company and, judging by the way he's looking at me, might like something more.

I listen to the clumping upstairs. They're likely in the big front hallway where Olive will be pointing to her paintings hanging along the wall. She'll be saying something like, "They're not very good. That's why I hung them up here."

"Not good?" One of them will likely say. "I think they're pretty damned great, if you ask me."

And on it will go. She'll show them all the pieces of raku that she has stored in one of the spare rooms. The trick with raku, she will tell them, is precision. The fire has to be at exactly the right temperature when you place the pottery directly into the flames. Then, using four-foot tongs, you carefully extract the piece and lower it into a barrel of sawdust. This process results in the burned and cracked effect in the bowl they saw on the table downstairs. She'll be telling them all of this while I'm leading John upstairs to my little room. If the tour continues as usual, I figure we'll have about fifteen minutes to ... to ... what's that he's saying now?

It seems that John has two children. He has just pulled their pictures from his wallet and is leaning close to show them to me. I like his smell. "Your kids are so sweet," I tell him, thinking how sweet he'd look on his back with his shirt undone and my fingers running down what looks from here to be a smooth and well defined chest. I'm betting he has dark silky hairs running down his belly. It's getting pretty hot here in Olive's kitchen. Maybe now is a good time to suggest we join the tour. We could go by way of the back stairs, by way of my old bedroom. I'll say something about filling in the part of the tour he missed, like my iron bedstead that's over a hundred years old. In mere minutes I might find myself holding onto the bars of the headboard while John kneads my breasts. I think he may have just asked me a question.

"I'm sorry, did you say something?"

"I asked if you have any kids."

My voice comes out in a croak. "One daughter."

"How old?"

"Oh, a little older than yours. Hey, do you want me to give you a tour up upstairs too?" I take a deep breath, and I can't believe I'm saying this but here it is: "I could show you where I sleep."

He looks at me for what seems like a long moment. Then he rubs his hands together and says it's likely pretty cold up there away from the heat. Then he starts talking about his wife, Crissy, who is a hairdresser, a colourist to be exact, and if I'm ever down their way I should get my hair coloured by her. She is part owner of the salon, he says proudly, and the name of it is indeed, "Crissy's." In fact, he'll make sure all three of us women get freebies for feeding him and his buddies today.

How to react? With as much dignity as I can muster. I tell him I'll certainly go to Crissy's, if I ever feel the need to colour my hair.

By now, the upstairs tour will have moved to the front stairway and down to the landing. Olive will introduce the group to her giant mural: a swirl of dark colours fall inward to what looks like a campfire.

"I call this painting, 'My Passion Well'," I hear Olive say. "But it's the only one I'll bring even part way down the stairs."

"You should bring them all downstairs," one of the men says. "I may not know art, but I know what I like and these are really good."

I hear Rena saying, "Maybe she wants to keep them for herself."

"You know, Rena, that is very astute of you. I suspect my family has become quite attached to seeing my paintings in the private part of their home."

"But you still let a bunch of strangers tramp through the private parts of your house."

"I've never minded showing my artwork to people who appreciate it."

"I used to feel the same way," Rena is saying as they come into the kitchen.

"Oh? About art?"

"No, about my private parts," Rena suddenly cackles, and gives Olive a solid punch on the shoulder.

One thing about Olive, I discover right here on the spot, is that she's not all that predictable. Like here I was expecting Olive to shy away from Rena like she was some sort of vermin. Or that she'd move to cover the twins' ears as they follow the linemen back into kitchen. But no, she starts up with her own brand of laugh, which amounts to a whole lot of snorts through her nose. And that, combined with Rena's cackle, makes them sound like a couple of old witches. Well, all of a sudden the men look pretty scared and I just stand there amazed until Olive shrieks, "I guess if I was really proud of my private parts I'd show those off instead of my paintings!" Now both of them are doubled over and falling onto the kitchen couch.

Funny how the linemen's visit ends right at this point. In spite of Olive's attempts to get them to stay for dessert, a chocolate pudding that would take mere minutes to prepare, they suddenly remember they have a job to do out there.

There's nothing for me to do now except hand John his sock. He reminds me to be sure to get my hair done at "Crissy's," and just before he goes out the door he plants a kiss right fair on my cheek. I blush at what was only meant as some sort of kindness. It sure doesn't take much these days.

On their way out, the men toot the utility truck horn and we women wave from the kitchen window. It has started snowing again — day three of the storm.

20. Escape

I T FEELS SOME GOOD to plunge the key deep into Billy's ignition. The truck roars for a second, then shudders before settling into a powerful purr. Overnight, it seems, the temperature has risen enough for the ice on the windshield to slide off easily with a tap of the scraper. For a moment there, this morning, the sun actually broke through the clouds, which caused everyone to cheer except me. Not because I wasn't happy to see the sun, but because I didn't want to appear too excited to be running away from Kyle House. "Which is exactly what we're doing, huh, girl?" I say to Suzie who is curled up beside me on the seat. I'm not quite sure how I'm going to accomplish this, since Olive has given me a long list of supplies to pick up at the Four Reasons. What gets me is what she has written at the top of the list in big letters: INVITE DANNY AND ALANA OVER FOR SUPPER AND BEAR JAMES TOO IF YOU SEE HIM.

Last night, I went up to bed as soon as the dishes were done — another mountain of them. How does one person generate so many dishes when serving leftover stew? Rena and I were kneeling side by side on the bath mat, our hands deep in the tub scooping up utensils, when Rena said, "Now, what do you suppose this is?"

"Parsley snipper," I said, wondering why the hell Olive couldn't have just torn off the few sprigs of parsley she needed to add to the stew instead of messing up this thing.

"This is a new one to me," Rena said. "I'll have to tell Tripper about it. He collects just about every gadget there is."

Now there was a name I hadn't heard in a long while. After Ricky Chase died I knew that Tripper had taken on Rena, or was it that Rena had taken on Tripper? In any case, I knew they lived in a tiny house near the marsh right at the edge of town. Alana used to say that, besides peacock feathers, there were two things you should avoid bringing into your home: Tripper O'Leery and Rena Dickson. "Cause he's sure to rip your man off, and she's sure to rip one off your man," she'd said.

It's probably been ten years since I've seen either of them since I hardly ever go to town. And suddenly here she was, Rena, kneeling beside me in front of a bathtub, and with just the mention of Tripper, they land back in my life. All thanks to Olive who is so desperate for friends she'll pick up anyone off the road. I wouldn't let her through my front door. Tripper either.

I think Rena must have read my thoughts just then because she said, "You know, he's changed a lot since he got the cancer."

"Who?"

"Tripper."

"Tripper O'Leery has cancer?" There was a time when people thought of Tripper O'Leery himself as a cancer. Once he took a .22 rifle out into the marsh and was gone for days. Someone said he'd told them he was fed up with everyone in town, so we all thought he'd gone and done himself in. And it's a terrible thing to admit, but there weren't that many sad to hear it, myself included. Even so, when he showed up a week later with a bunch of stinking muskrats tied to his belt, there was an odd mix of disappointment as well as relief around town. Tripper O'Leery may have been bad news, but he was still one of ours. I heard myself say, "I'm sorry to hear that. How's he doing with it? I mean, will he be okay?"

"Okay?" Rena shrugged. "That chemo is awful. You ever have it?"

"Uh, no, can't say that I have."

"Me neither, but there's so much cancer going around we probably will some day."

"Nice thought."

"Funny, huh?" Rena laughed. "When you think of all the poison we used to do on purpose."

Let me tell you, my head snapped up then, and I looked out to the kitchen to see if Olive may have heard that. But she was sitting at the table next to the kerosene lamp, her head still bent over her hooking project. Rena poked me with her elbow and whispered, "I bet that one over there never got into the kind of stuff we did."

I shrugged, like I couldn't care less, but just hearing her talk about the kind of stuff we used to do made my mouth go all dry and suddenly I felt a need to run to the toilet.

Recalling that conversation is enough to make me run Billy out of the ruts in Olive's lane. It's a high lane, and I jerk the wheel away from the edge just in time. Oh, that would have been good, Trish, landing Billy in the ditch.

As I turn onto Thunder Hill Road, I'm surprised to see it's not as rough and icy as I imagined. It's even bare in spots. All morning, the sun has been breaking through the clouds over Thunder Hill. Bear must be at home in his cabin because a plume of smoke wafts up through the trees. I picture him tending his fire, the way he putters around his yard collecting wood, squatting in front of the hearth to light the kindling. Oh, look, his clothes have gotten wet, so he's taking them off there in front of the fire. His body looks golden in the light, and the heat or something has given him an erection.... Oh, Trish, where are you going with this? Because now he has it in his hand and he's got this thoughtful face on because he is thinking about ... about ... you, of course, and his missed opportunity on the pool table. Easy girl, I'm thinking, you're almost at the Four Reasons and you probably shouldn't go in there all flushed and panting. Alana once declared that men have an unfair advantage over women, starting when they get their first erections and learn to think about other things to keep it in check. They have a whole lifetime to perfect the idea of mind over matter. We women go through life oblivious to this learned skill. We all laughed when she came out with this idea. Now I'm thinking maybe she was on to something, because I probably look like I'm burning up. Quick Trish, you're rounding the final corner before the Four Reasons. Who knows, maybe Bear is there in the store right now. Think about something to calm you down. Think about Olive's grocery list. What did she want me to pick up anyway?

A box of raisins, for all the oatcakes she'll bake.

Vegetable shortening for the pies.

Lemons to go with the gigantic salmon that has thawed and must be eaten tonight.

Batteries, toilet paper!

Candles, bread and butter pickles for the kids.

Extra dog food in case the storm picks up again.

Bear really is hot.

That does it. It's time to get some expert advice on this whole matter.

21. Angry Alana

JUDGING BY THE WAY Alana is snapping apart the wooden vegetable crates and stuffing them into the stove, I gather that now might not be the time to ask her about anything. It's a pretty feeble fire she's got going; it barely takes the chill off the place. And knowing Alana, she's too stubborn to leave the store to go across the road to the Bradley Farm where there's a generator and warmth.

"Have you thought about what you might burn next?" I say, looking around the store.

Alana straightens up and places her hands on the small of her back, which is a sure sign that she's stressed. Or pissed. Or both.

"Yeah, I'm thinking of burning down the store. We'll go out with a big bonfire at least."

"Right," I say. "Where's Danny anyway?"

Another sore point — I can tell immediately by the way she cracks the last slat over her knee. I open the stove grate for her and she pops in the pieces.

"Danny took it upon himself to go all the way up Thunder Hill to collect fallen branches around Bear's house. So he borrowed the Bradley's truck yesterday afternoon and nobody's seen him since. Including the Bradleys."

I say the appropriate things, like, isn't she worried? But all the while I'm processing what it means that Danny has gone up to Bear's. Would Bear tell him how I was practically humping him there on the pool table?

No, Alana tells me, she's not worried, she's pissed. She figures he spent the night getting drunk with Bear, who always has a stash of rum. And, she can't wait to get her hands on him when he walks through the door.

"I told him not to go in the first place, because I knew that road would be too slippery to come down, but you know Danny...." She slams the stove's grate shut. "And so I've got the Bradleys wondering where the hell their truck is, and here I am burning furniture to keep warm. And I don't even have any rum!"

I think maybe I should offer to trade places with Alana. She could run Billy back to Kyle House and get warm and drunk while I wait here for Danny. There's a good chance he'd bring Bear along too. Then what would you do, Trish? I realize I'm shivering now. I wonder if that's due to the thought of seeing Bear, or simply that it is real fucking cold here in the store.

"Screw Danny. In fact, screw all men!" I say, raising my fist in the air.

"No. One is quite enough," Alana says, slumping into her chair, her elbows on her knees, her hands dangling towards the floor — Alana's classic "I give up" pose.

"Hey," I say. "What happened to 'it's okay to have somebody waiting in the wings'?"

She waved her hand at me in disgust. "You haven't reached the stage where you realize all men are pigs."

"Oh, come on," I say. "Danny's just pissing you off today."

"Yeah, like Ray always pisses you off too. He called yesterday, by the way."

"Oh?" I say, surprised that for the first time in a year this news is not making my heart jump. Jiggle maybe, but not jump. "What did he say?"

"Not much. He's still stuck down there in Newville."

"Did you tell him about...?" I was going to say the flue fire, but she jumped right in.

"Tell him about what? You and Bear on the pool table? No, I thought I'd let you do that."

She is enjoying this, I can tell. And here I'd come looking for advice. You'd think she'd be more sympathetic, given that she was the only one who knew what I went through when Ray left me for Newville. I've never been much of a crier but for four solid weeks, I could hardly say his name without my eyes misting.

Back then, Alana tried her best to help. I'd stop in every night after work and the second I walked in the door she'd hand me a shot of rum. Anesthesia, she called it, and I have to say, it helped. In between customers we sat in the back by the stove and she'd listen and I'd talk, and talk, and talk. Sometimes I felt so angry with Ray for walking out that I'd spend the whole time trashing him.

"You know how everybody thinks he's such a nice guy, always ready to help? It's bullshit. He thinks of kindness as an investment, like how that person is going to help him out some day. Deep down, he only cares about himself."

"Doesn't everybody?" she'd said. "I mean the only reason anybody helps anyone else is because there's something in it for them. Even if it's just because helping others makes them feel good about themselves."

A little later, I said, "He could have said something to me, you know. I mean, I was always honest about all the things that bothered me about him, but he'd never say a word about what bothered him. So he'd just let it fester and fester. I don't think that's fair. Do you?"

"No, I don't think it's one bit fair. But maybe he was afraid to say anything to you because you'd get so defensive. I've seen you Trish. You've got an awful bad temper."

"So? So do you."

"We're talking about *you*."

Somehow Alana wasn't giving me what I'd grown to expect from her, my best friend — that little thing called "sympathy."

I took a different approach. "I guess I don't blame Ray for leaving me," I sighed. "My hair is practically grey, I wear flannel to bed, and let's face it, I'm not as pretty as I used to be."

"So, who is?"

"And I shouted at him a lot."

"That you did."

"And I took him for granted."

"Yep."

"No wonder he left me."

"Trish," she said. "You're allowed to take your mate for granted, up to a point."

"And you think I went beyond that point?"

She shrugged. "All I know is that this sort of thing happens to the best of couples."

"Yeah, well he took me for granted too," I said. "And I'm beginning to think we just got bored with each other."

"Tell me about it," she laughed, and then went on to say that even she and Danny were far from immune and that they had to work hard at keeping it fresh. Sometimes they had to work hard just not to kill each other. This was supposed to make me feel better? How could Alana dismiss my marriage to Ray so easily? We were talking about Trish and Ray here, not just some Jane and Joe Blow. I vowed right then not to allow my marriage to end. I would pour my heart into it.

After that first weekend he came home, I phoned him every night. I kept those calls short, and I drew upon the power every woman has over her man. What did I talk about? Nothing relating to our marriage, or to our child, or to our history together. Instead, I whispered things into the phone that were sure to make him hard. I'd start with a husky voice. I'd say, "Guess what I'm doing right now," and let him run with it from there. At first I was afraid he might hear the desperation in my voice, but it seems Ray liked to talk about sex over the phone. It was new to me too, and I surprised myself with how worked up I could get.

I kept this up every night for a week or so, until he got good and used to a dose of this sort of talk just before falling asleep at night. Then I stopped the calls cold. I even took to popping Gravol early in the evening so that I'd be sound asleep by telephone time and therefore not tempted to hear his voice. I did this for three nights. On the third night, the ringing phone eventually found its way through to my consciousness. When I picked it up, there was a desperate Ray who wondered if maybe he could come home the next weekend too.

From that moment on, I went around acting as if everything was fine and dandy between Ray and me. If Alana asked me how we were doing, I'd say that what happened on Gayl's birthday had been a serious blip in our marriage but that we were cool now. There were times when I even managed to convince myself of this.

I look out the window and up the road. "He'll likely be coming along any minute."

"Who?" says Alana. "Bear?"

"No, Danny, of course."

"We weren't even talking about Danny. We were talking about Bear."

"We were?" I said. " Well then, maybe Danny will bring Bear along."

"You know what? I don't even want to see Danny. Maybe I should just close up shop and go over to Olive's with you. How's it been over there, anyway?"

"You would not believe it."

"That bad?"

"She cooks all the time and uses up every dish and pot in the house. And guess who does the dishes?"

"After all the canned spaghetti we've had lately, I wouldn't mind having one of Olive's meals." Alana sighs again.

I try again. "Guess who's in charge of cleaning up!"

"I'd gladly do the dishes."

"Maybe you wouldn't if you knew who I've been washing dishes *with*."

"The twins?"

I shake my head.

"Olive?"

"Weirder."

"Weirder than Olive?"

"Try Rena Dickson." Now I would have thought that would stop Alana in her tracks. But all she said was, "Oh, really?"

"You don't seem all that surprised."

"I knew she was opening the Chase cottage," Alana says, sinking into her rocker and biting her lip. "So it's true then. She's going ahead with her idea of opening an ice-cream stand."

I almost choke on my tea. "Ice-cream stand?"

"She came in the day before the storm for a reading. She wanted advice. Don't look at me like that. What was I supposed to do? Tell her she shouldn't open an ice-cream stand in our neck of the woods?"

I shake my head. I'm getting that feeling again, like I've entered some alternative world like you see in sci-fi movies, where everything has gotten twisted around somehow. Like the fact that I'm suddenly hot for my old friend Bear? Like the fact that Alana likes cats all of a sudden? Like she's now inviting Rena Dickson back into our lives?

"You actually advised Rena Dickson to move out here and open up an ice-cream stand?"

"Why not? I don't mind a little competition."

"Gee. That's very generous of you," I say. "Considering how you once vowed to kill her."

Alana laughs. "I mean competition in the ice-cream business. I somehow don't think of Rena as a threat in the other department."

"Why the hell not? Remember the time you caught them in the act and him trying to convince you that blow jobs didn't count as cheating? And then her having the nerve to take advantage of Ray when he was so drunk he could barely stay seated on the edge of a bath tub?"

"Oh right, like she took advantage of all our poor innocent men."

"Okay, okay. But what makes you think she's changed?"

"Because that was a long time ago, Trish. Sometimes you have to let this kind of stuff go.

"Why does everyone keep telling me that?"

Alana is smiling at me like I'm about thirteen.

"Quit looking at me like I'm thirteen," I say. Since I'm feeling pretty weak in the knees, I sit on the stool next to the stove and stick my chin in my hands. "lately I feel like I'm about thirteen."

"So I've noticed."

"Really. It's like you said, about the past staring at me in the face."

"You mean seeing Rena again?"

"No. Not Rena."

"Well who then?" Her breath catches. Then her eyes narrow and she studies my face until I blush. "It's Bear! I knew it."

"You did not," I say, but I can feel a guilty smirk invading my face. Of course, Alana picks up on this and suddenly her mood perks up.

"I knew something more than sleep happened on that pool table!"

"No, not really, but..." It bursts out of me and I can't seem to keep everything from gushing out. I tell her about Ray and how I feel we really have come to an end. And that what's been going on with me these past few weeks is me trying to come to terms with this fact and that maybe what happened on the pool table at Hog Holler happened for a reason.

"But what happened on the pool table?"

"Nothing happened. It's really what *didn't happen*."

"Tell me!"

So I tell her about Bear rubbing my feet to the point where I was practically jumping out of my skin. And I tell her every detail about the cuddling and even the kissing on the pool table.

After all, as Alana once said, what is friendship between women about, besides details?

Then she says, "So? Then what?"

"So nothing. We went to sleep."

"Really. You fell asleep," Alana is saying.

I look out the window. The sun is still shining out there. The spots of asphalt on the road are growing larger. I realize that Alana hasn't said anything in a while, which is quite unlike her, so I turn and see that she is staring at me like I'm holding something back from her, like I'm a total stranger. She's not the only one who has been looking at me this way lately.

The weekend before Ray and I had the big fight about me finding the acorn in his pocket, we'd had another fight. We'd been drinking all evening at the Four Reasons and when we got home I was pretty much hoping we'd go right to bed since Ray had been in Newville all week. I must have been expecting to have that drinking and smoking weed kind of sex, except Ray said he wanted to watch TV and that he'd be up to bed later. Naturally, I reacted badly. By that, I mean, I started going on about how he'd just made me feel like the ugliest girl in the world.

But when he picked up the TV remote and said, "I just want to be alone for a change," the booze in me came right back and I got all pathetic then. Lost any sense of dignity. "So what is it, Ray, you gonna watch porn videos after I go to bed? Is that what you do down there in Newville? Jerk off to tits and ass on the tube? Or is it some real live slut you got going down there? That it, Ray? That why you don't need *these* anymore?" I think that's when I pulled off my shirt, pointed my tits right at him.

"I have a question for you," he said, as calm as can be, looking past me at the TV screen. "At what point in our marriage do you think you turned so sour?"

I sat down on the footstool then. I looked at the man who I've loved for the past twenty years and realized I no longer recognized him. On the television, a lion was pulling down a wildebeest. The sound was off but you could see the poor thing bawling. I grabbed my shirt and went to leave the room, but not without a parting shot.

"Let's just say I turned pathetic the day you abandonned us to go to Newville."

He was still ignoring me so I threw something then, a glass bowl that had sat for years on a side table. It hit the footstool and bounced intact across the rug so I picked it up and threw it again, this time against the radiator. There was a satisfying smash that ended in about a million little shards. I know this because I cleaned up the mess the next day, and three weeks later, I'm still finding pieces.

"You're fucking crazy," was all he said.

He must have fallen asleep on the couch after I went upstairs. I was sick in the bathroom, I guess from the booze and the rage, and when I woke up the next morning, my head and heart pounding at the same rate, I could tell he'd left for Newville before I even got out of bed. Not a good sign, I thought, if we can't spend a weekend together without him ending up on the couch and leaving the next day. You'd think I might have learned a lesson from that, but no, the next weekend went pretty much the same way.

A big black police truck now pulls up to the pumps. Alana bunches her fists on her hips. "What do they expect me to do out there with no power? Siphon the gas?"

I say, "I wonder if this means the road to town is finally open."

Alana goes storming out the door before the driver even turns off the engine. I watch her approach the police vehicle, fully prepared to do battle if anyone so much as dared to ask for gas.

"What the hell?" I say, from where I'm standing at the window, because she is out there hugging whoever has stepped out of the truck. It's ... Uncle Leftie? Now what would he be doing all the way out here? I can't even remember the last time I saw him, especially since he retired as police chief. The back doors open up and who should jump out but Gayl and Biz. More surprises. More confusion. Just what I need.

I open the door for them and say to Gayl, "What are you doing here without my car?"

"I'm so glad to see you too, Ma," Gayl says, as she stomps the slush off her feet.

"Sure you are. The girl who can't wait to leave home," I say, but she hugs me and I find myself drinking in the smell of her because, after all, she is still my baby. "The road's open now," Uncle Leftie is saying to Alana. "But barely."

"But why are you kids here?" I ask. "What about your grandmother?"

"Olive didn't tell you she phoned us?" says Gayl. "She said you guys wanted us home. So when Leftie came by, Gran said we should come out with him. I guess you didn't miss us that much."

"What I miss," I say, "are the things you left back in town, like a hot bath and running water. And then there's the matter of my car."

Now they're all looking at me like I just said something totally irrational. I feel like asking them just what their problem is, but, instead I say, "Well, seriously. Why would you three leave the comforts of town to come out here?"

"Maybe to make sure you were okay?" says Gayl, sternly adding, "Mother."

"You all felt you had to come to check on us?"

"Olive said we should all come."

Olive, of course.

"You could come back to town with me if that's what you want, Trish," says Uncle Leftie. "Your mother would appreciate it, I'm sure."

He says that like all my mother's family does, as if I neglect her or something.

I mumble something about there being no point now that Gayl's here, but just how soon is he planning on heading back to town, anyway? In case I decide to go in to see my mother. After he drops the kids off at Kyle House, he tells me, but first he'll see if Olive happens to have her famous oatcakes on hand.

"Although I guess without power she might not have been able to bake," he says, looking forlorn.

"You don't need to worry about that," I tell him. "She's got a molasses tub full of them."

Uncle Leftie is famous for his sweet tooth, and sure enough, he's licking his lips at the very thought. I'm about to mention the blueberry pie she's making but I check myself in time. If I want to catch a lift in with Uncle Leftie I'd rather not mention the pie or he'll never leave Olive's. I like my Uncle Leftie okay, especially after what he did for us the night the farm collapsed, but to this day he still looks at me like I'm something to be pitied, so it's not like I want to spend a lot of time with him.

But Olive has said she gets a kick out of his old fashioned manners so I can just see her trying to convince him stay for dinner or even the night.

"Well, it's about friggin' time," Alana says from where she's standing by the window. I look down the road in time to see the Bradley truck making the corner from Thunder Hill. Before I have a chance to see if maybe there's more than one person in the cab, it turns down the Bradley's lane and drives behind the barn.

Suddenly, I'm so busy thinking about coming face to face with Bear any minute now that I can hardly hear what anyone is saying. Gayl is offering to drive back to Kyle House with me, but I say she should go on ahead with the others. "I have groceries yet to pick up and, and ... I'm wondering if I should get over to our house to check on the cat and shut the water off before the pipes freeze."

"Have you talked to Dad lately?" Gayl asks.

"That's the other thing I have to do while I'm here," I say. "Go on to Olive's, I'll be there soon."

First, I try sitting on one of Alana's stools by the counter. I position myself in what I hope is my most attractive pose. In a minute Bear could walk through that door. But when Alana tells me I look all fidgety, I decide to gather up Olive's supplies. The bell over the door clangs again and when I dare look over it's to see Danny. Alone. I peer over his shoulder to see if Bear is behind him. "Expecting someone?" says Danny, looking behind himself. So much for being subtle.

"No, no, not at all."

He drops an armload of birch branches in front of the stove. "What brings you here?"

"I had to pick stuff up for Olive and I thought I should get over to my place to shut off the water."

"No need for that," Danny says. "Bear told me he went there yesterday and shut it off for you."

"Bear shut off my water?" I say, hearing wonder in my own voice. That means Bear came looking for me after he woke up alone on the pool table. I say, "He must have wondered where I was. I mean, when he got to my house."

Danny is studying me far too closely. "I told him you'd gone over to Kyle House. He also said to tell you he put out more food for Carrie in the barn, so she's okay."

"Oh." I straighten out a row of chocolate bars on the candy rack. "So what's he up to then?"

"He said something about going into town for TV bingo."

"That's right! It's TV bingo tonight!" I say. "Alana! We have to get to town!"

"Um, Trish?" says Alana. "TV bingo is the last thing on my 'to do' list."

"But we haven't missed TV bingo in three years!" I say. This is true. If there is one thing that's sacred it's the bunch of us driving into town on Monday nights to play bingo via cable TV. Even our kids have joined us there at the tavern table with their very own daubers. Of course, to them, it's a joke, like we're a bunch of pathetic old fogeys. TV bingo was something we started going to town for after the collapse of the farm. We called it bingo therapy. It made us feel so normal; something we suddenly felt we needed.

Alana takes hold of my shoulders and turns me away from the window, telling me in a calm voice that everything's going to be fine. "I think what's needed here is for things to return to normal," she says in a slow voice, like she's read my mind.

"Normal," I laugh, and as I do, I notice how much I sound like my mother. "What's normal, Alana? Do you know?"

"No clue. But by the way," she says. "Ray said to tell you he's been working double shifts. He wants you to phone him."

Ray called. TV bingo. Bear James in town at TV bingo. Ray called to say what? I feel like I'm being sanded and salved all at the same time.

"So why don't you phone Ray right now?" says Alana. "It might help you to put things into perspective."

22. Hope

HOW QUICKLY SNOW MELTS in an April sun. The road back to Olive's is almost bare now. Bright green grass pokes up in spots through the fields. Alana's right. Life will return to normal.

The first thing I'll do when I finally get home is to make a cup of tea. I'll steep it in my very own mug. Next, I'll run a long hot bath in my own tub. That reminds me; I'd better pick up that new piece of stovepipe and get it installed before Ray gets home. Yes, Ray is coming home. He's not sure when, but he's going to leave Newville as soon as the road clears. I phoned him from the Four Reasons, and when he said all this I was so surprised I didn't even stop to think about the toothless wonder I've pictured him with too many times. All I know, or care, is that the storm is over and Ray is coming home to me and our old wooden bed with its jumble of quilts and pillows and a few thousand memories. I'll soon be digging through the mess in the front bedroom to locate the summer sheets. It's amazing how a person can forget something like where she put her summer things, let alone what they might look like. It's the same with my clothes. I'll pull out the box from the back of my closet and be surprised to come across my white muslin skirt, the one I wore way back in the farm days. I bet I can even fit into that old skirt since I've lost so much weight this past year. I am feeling positively silly.

I turn off Thunder Hill Road onto Olive's lane and it is some mucky here alongside the lilac bushes. I roll down my window to feel the sun on my face, and is that honking geese I hear? They are headed in what looks like the completely wrong direction; but no, they are flying to Kincaid Lake, their annual resting stop. I shield my eyes from the glare of the sun. Beyond the bare lilac bushes lies a field dotted with rotted potatoes that the harvester overlooked last fall. The smell hits me fair in the face. All of my surroundings — land, water, sky — seem to ooze with spring.

On the radio, Stevie Wonder sings, and I join him. "*You are the apple of my eye, mmm, mmm, forever you'll stay in my heart.*" I was almost surprised when Ray answered the phone at the boarding house. I don't know what I'd been thinking, that maybe he'd disappeared from Earth? He told me he was working the night shift until the end of the week. He said he was planning on coming home. He said all of this like there was nothing strange about the fact that he hasn't shown up for the last three weekends.

Then he asked how I'd managed to end up at Olive's.

"Oh, it's a long story."

"So I hear," he said. "It was a dark and stormy night there on the pool table with Bear James."

"Who told you that?" I almost swallowed my words.

Apparently, just about everyone Ray has spoken to in the last two days told him about Bear and me being storm stuck at Hog Holler and sleeping together on the pool table. This, I guess, is far bigger news than any old flue fire, because he didn't even mention the fact that it was the flue fire that led to all this in the first place.

"Have you spoken to Bear since then?" I tried not to squeak.

"No, why?" he said and laughed. "Old Bear try to jump you or something?"

I didn't know if I should feel defensive or insulted because I wasn't sure if it was concern or amusement I heard in his voice. "Don't worry," I said.

"I wasn't worried," Ray said. "Do you want me to be worried?"

I cleared my throat and said, "I think most husbands would wonder, given Bear's track record."

"True. He'll jump anything that moves," he said, as if he took some pride in Bear for this.

After a little cough I said, "Oh, come on, everybody slows down with age. Even Bear, I bet."

"Naw. Not Bear."

"How do you know?"

"I'm his closest friend."

"He tells you everything?"

"Pretty much. Why? What are you getting at?"

"Oh nothing. Do you ever talk to him about us?"

"Never about us."

I wanted to say, then who *do* you talk to him about? Your hot one down in Newville?

He said, "Anyway ... we should talk about Gayl."

He's been in touch with her these past few days. Has it only been days since the storm began? Gayl talked to him about her plan to move into town with my mother long before she mentioned it to me. This is so typical of Ray, how he avoids sticky issues by switching topics. I was wondering if I should call him on this when he said, "I told her it would be okay with me if it was okay with you."

When I didn't answer he said, "From what she tells me, you two are at each other's throats most of the time so I assumed you'd okay it too."

I should have felt genuine rage coming on here, thinking, it's fucking great of you to think you can run my life from Newville, but instead my voice kind of cracked, and I found myself saying, "no matter how much Gayl and I fight, no matter how much I can't stand her dirt and mess and noise, I'd feel too sad without her here."

I could have said the same thing about him, but there was no way in hell.

He was quiet for a minute. Then he said, "You know, Trish?

Sometimes you just have to let things go."

"What's that supposed to mean?"

He sighed. "Like maybe it's time for all of us to move our lives forward."

There it was, confirmation. My heart sank like it had been tied to a stone and tossed off a bridge.

"She's growing up, Trish. And going to your mother's might be a logical first step. As soon as I get home I want us all to sit down and discuss what her moving to town would mean. You know, what her responsibilities would be."

Home? Funny how, just like that, my heart bobbed back up to the surface. And that's where we left it, with him repeating that he'd be coming home soon. I simply said, "Fine, see you then." It struck me how completely out of my own control life has become.

23. TV Bingo

I'M STILL REPLAYING THAT conversation with Ray as I drive up the lane to Kyle House. I swing Billy around to the yard in front of the kitchen and just like that, I realize just how nuts I have become. There, parked right next to Uncle Leftie's police truck is Bear's Rover, and *poof,* all thoughts of Ray go flying out the window. How out of control is that?

I park as far out of view of Olive's kitchen window as possible, which means no one will be able to see me out here in the yard. I plan on sitting here taking deep breaths for as long as possible. Oh hell, there's no use putting it off anymore. I'll be face to face with Bear James in a matter of moments.

I slog through the slush until I reach the door to the summer kitchen. What happens next feels like slow motion. I open the door into the main kitchen and the first people I see are Olive and Leftie. They're standing over by the table, where Olive has spread out some old photos of my parents that she'd found in a bedroom cupboard. It's amazing how twenty-five years after my parents moved out of Kyle House, little bits of them still remain.

"Hi," I say.

"Look who finally made it back!" says Olive. She actually winks at me. "Look Bear, it's Patricia."

I glance into the pantry and there's Bear, arranging lemon slices around a large filleted salmon. He looks up quickly and then back down at his task. "Hey, it's Trish."

"Hey yourself." I look down at the salmon whose eye seems fixed upon me.

"That's all you have to say to each other?" Olive says, swooping towards us, causing me to step into the pantry until I'm standing so close to Bear I can smell his homemade beer shampoo. Then Olive is between us, her arms draped around our shoulders. She calls out to my uncle, "Say, Leftie, did you hear about the adventure these two had the other night?"

"Can't say that I did," he grunts, like it's the last thing he'd be interested in. I know my Uncle Leftie though, and he's recording every word Olive has said about me so he can tell my Aunt Sybil later.

So Olive goes back out there to the table and tells him all she knows about our night at Hog Holler, about how we'd gotten so cold we'd been forced to cuddle up on the pool table. She's laughing about it the whole way through, like it was the cutest thing in the world.

I can hear my uncle clear his throat. He is the straightest man in the world and wouldn't see much humour in my being at the Hog Holler, let alone spending the night with Bear James on a pool table. I can just hear him and my aunt agreeing that it was no wonder Ray took that job down in Newville.

I feel shame colouring my face as I stand here in the pantry, not knowing if I should go out there and defend my actions or if I should run outside to Billy and drive away never to return to Thunder Hill for all time. And then Bear suddenly grabs me by the shoulders and kisses me on the cheek. I freeze, and he laughs.

"Gayl says she saw you over at the store," he says, turning back to his fish. "I bet Alana was some pissed off when Danny got home."

"You've got that right," I manage to say.

"Those two," he shakes his head and looks at me, one eye hidden by that forelock of his. "You'd think after all this time she'd know."

"Know what?'

"That he's just being Danny."

"Oh, I see. And because he's Danny he gets to get drunk with you while she's freezing her ass waiting for him to bring some wood?" I drop my voice. "She was starting to burn the furniture."

"Well, I didn't force him to start drinking," Bear says, looking up from his fish. What I see in his eyes is a blend of guilt and humour. And I start thinking that for a man, Bear really is different in how he sees the big picture of what goes on between men and women.

He says, "How's it going with Gayl? Did you speak to her any more about her moving to town?"

"No. Not really. I think it's because a part of me thinks it would be good for her, and but another part of me just can't imagine life without her. Not yet anyway. Not now." I say this like I'm the only parent.

He rearranges his lemon arrangement for a minute before wiping his hands on a dishcloth and saying, "Ray know about it yet?"

"About?"

I must look really distressed about his question because he quickly adds, "About Gayl wanting to move to town."

"Oh that. Yeah ... He knows. He thinks it's a good idea. Easy for him to say isn't it?"

He clears his throat. "So you've talked to him? Lately?"

I nod. "Today."

"Today."

"Yeah. I guess he'll be staying in Newville all week."

"Interesting," he says. Now it's his turn to nod. He looks at me and I try to read his face again, but Olive chooses this moment to come barging back into the pantry.

"Oh, look at this salmon!" she says, picking up the platter. "Bear, you are a master at filleting. Among other things, I'm sure." She has some nerve to wink at me again.

He bows. "At your service." Then he winks at me too and I feel like melting into the floor.

Here I am, washing up the dishes in the bathtub, again. My wine glass sits next to the kerosene lamp. In front of me, a tower of pots and measuring cups and odd things like lemon squeezers threaten to topple over. Olive refuses to let Rena "lift another finger," since she'd helped out so much while I was gone. So Rena's out there at the table sucking back her cranberry juice as fast as Bear and Olive are drinking their wine. If I lean back from my position in front of the tub, I can see them out there at the table. They all look pretty relaxed in their chairs. The talk has turned to my uncle. Olive is asking him about his miniature boat carvings, which have become very popular in the tourist stores around town.

"Not as exciting as police work, but at my age you start looking for ways to calm yourself down instead of trying to rev things up."

In the candlelight, my uncle looks twenty years younger and so does everyone else. Excepting, of course, the kids, who don't age in even the harshest of lights. I can't help but notice how the candlelight magically fades the lines usually etched across Rena's face, and she looks almost as fresh as she did back when she was busy messing around with practically every man in town.

"Now, where did you catch this salmon?" Leftie had asked Olive awhile back, when we'd all been seated around the table. Biz and Gayl were saying how cool it was that the only light for miles was coming from the candles on the table.

"Actually, we caught it out in the snow!" Olive said, as she poured the wine. "Right Rena?"

Rena nodded. "She had to use a fishing rod to get him out."

Olive's eyes sparkled. "He gave us quite a struggle, but we managed to reel him in."

Then she explained how, yesterday, we'd had to move everything from the freezer, including the salmon, out into the snow.

And that's when she started listing off all the wonderful things Rena had done today. It seems she'd brought in three armloads of wood, made a salad, peeled potatoes, scrubbed out the bathtub, and on top of all that, washed some of the twins' clothes. All of which were now drying nicely above the stove. Did we think Olive could convince Rena to move into Kyle House permanently? Rena grinned as she piled rice onto her plate, saying that keeping busy helps to keep her mind off her problems.

I excused myself then, saying I wasn't very hungry and that's why I'm now looking at this mountain of pots and unwashed dishes from lunch. And I'm thinking I should get Gayl in here to help instead of her sitting out there drinking and eating like being stranded at Kyle House with no running water is such a lark. But then that would mean I'd have to go out and sit at that table instead of being safe in here alone.

There's a scrape of a chair and I hear Uncle Leftie say, "Well, I'll be heading back to town right after I have a piece of Olive's blueberry pie. I can give anybody a lift in if they want."

"Oh, no," says Olive. "Stay here tonight. Everybody can stay!"

Is she serious? I look around the corner and see them all sitting there like they're actually considering it.

Bear says, "I'm heading into town too."

Like an idiot, I rush into the kitchen "You are?"

Bear laughs. "It's TV bingo night. Can't miss that, now can we Trish?"

"Uh, not if we can help it," I say, wondering if this is an invitation.

Olive says, "But isn't the road still blocked?"

"The RCMP were taking down the barriers when I went through," Uncle Leftie says. "The salt trucks would have been right behind them."

I'm sure I'm standing here looking like I don't know what to do next. Which happens to be true. Okay, now, all I have to do is walk up the back stairs, grab my things and drive to town with Bear. And while we drive we'll talk about what happened the other night. I wonder how I should react when he confesses that although he'd always desired me back when I was young and pretty, it was only after earth's gravity and time's mischief had done their work that my inner beauty began to really shine for him. Back there on the pool table, he had made a conscious decision to hold himself back in spite of the efforts of a certain someone by the name of Trish. Congratulations, Trish. You have completely grown out of maturity and back into adolescence. Next, you'll be blushing and giggling at the very thought of you and Bear doing the deed.

Someone mentions the time and Bear says, "We'd better get a move on Trish if we don't want to miss it."

He's right. By now everyone at the Roll-a-Way Tavern will have been served their fish and chips. Bingo cards and beer bottles should be cluttering up the tabletops. Soon, hands clutching daubers will be poised above bingo cards as Dennis the bartender reaches up to turn on the television. There's no way we'll be on time. We'll enter the tavern and act all pissed that we missed it after all. The road was still bad? Terrible. We'll carry on as if we are still just good friends and not the two people who pulled off the side of the road just so Bear could fill me up to the brim and beyond.

Bear pokes my foot with the toe of his boot. "You coming then?"

I blush. But I stifle the urge to giggle and casually ask, "Got any bingo daubers in your jeep?"

"Daubers I got plenty," Bear says, pushing his chair back from the table.

Leftie places his coffee cup onto his saucer and says, "I gather you're all coming in with me, then?"

"Thanks anyway, Uncle Leftie," I say. "I thought I'd catch a lift in with Bear."

"Doesn't look like Bear's driving anywhere tonight."

Bear and I glance at each other before we sit back down like two naughty children. Uncle Leftie may have retired from the force, but to us he will always be Chief of Police. Bear has just finished four glasses of wine and Uncle Leftie is looking at him exactly like he did that night we got busted. That is, he's looking at us like he would a couple of criminals. I am feeling dizzy. So dizzy in fact, that I slink back to my spot in front of the tub and make like I'm washing more dishes.

24. Nurse Trish

"**N**URSE!" THAT WAS A familiar call weeks before the collapse of the farm. "Nurse! We need you now!"

We were practically delirious the night that Rena Dickson and Tripper O'Leery knocked on the door. While I got Gayl ready for bed, the others whisked Rena and Tripper upstairs to set things up. They were waiting for me because they thought my hits almost never left a bruise. When I think now of the things I prided myself on then.

Gayl was almost two at that time. Everyone at the farm had become horribly unhappy. Suddenly, the bills for food and power and phone had our men finding jobs like clearing brush from the sides of roads, or worse, scooping blueberries for my father. In the evenings they came home to us women, some of whom had been with babies and kids all day long and were looking for a little male attention. The men got grumpy and we women got bitchy. They wanted to drink beer and play cards at night while we sat in the kitchen fuming about them. All those dreams of life on a communal farm suddenly seemed pretty shallow. When I look back, I see how willing we were for something to bring us all together again. That "thing" turned out to be what nearly destroyed us all.

"Nurse!"

The voices were more desperate. I buttoned up Gayl's little bed sweater and tucked the covers around her neck.

"Night-night, sweet pea," I said as I closed the door.

October was upon us the day that Rena Dickson and Tripper O'Leery arrived at the commune, and the days were growing shorter. Bear's crop had been drying in the barn for over a week, and he was bursting with pride. Those who'd helped him harvest the plants later told us that he was almost crying out there in the field when it came time to cut down his babies. But, as a result of Bear's careful devotion and care, there'd be enough weed to sell to make the mortgage payments.

As if growing and selling weed wasn't risky enough, some of us had also picked up the bad habit of dabbling in speed. It was pills at first, then snorting lines. Then Tripper O'Leery introduced us to needles. "Well, at least it's not heroin," Danny had said at least twice in the past six months. "That stuff is fucking addictive."

Besides Ray and me, there were Tripper and Rena, Alana and Danny, plus the American couple, Sly and Sheena. So that night, after Alana got her kids to bed, and I had finally gotten Gayl to sleep, they started calling for me.

"Nurse! Nurse!"

I ran down the hall.

As soon as I entered my bedroom, I could tell they had my work cut out for me. I took one look at the tracks on Rena's arms and said they looked infected, so there was no way I was going anywhere near those.

"Oh for fuck's sake, give me that," said Tripper, taking the hit from my hand. "Now watch carefully. Rena sweetie, take off your pants like a good girl."

Rena dropped her jeans to the floor and we watched him snap his finger at a vein on her groin. After, as she flailed around on the bed, groaning from the rush, Tripper grinned and said, "See? I told you it was good stuff."

He divvied up our share. We smacked our lips in anticipation. I'm sure Tripper could tell how hungry we all were too, because he took his sweet fucking time spooning those crystals onto a mirror and dividing it into lines. *Click, click, click* went the razor blade. He laughed while he did this, knowing full well the power he held over us all. I'm sure our teeth were grinding in total agreement.

A sudden knock on the door made everyone jump about a foot. We were some jittery bunch.

"We got any more baggies, Trish?" Bear said from the doorway. I told him no, that he'd have to use tinfoil to separate his ounces. He stood there watching us for a minute before saying, "You guys are fuckin' nuts, you know."

None of us had slept for days. Ray was pacing the floor, making these little ticking sounds in his throat that normally only occur in his sleep. Tripper was tightening a belt around one of his own arms while I tied off the other. He wanted to try something he'd heard about called a "double-barrelled shotgun." Really, I think we all thought he was being greedy for taking two hits at once, but it was his stuff and we were grateful that he'd decided to share it with us. He could have stayed in town and sold it on the street for a far better price. We knew he'd come all the way out here because he thought we were cool.

"Just don't blame me if you overdose," I remember saying as I pushed both plungers at once. Tripper's eyes opened wide as he lurched forward in his chair. We all held our breaths.

"Fuck, Trish, you're good," Tripper croaked, before he fell back into the chair. A huge grin appeared on his face. "God, I love all you guys!"

We exhaled.

I guess it was just about then that we heard Bear's voice croaking from the kitchen. "Narcs, you guys! Narcs!"

Just like that, we were busted.

When we heard the word "narc," there was a scramble to gather up spoons and syringes. Tripper began hyperventilating from the shock and the speed, and, banging his fist against his heart, shouted, "Help me! Nurse!" In that moment I saw my future flash before my eyes. Trish Kyle: in prison for having administered a fatal dose of speed to Tripper O'Leery's heart.

Concern about Tripper's heart all but disappeared when I realized what had brought the RCMP down our lane in the first place. As it turned out, they hadn't come down to bust us at all but rather to make a delivery. When I peeked out the bedroom window and down into the yard, I saw the cruiser open and the light come on. In the back seat was a policewoman with a kid in her arms. Even though it was dark, I could tell it was Gayl because she was wearing her little yellow bed sweater. I cried out before running down our stairs so fast I slipped and skidded down the last few steps on my spine.

In the kitchen, the cops were busy busting Bear for the pot. One of them made a move to catch me as I raced for the door, but then he must have realized I was Gayl's mother because he turned his attention back to Bear. Bear, I knew, was in deep shit since he already had a possession conviction.

Out in the yard, the policewoman rolled down her window and put her finger to her lips, saying, "She's asleep. It's probably best to keep her this way."

Later, I would learn the RCMP had received a call from Jean and Vern Bradley who lived down the road, saying there was a lost little girl named Gayl sitting in their kitchen. It seems the biggest yahoos in the county, none other than Clayton and Perry Card, had found her wandering in the woods, and not knowing who she was, had taken her over to the Bradley Farm. Later, those boys were hailed as heroes, even though everyone knew what they'd been up to with their flashlights and hunting rifles. Deer jacking, as far as we were concerned, was a far greater crime than growing marijuana. What if they had shot little Gayl?

Meanwhile, the yard was suddenly filled with more RCMP cars than I thought existed in the entire county. By now the narcs had been called in. They roamed around the house for an hour or so before packing four hostages into their cars. One was Tripper who kept insisting they send him an ambulance. Instead, they kept him in the back seat of a cruiser. They let Rena ride with him, I think to convince him that he wouldn't be dying that night. Ray was put into the third cruiser. While I'd been out in the yard, shivering with fear at the sight of Gayl in a police car, Ray had stepped forward to claim the weed as his own. Ray had just saved Bear's hide.

I didn't know any of this as I watched a cop duck Ray's head into the cruiser. Everything seemed to be happening quickly. It was still warm out, and I remember this because the crickets were screeching in my ears.

"Where are you going with her?" I said, as one of the officers slid into the driver's side of the car. "I have to put her to bed."

"We'll take her into Children's Aid until things get sorted out," said the policewoman. "Does she have a special toy we could take?"

"No," I said. "No, you can't take her."

A fresh set of headlights bounced down the lane just then and like a miracle my Uncle Leftie appeared in front of me. I guess he'd heard on the police radio that we were being busted and decided to drive out here in case his sister's kid needed help. That was probably the only time in my life that I wrapped my arms around him and stayed there while he worked something out with the officers. They agreed to follow him to my parent's house in town where Gayl could stay until things got sorted out.

"Don't worry," my Uncle Leftie said. "We'll get her back to you."

When I saw how teary his eyes were, I broke right down. Next thing I knew, I was being held by Bear and he wouldn't let go until the taillights were lost to the highway. And then a thought struck me stronger than any jolt of speed could have — I had just managed to lose my entire family. Bear sat with me at the kitchen table while I sobbed. My life was over.

As it turned out, I was able to pick up Gayl at my parents' the next day. She didn't seem at all traumatized by what had happened the night before, although she did say she got scared in the cornfield when she thought she'd lost the kitty. The story my parents had managed to get out of her was that she had heard a kitten crying and had simply gotten out of bed and went down into the yard to help it. No doubt the kitten, knowing full well what Gayl's idea of "help" was, had scampered into the cornfield.

That day I sat with Gayl in my lap in my parent's' living room and admitted I'd made a terrible mistake. My mother drank while my father paced and ranted. He said there were mistakes that people made in life and then there were criminal acts. What had happened out there, last night, was criminal, plain and simple. Things were going to change, he said, because he vowed he would see to it that his granddaughter never found herself in the back seat of a cop car again in her life. For starters, he had already called his lawyer Bob Morton who would see to it that Bernie Kyle's granddaughter's father stayed the hell out of prison. I didn't even try to argue. There are times when you have to admit to being wrong and during those times, you don't turn down help. I also had to promise to throw everyone out of the farm and turn it into a normal family home.

Even though the RCMP had had no warrant when they stumbled upon Bear's crop it was still considered admissible evidence. My father's lawyer managed to have the charge of cultivation for the purpose of trafficking reduced to a possession charge. The parade of good citizens who testified on Ray's behalf, plus the fact that he had a clean record, helped to keep him out of jail. We didn't stay out of the papers though, and for weeks Thunder Hill Road seemed to be the most popular drive in the county. Family cars crept by our lane, children's faces peering wide-eyed from windows, their parents, no doubt saying, "Imagine, letting that little girl wander around at night. I'm surprised they let them have her back!"

Today Gayl knows all about the farm, how we did try to live a dream where people could live happily in a world made of home-grown food and free-range animals. She also knows that homegrown marijuana was a part of the dream as well.

A few years ago we told her about how she slipped out one night without anyone seeing her. At the age of two, kids are like that. We even told her about the bust. We talked about how dumb Bear was to have the entire crop on the table that night, and even dumber that he had the Grateful Dead up so loud he couldn't hear the dogs bark when the RCMP cruisers drove down the lane to bring a lost little girl home to her mommy and daddy. We were quick to tell her how it was the sight of our little girl crying for us from the back of the police car that made us realize she was our most important reason to be on this earth.

She also knows all about Ray taking the rap for the pot, that he has a police record, that they have his fingerprints. Even after all this time, there are *still* repercussions. Ray lost his job as a school bus driver just last year because some uptight parents who had moved here from the city heard about his record and caused a big stink about it, even though it had happened more than fifteen years ago. We told Gayl that the bottom line was that we had been sometimes very foolish in our youth and that we've paid the price ever since.

But when it comes to telling her about the other stuff, that's where we stop short. There are some things we'd rather forget. It's one thing for a little girl to slip out of the house at night when her parents are busy in another part of the house, and it's quite another that we were too busy poking each other with needles to notice she was missing. And now, looking out there and seeing Uncle Leftie and Bear and Rena all sitting at the same table as my grown-up daughter, I realize that no secret is ever safe. And here I'd thought the past was something that could be locked away, like a diary you can open to revisit, but still manage to avoid other sections altogether.

25. The Showdown

"**T**HEN THAT SETTLES IT." I hear Olive announce to everyone in the kitchen. "No one's going to town tonight. Bear can stay here and Leftie you can too. We'll have a big sleepover."

Well, that sure blasts me back from the past. I look out to see Uncle Leftie wiping his mouth and putting on his police voice. "Count me out. I have to get a move on."

What he means is that he'd rather risk driving through any kind of weather than to have to greet the storm waiting for him in the form of Aunt Sybil.

"Oh stay, Leftie," says Olive. "It's late and I think we should do something fun. How about charades?"

She smiles at her guests sitting back in their chairs, their bellies full of salmon and wine. Everyone is looking at Olive like she must be joking. She's not, I could tell them. Don't they know they'll have to pay for this meal by joining in the activities at Olive's refugee camp?

"I wonder what the weather's like out there now," Rena says, twisting around in her chair to peer through the window. "Hey look! There's the moon."

She gets up from the table and slips out through the porch without saying another word. We hear the outside door latch close.

"What an excellent idea!" Olive says. "We should get those children to come downstairs and go outdoors as well." She calls up at them from the stairwell, "Girls, come down here, we're all going outdoors. You too, Byron."

Next thing you know we're gazing up at the moon on the warmest April evening anyone can remember. The snow has already melted in large patches where the sun has beaten down all day. It's like we're watching it disappear right in front of our very eyes.

In the middle of the yard, Gayl and the two little girls squeal in delight at having their coat sleeves nipped at by the pups. All the while, Suzie barks and then barks even more at the sound of her hollow echo bouncing back from Thunder Hill. Finally, Gayl declares she's chilled and says she's going into the house to find Biz. Thankfully she is followed by the twins, the pups in tow. A blanket of silence settles around those of us left in the yard. Suzie's not the only one who seems glad to have seen the last of all that energy. From where she lies on a patch of snow she raises her nose to catch all the news the breeze has to offer. All I'm able to detect is the smell of rotten leaves and grass. Every so often a whiff of salt water drifts up from the strait. Under a full moon, everything in the yard glows, until Olive's voice slices through the quiet with, "Is this not the most amazing night?"

She hauls up her coat and skirts with one hand. With the other she reaches for Uncle Leftie's hand and tries to get him to ... what the hell is she doing now? Skipping? Olive is actually trying to get Leftie McKinnon to skip down the lane with her.

"Come on, Leftie! Doesn't this spring air make you want to sing and skip? *Skip, skip, skip to my Lou. Skip to my Lou, my darlin'.*"

I can't believe what I'm seeing with my own two eyes. My Uncle Leftie tries a skip or two before holding up his hands in surrender. The next time I write to my cousin Nancy, I'll be sure to tell her about her father skipping. She won't believe it either.

Giving up on Leftie, Olive grabs Rena's hand and pulls her along. We watch them skip down the lane, Rena keeping up the best she can. Before she left the house she'd stuck her feet into

Arthur's rubber boots and now she's galumphing down the road. In the light of the moon, Olive's tall figure twists and bends while her free arm waves at the air. Meanwhile, it looks as if Rena has traded in skipping for a hopping run.

"Would you look at that!" Uncle Leftie says, shaking his head. "That Olive sure does get things riled up, doesn't she?"

Uncle Leftie has a fascinated look on his face that I've seen on other faces. What is it about Olive that causes such amazement, when she bugs me so much?

Pulling his keys from his pocket, Leftie heads to the police truck. He turns to me and says, "You coming to town with me then, kid?"

I look at Bear, who is scraping the bottom of his boot against the clothesline pole. He keeps bending over to examine his boot and doesn't even look up as I debate Leftie's question.

A part of me is thinking, get into that car with your uncle, you fool! It is far too dangerous to be standing next to Bear James. What if what happened the other night happens again, or maybe even worse, what if what *didn't* happen, happens again? And judging by how much you're sweating by just standing next to him, the faster you get out of range, the better.

Think practical, Trish. With or without Bear, there's TV bingo to think of. And your mother's house has a nice hot shower and television and a warm bed and most likely some leftover pizza in the fridge. Tomorrow you could even go down to Canadian Tire to pick up that piece of pipe for the stove and get it fixed before Ray comes home. Because, Trish, the question before you goes like this: Do you keep trying to save your marriage, or are you ready to lose your family again?

Try picturing the first scenario. When the power returns you go back home and to work at Foghorn Pewter. You can even rekindle that little fantasy thing you've got going with Kelly, your boss, because, bottom line? That little thing for your boss is safe because it'll never go further than your mind. When Ray comes home you'll talk as though you believe your marriage is worthy and strong. And if the talking doesn't work, you'll get him to bed and do your convincing there.

And what if you let it all slip away? That would be like stepping off a cliff into the fog, now wouldn't it, with no idea how far you'd fall before hitting bottom. Falling would be the easy part compared to what it would take to crawl back up to that edge. Unless ... unless you somehow learned how to fly on your own.

All this thinking is going on while I wave goodbye to Uncle Leftie. Bear and I are standing here watching the truck bounce down the lane until the brake lights flash when Leftie reaches Olive and Rena.

"You suppose Olive might yank him out of the car and make him skip some more?" Bear says.

Sure enough, Olive's voice carries all the way up the lane. "Shame on you, Leftie! No sneaking away allowed."

But Uncle Leftie would never take the chance of having to listen to Aunt Sybil give him shit for the next six months if he ever tried to pull off the old "the roads were bad so I decided to stay over" routine. My Aunt Sybil keeps Leftie on a short leash, and while he'd never admit it, everyone knows he needs the security of Sybil. I wonder if most men are like that. Mine acts like he is the exception.

So there goes Leftie, out of danger. I can hear his tires crunch on the gravel just before he turns onto the road to town. That moon is so bright I'm able to make out the figures of Olive and Rena down at the end of the lane. The wind has dropped so I can hear their voices floating up the lane as well. The storm has finally moved out. Spring has returned, and I'm feeling a weird sort of calm about what might happen next.

I sneak a peak at Bear's profile. I've never really looked at him in this way. Like a lover, that is. I can't help wondering, or maybe hoping, that what I feel towards Bear means it's time to accept that Trish and Ray are finished and it's time to reshuffle the deck.

Hmmm, living with Bear on top of Thunder Hill with his

wonderful summer bathtub. On the negative side, there's that two-seater outhouse to consider, and in winter a chemical toilet behind a curtain. But, hey, if he gives you the right kind of love you could live with that and more. You and Bear would keep throwing those great big "end of summer" parties and who knows, maybe Ray would show up from time to time, with his *hot one*. She's probably not much older than Gayl, someone who looks up to Ray as being so smart, so sweet, and so ... so ... devoted. Probably like I used to.

Stop it right there, Trish. Stick to your own fantasy, not Ray's. Because you would be with Bear, right Trish? Maybe this nightmare of a journey you've been on these past three days has led to this very moment here in Kyle Lane.

If this is the moment, then you should probably act on it now. Say something like, "What do you suppose that was all about the other night?" or, "That was an interesting time there on the pool table, don't you agree?" At least then it will be out and he'll be forced to respond to a mature and direct question.

I start by asking, "Was that dog shit I saw you scraping off your boot back there?"

"Sure was," Bear says. "I guess I should have gotten you to clean it up."

"Me? Why me?"

"Because it was Suzie's shit."

"Come on. It could have belonged to one of the other dogs."

"No, it was Suzie's."

"How could you possibly know that?"

"Hey, you don't live your life in the woods and learn nothing about shit."

"You're the one who's full of shit, Bear James. Are you sure it wasn't your own?"

Bear laughs and reaches into the inside of his jacket for a joint while I fumble in my pockets for a wooden match. He leans towards me with the joint between his lips and murmurs, "You know, your Uncle Leftie's an okay guy and everything, but I thought he'd never leave."

Hmm. I run my thumbnail over the match head a few times until it lights.

Bear whistles in appreciation. "Very impressive. You must have gone to match lighting school. I suppose you can hold a cigarette butt between your teeth and flip it into your mouth too."

"Yes. As a matter of fact, I can."

"You are one talented human being, now aren't you?"

We smoke the joint and watch as the world around us slides into an altered space. The tops of the spruce tree hedge my father planted so long ago stand crisp against the night sky. Far down the lane we can make out Olive and Rena's figures moving closer to us in the moonlight.

The night is so quiet now that Bear and I are standing here in the driveway listening to the drip of melted snow and ice running off the eavestrough. The surf sounds far away, like low thunder. It's time to take a deep breath and face the truth.

"Bear?"

"Yeah?"

"How are you feeling?"

"You mean do I feel sick or something?"

"Maybe I shouldn't bring this up, but you know the other night? At Hog Holler?"

"Yeah? What about it?" He taps the end of the joint and tucks it into his pocket before turning to face me.

"I was just wondering," I say, feeling my mouth go suddenly dry. "Did Clayton ever wake up? At Hog Holler? In the morning, I mean? After I left?"

"Were you still there when he fell off the couch?"

"No."

"You should have heard the sound his head made when it hit the cement floor." Bear raises his voice like he's telling the story to several people. "I looked over there expecting to see his head look like a smashed pumpkin."

I give a little laugh and clear my throat. "I'm not sure I remember much of that night." Then I act as if maybe the moon has distracted me and that's why I'm staring straight up at the sky. "Do you remember much?"

"Nope. Not much. Do you think we missed anything?"

I look at him and he looks at me, his eyes steady and calm.

That look, more than his words, make me feel like earth's gravity is pulling even harder against any influence a big bright moon may have had seconds ago. When my teeth get to chattering, and Bear turns to me, it's sad to think he won't be wrapping his arms around me like the friend he used to be. So when he too, starts staring up at the moon, it feels like an invisible stop sign has just sprung up between us.

Right then, a set of headlights suddenly sweeps around the curve on Thunder Hill Road and heads up the lane to where we stand.

26. Blue Grass Badly Played

IWAKE UP TO what sounds like a bluegrass band playing badly. My eyes pop open to darkness broken only by a tiny flicker of light coming from somewhere. Never mind *where* am I? *Who* the hell am I? A pair of hands slap down on either side of this body and this head turns and these eyes watch that faint flicker of light coming from a spot on the floor. A faint smell of dried flowers, mostly roses, and the music suddenly stops. Voices, male and female. Then just as clear as a bright winter's day, the sound of Alana's voice. Yes, it's Alana, who after many drinks sounds as familiar to me as my own mother.

"You think someone should check on old Trish?" she is asking.

Thank you, Alana. You know those fast motion films of a tide rising and falling in the space of a minute? That's how it feels to catch up with myself. For a moment I savour the relief until I start to piece it all together. Like how I came to be lying up here in the room of my childhood. I can hear Suzie licking herself under the bed. It's late evening and I'm waking up from sleeping off Bear's frigging wheelchair dope on top of a stomach full of Olive's wine.

I can't say I was all that excited to see that the visitors behind the headlights last night in the yard were Alana and Danny. Danny must have gained Alana's forgiveness by getting her liquored up and was she ever. Over the years, Alana has picked up this sloppiness in her face when she drinks. Her skin seems slacker than usual and her eyes get all puffy and red. Olive hustled them into the warmth of her kitchen while I was wondering when this party would ever end.

"Of course you're staying. You should have come over here days ago," Olive said, taking their coats and handing them to me. By the time I hung them on the hooks behind the door and turned around, Danny and Alana were settled at the table. The fish and vegetables were popped back into the oven to warm up and a bottle of wine was uncorked. Thank God I hadn't gotten around to washing up all the serving bowls because Olive simply filled them up again and brought them to the table. "I wish you'd come earlier," she said and then she turned to me. "Patricia, you were supposed to invite Danny and Alana for supper!"

"I did."

"But you should have brought them earlier!"

"I didn't think it was my job to physically drag them here."

Olive placed her arm around Alana's shoulders. "But they're Danny and Alana. Of course it was your job to drag them over."

Gayl and the twins suddenly burst through the back stairs door, followed by the pups. Now there were so many people and kids and dogs in the room that the windows fogged right up. The girls were jumping up and down and the dogs were barking and it was just as Olive was setting down the salmon platter with the accompanying herbed potatoes and fresh parsley garnish that I started to feel the whirlybirds.

Maybe it was the way she was fussing over Danny and Alana — fetching napkins, spooning vegetables onto their plates — like they had survived some horrible ordeal and had just been rescued, but I honestly thought she was going to spoon-feed them next.

I looked at Alana to see if she was wise to this, but she seemed just as happy as Danny to be fawned upon. What is wrong with these people? Why can't they see through Olive?

"Now where's my official wine tester? Patricia?"

"No more wine," I said, placing my hand over my glass.

Danny held out his glass and shouted, "Since the official wine tester has done far too much testing for tonight, I don't mind substituting."

"It's a lovely Merlot, don't you think?" Olive smiled. "Not too dry. How would you describe it, Danny?"

Danny put on the air of a snooty wine taster. He swished it around his mouth, pretending that it was filling up his mouth to the point where his cheeks bulged and his eyes looked ready to pop out. Olive found this hilarious.

Alana didn't. She elbowed Danny in the ribs. "Swallow it for Christ's sake!"

Danny swallowed. "Ahhh."

"What do you think?" said Olive, so excited she held her fists up against her chest.

"There is only one word to appropriately describe the boo-kay of this boo-tay," Danny said, loudly smacking his lips and pausing for the longest moment. "Moist!"

Olive clapped her hands. "Wonderful!"

"Brilliant!" said Alana, banging her glass onto the table as she often does at this point in her drinking. Olive has obviously noted this about Alana in the past because tonight she has served her wine in a sturdy Irving station mug.

"This," Olive said suddenly, smacking both hands down on the table, "is exactly what I love!"

We all looked at her. *What?* What did she love? The wine? Danny's jokes? The weather? Everybody's faces seemed to shine with expectation.

She drew in her breath. We probably did too.

"*This*! Friends and family gathered around the table, drinking wine and eating good food, as people have done since the beginning of time." She raised her glass. "To power failures and candlelight. And ... and ... our collective consciousness!"

Everybody just sort of smiled as if wondering what the hell

she was talking about. *Collective consciousness?* Olive is so full of herself I wanted to shout.

"I want to make a toast," Kyla pouted.

"Go ahead, lovey," Olive said.

Kyla raised her glass that Olive had filled with cranberry juice and a touch of wine. "Here's to no school!"

"Here! Here!" said Bear.

"This is fun," Olive said. "Danny? What's your toast?"

"That's easy." Danny slapped his hand on the bottom of the empty bottle as he held it over his glass. "Here's to more wine tasting!"

"I'll drink to that," Olive said, reaching to her sideboard for yet another bottle. "Bear? Do you have anything you'd care to toast?"

"He's already toasted," Danny said.

"I thought he might have something to say about pool tables," Olive said, winking at him and smiling pointedly at me. When does she ever stop? I looked at Bear.

"Sure. Why not? To pool tables!" Bear thrust his glass out like he'd been planning all along to make this toast. "Where you meet the nicest people on a Saturday night! Right, Trish?"

"Ha Ha!" all those collective faces laughed.

Could this night get any worse?

"Why are you turning so red, Trish?" Danny teased.

That did it. I grinned so hard my cheeks ached, while I raised my glass high in the air. "And here's to Bear for rescuing me. Cause there's nothing warmer than a nice big bear rug on a cold, stormy night!"

"Here, here!" Bear said, clinking my glass with his own and giving me this big exaggerated grin. And just like that, our night on the pool table had officially become a harmless event, now plopped into the collective joke pool.

And that's when the room began to seriously rotate. I said something about them having to find someone else to do up all the dishes because I had to go upstairs to lie down.

I had Alana's attention now and I felt like she was zeroing into my brain. "You okay, Trish?"

"Yeah, sure, why?"

"You look scared or something," said Alana

"You do look a little strange," Danny said. "I mean, stranger than usual." Their laughter followed me all the way up the back stairs. "If I look scared, it's because I am scared," I shot back, but not loud enough for anyone to hear.

My feet felt heavy, and that's the last thing I remember before falling face first onto the bed.

Now that I know where and who I am, I slip out of bed and crawl across to the floor register. I slide the grate open and peek down just as the "band" starts up again. Olive is squeaking away at what might be "Rocky Mountain Breakdown." I see she has forced everybody else to take up instruments too because Bear and Alana are pretending they know how to play the spoons and Danny is drumming away on a tiny set of bongo drums. And what's that other sound? A kazoo? I crane my neck so I can see the kitchen couch. Rena's there, blowing into a comb. She has tucked a napkin behind it, and judging by the way her cheeks bulge out, she must think she's playing a tuba. And there's Gayl looking happy to be squeezed between Bear and Alana on the couch. In fact, everybody looks plain cheerful. Just look at Bear, reaching out to squeeze Olive's elbow when she screeches out the last note of the song and everybody's whistling and clapping for Olive, who's acting like she's some sort of rock star the way she laughs and tosses her hair when she bows. The only one missing from the happy scene is Biz, who maybe like me, is turned off by this Olive love-in and is likely in his room staring at his ceiling and wishing he was somewhere else.

I watch the musicians down in the kitchen while I lie here on my elbows with my hands over my ears to drown out the sound. Finally there's a lull, but that quickly ends when the twins start pestering Bear and he starts tickling them until they start up with their ear-piercing shrieks. Over the noise Olive is shouting something about playing charades again. Rena seems to have picked up on the fact that one way to divert Olive is to distract her. "Hey, Olive, why is that dog shaking its head so much?"

"Oh, no!" Olive says, making a grab for one of the pups. "I hope it's not another ear infection. Rumi, hold still and let me look at your ear."

Now I hear Bear say to Alana, "I thought you said you were going to go check on Trish."

I can tell by the way Alana's curled up at her end of the couch that there's no way in hell she's about to give up her spot. Sure enough, she says to Bear, "Maybe you're the one who should go check on her. Now that you've become so close...."

"Right. Like anyone would dare get that close to Trish these days," Bear snickers, and suddenly shouts, "Hey, what happened to the music?"

I back away from the register like it's suddenly on fire. I have to get out of here *now*.

There was a time when Suzie monitored my every move. It got to be annoying even, having her right at my heels no matter what I was doing. But now as I leave the bedroom she is so busy snoring under the bed that she doesn't even notice. Maybe she assumes I'm heading for the bathroom. When I reach the bottom of the stairs leading to the front door, I notice a flickering light in the parlour to my left. Now, who the hell left that candle there to burn the house down in our sleep? I turn into the room and walk toward the candle on the mantelpiece but stop in my tracks when I see my father's face clearly reflected in the mirror that hangs where it has always hung, over the mantelpiece. A chill rips through me as I take in his profile, complete with that silly cowboy hat he once brought back from a trip to Calgary. In that second I decide there are two possibilities. One is that I'm seeing my father's actual ghost, or, two, I'm still upstairs dreaming. Maybe that whole music scene in the kitchen was a dream. In fact, I bet that if I look away from the mirror and over by the window, I'll see my father standing there. Maybe I can talk to him like I have in other dreams. I often feel like we're trying to apologize for something, except neither of us seems to know what we're sorry for. So, yeah, why not turn now and face your father, Trish? Maybe this time you'll know what to say to him.

This all happens in a second, of course, so when I turn my head, slowly, because even in a dream it can be startling to see one's dead father, my mouth drops open. This is no freaking dream. There's Biz, standing behind one of the armchairs. And now I do feel like screaming because what hits me worse than a nightmare is the instant proof that Olive is my half sister. None of those DNA tests are needed here, no private detectives. A reversed Biz's face reflected in the mirror shows my father's sloped forehead, his same strong chin. A smaller nose, maybe, but the resemblance is there, all the same. He is approaching the mirror now, his fingers adjusting the brim of the hat, his face turning this way and that. He hasn't noticed me standing there. It's going to stay that way too, because now I'm rushing out the front door of Kyle House.

27. Heading for the Nearest Cliff

THE AIR HAD BEEN as still as an ice pond all evening, but the tide must have just turned because the wind is picking up. I clutch at the shawl I had the good sense to grab from the porch. And after what I just saw there in the parlour, it's a wonder I thought to slip on Olive's rubber boots before making my escape. With my hair flying every which way, I probably look freaky tearing out of the house like this. Except for a scattering of clouds scuttling in front of the moon, the sky is clear and bright. At least I'm not feeling sick any more, I mean, not the stomach kind of sick.

The path to Kyle Point runs through the cemetery and that's where I'm passing now. I can hear bits of melting snow drip from the aspen branches onto the headstones. Most of the stones sit over the bones of the first settlers to the area and are more than a century and a half old. My father has no business being buried here. All of our ancestors came from the bay side of Thunder Hill and the cemeteries there are packed with Kyles. But as far as Bernie was concerned, he was important enough to be planted anywhere he chose, provided, of course, my mother would let him have his way. I keep my head down against the wind and I realize my thoughts must be passing by his plot as surely as my feet are. The creaking branches of the aspens sway high above me, their shadows flitting across the gravestones. Bare rosebushes clutch at my shawl. I have to keep yanking it free from what feels like sharp little claws, and so I'm almost surprised when I reach the edge of the cliff.

The cliff doesn't seem quite as high as it did when I was a kid. I'm not sure if this is because I was so small then, or if the sandstone face could have eroded that much over the years. I suppose the stone stairway my father made down to the beach is long gone. As a kid, I'd burst out of bed in the mornings just to race to the cliff and down those stone steps to my own private wonderland of red ledges of rock and clear tide pools. All of this could have, should have, been mine.

Now as I stand here on the brink, I look down at where I think the steps used to be and I'm wondering if I can still make my way down. It would be less windy down there. I could climb down to watch the tide come in under a full moon. I can't remember when I stopped doing this sort of thing, this roaming about by myself. Had it ended when I met Ray? Ray, who made my world make sense. Ray, who relied on me to make good decisions, even if he didn't agree with them. He seemed to have this blind faith in me. When had all that changed? Had he just decided one day that maybe I wasn't so right? Had he just one day fallen out of love with me?

Ray doesn't love me anymore.

I feel a fresh wave of panic. Over the years, there've been times when I was convinced that I no longer loved him, but the thought of him not loving me? Even when he moved to Newville I felt he had left me out of frustration or possibly even anger, but until Olive suggested there might be someone else I really believed there could never be anyone else for Ray but me. A coldness like I've never felt before enters my body, and I feel as though I must be falling. Falling even as I stand straight against the wind.

The water below is tossing about pretty good tonight. I can see the swells rising and falling against the cluster of rocks just down the beach. I try to match my breathing to its rhythm. In and out, up, and then down. It's calming to breathe at the ocean's pace. Damp salt air rushes in and out of my lungs and best of all, the clutter in my head starts to fade. I haven't felt this clear since the last time I had a soak in Bear's mountain tub. *Bear.* My breath catches with the thought of him, and it takes every bit of effort to push it away. Again, I focus on the swelling tide only to find that breathing and meditating have become a struggle to harness. I work and work at it, and just when I'm feeling calm again, thoughts of Ray come barging into my brain like they have some right to be there. I'm trying to force them away when something cold and wet slides into the palm of my hand. I almost jump out of my skin, but a stronger instinct reminds me that the edge of a cliff is not the best place to make any sudden moves.

Suzie's wet snout is in my hand.

I look around, wondering how the hell she got here but I don't see a soul. I pull at a burr stuck on her ear and that gets me thinking about instinct and how it just saved my skin. So when did I stop trusting *my* instincts? How can I trust a feeling that one minute screams at me to hold on to my mate, but in the next heartbeat makes me want to fuck his best friend? Maybe I don't need Bear or Ray at all. What if it's true that men are only necessary for a certain time in a woman's life?

That gets me thinking of my mother and how she's slowly drowning in rum. After my father died, I bugged her to start dating other men and she tried for a bit. First, there was Darby Hargraves, who owns the biggest farm machinery outfit in the county. Then, there was Keith Sparks, who I thought she might take to because he sings in the church choir and she has always loved the sound of a man singing. I'd just assumed things didn't work out with either man was because they could never compare to my father. But, one night, she told me she had no interest in taking care of another man, because at her age, that's all she'd end up doing. At the time I found that such a depressing thought, but maybe it makes sense. Ray just seems to hurt my heart. And Bear? Turns out that our friendship is more important than our lonesome body parts.

I look over the edge of the cliff. Now, where are those old

stone steps ? I'm feeling such a strong urge to go down to the rocks below. But then I hear someone hurrying up the path from the cemetery. Whoever it is, they're wearing a dark cape. Now, I can tell by the way the arms reach out for balance that it is Olive. She lifts her face so she must have spotted me because she picks up speed and stumbles so much coming up the path that I reach out to grab her before she knocks us both off the cliff. By the way she pulls at me with all her might I can see she thinks she's saving me from jumping. Her face is full of fear.

To calm her down I say, "Isn't it beautiful out here at night?"

She screams, "Have you been standing out here this whole time?"

I admit I'm a little shocked when she tells that I've been out here for almost an hour. It has felt more like five minutes. She tells me how she first went into my room and spoke my name, but since Suzie was thumping her tail under the bed, she went back downstairs thinking I was asleep under all those covers. Then awhile later she heard another thumping sound and went back upstairs. Suzie was scratching at the bedroom door. Suzie must have finally figured out I wasn't in the room. So while the rest of them were caught up playing charades, she and Suzie had slipped out to find me.

I feel her tighten her grip on my arm. The path here narrows to where it runs through the wild rose bushes and we walk along in single file until she stops all of a sudden. She wheels around and stands so close to my face I can feel the warmth of her breath. I take a step back and make a move as if to continue along the path. She blocks me, saying, "Look. If you want to talk about it, I'm here to listen."

"Talk about what?"

"Anything." She takes a deep breath. "Like you and Ray."

I keep on walking. We've reached the cemetery now so the

path weaves through the time-blackened headstones of the earliest settlers. We're far enough back from the cliff that the sound of surf has fallen away and all we can hear is the melting snow dripping from the trees. The moonlight pours down on us when we reach a small clearing not far from my father's grave.

She says, "Sometimes it helps to talk to someone to put things into perspective."

She stops beside a child's headstone and trails her finger over a granite lamb. It's too dark to make out the words on the stone, but I remember them well. *Here lies little Bella.* She was only two years old when she died in 1895. When I was a kid I felt sorry for this little girl, for not having a chance in life. Now I'm thinking this little girl was lucky to have been spared life's awful truths.

"Marriage is a funny thing." Olive is gazing into the distance. "Just when you think it's solid and secure, something comes along to shake it up."

I feel my lips tighten at this. Next she'll be saying that this is what makes it all worthwhile. Meanwhile, we've reached my father's grave with its little granite stone next to Olive's big red monstrosity.

"Ray and I have our problems but we're going to be just fine," I say, just to head her off at the pass.

"I know you're going to be just fine," she says. "Everybody thinks you'll be fine."

"Everybody?"

"Well it's not exactly a secret that things between you and Ray haven't been normal in a while."

"Normal?" Maybe it's because of where my head is at here in the middle of a cemetery in the middle of the night that makes me feel brave enough to suddenly shout, "Who made you the authority on what's a normal marriage?" I can tell by the shocked look that I've got her attention here. I bet my face looks just as shocked as hers, but off I go anyway, saying, "How can you talk about normal when your own husband spends more time in Toronto than he does with you!"

When she slaps her hand over her mouth like she's holding back vomit, you'd think some compassion might kick in here on my part, but no, I've got some vomiting of my own to do. Because if I've learned some big lesson these past three days it's that I'm running out of things to lose. And standing in front of me is the one person in the world I don't mind losing one bit. I shout again, "You say you want to be my sister? Then let me tell you something, sister. Your man goes around looking like a kicked dog half the time. And your son does too!"

God that felt good to say. I feel like something has been pried loose inside of me. I feel like screaming at her for making me feel so ... so ... fucking inferior every chance she gets in that way she has of fooling everyone into thinking that she loves me when secretly she *hates, hates, hates* me.

Olive has dropped to her knees in front of my father's headstone and she's weeping onto the stone. Well, the sound of Olive crying is a lot like a rabbit when it's caught, and the sudden sight of her draped over the headstone causes something to hurt in my heart so much that now we sound like two caught rabbits. I find myself rubbing her shoulders, pushing my thumbs into her back like I used to do for Gayl when she couldn't sleep.

I hear myself blubbering, "I'm sorry, Olive. And here you came looking for me...." And it's not like this is the first time she has come to my rescue. There was that night at Hog Holler and, come to think of it, ever since Ray left she has been poking her face into my life every two seconds. She is saying something to me now; something about Toronto.

"I'm sorry," I say looking for something to blow my nose into. "What did you say?"

Olive says, "He's moving back to Toronto."

"Who? Arthur?"

"You're right. Things aren't working out for us. " She looks up at me with tears and snot glistening in the moonlight. "Arthur's giving up the country life."

"What?" I shake my head like I haven't heard right. "Are you sure? I mean, why?"

"Oh, I'm sure. When he phoned to say he couldn't make it home because of the storm, he..." She chokes here, a cough really, and I speed up my thumb action. "We've been talking about it for a while now, that maybe he and Byron should move back up there and that I'll stay here with the girls!"

"But, what will you do?"

"I've decided to get a job." She sniffs, and draws in a deep breath, as if this is the first time she's ever considered employment in her life. She starts going on about how she'll never abandon her art, but that she'd reached the conclusion that her art will never support her.

"Here?" I say. "There aren't too many jobs around here. Except the pewter factory, I suppose."

There's a thought — Olive working next to me every day.

"I thought of that, and I've even talked to your boss, and he said the job you turned down might still be up for grabs. So I thought maybe I'd..."

I abandon the back rub and move around to look her right in the face. "Wasn't it you who said Kelly wasn't offering me nearly enough money?"

"Well, after you turned it down," she says, stressing the "turned down" part, "I had a talk with him and I pretty much convinced him it would be in his best interest to pay someone well to do a good job."

"And that person would be you?"

She sniffs. "Well, I have to start thinking about my future, now that Arthur's leaving."

"But what about me?"

"What about you?"

"I'll need more money with Ray gone."

"Is he gone?"

I lean against Olive's red monstrosity to think about her question. Ray said he was coming home, but who's fooling who?

During this past year his visits have added up to what has felt like a bunch of Band-Aids trying to close a gash the size of a canyon.

"Yeah, I'd say he's gone. Or going. Pretty much gone." I can't believe I just choked that out.

"Then I guess we're in the same boat, now, aren't we?"

"Kind of looks that way."

Now I'm crying for letting my own marriage slip through my fingers. I wonder if Alana was right when she said sometimes women reach a point when they turn on their men, forcing them to run away.

I go back to standing behind Olive, again rubbing her shoulders. I'm doing it because I have to think about us running our men off and in order to think I need some quiet. And it is some quiet here in this cemetery, except for the snow dripping from the trees, and our sniffling, and Suzie's rustling around in the underbrush. Maybe there's something I need a whole lot more than a man in my life right now. Maybe it's time to move forward and allow the past to fall away.

Olive now says, "I've been so happy getting to know you as a sister, and in doing so, I feel I've gotten to know our father better too."

Now two things hit me, both colder than snow thrown in the face. There's a chance Olive could decide to move back to Toronto too. And now here comes a thought that surprises the shit out of me: Olive disappearing from my life doesn't exactly thrill me as much as I thought it would.

I say, "Well, maybe you'll both change your minds once summer comes and it's so beautiful here."

"He doesn't want to be here," Olive says, her voice suddenly so cold my thumbs freeze between her shoulder blades. "That's one thing we agreed upon when we made this move — that we'd be honest with each other. And the last time I spoke to him he confessed that he'd rather be back in Toronto. And that goes for Byron too."

She drops her head back down onto her arms again and this is where we're at. My thumbs are feeling stiff now, both from the constant movement and from the cold. But I don't dare quit for fear she'll come up with something even weirder to tell me on this night.

"You know, when I heard that I'd inherited the house, I looked at it as a sign or as a gift that had fallen out of the sky. Arthur and I had been drifting further and further apart and I was hoping we'd have one last chance to reconnect."

The moon has been hiding behind a cloud these past few minutes and now it reappears, casting shadows from the aspen branches onto the snow. In this new light, I can almost make out the inscription on Olive's marble monstrosity.

"The stone is handsome, isn't it?" she says, reaching over to brush it with her hand. "I hope he likes it. It was important to me to make an overture to my father. I mean, our father."

"Our father who art in heaven," I say, and now she's laughing like I just told the funniest joke she's ever heard.

Then she says, all wistful, "He *was* kind of like a god to me, or at least a mythical hero. When I was a kid, I'd run to the front door every day in case there might be a letter from him."

I am starting to doubt that Olive has any idea how deeply his rejection of her went. She once told me she was envious that I had grown up with him. Now I wonder if I should tell her my little story about our father, about the last time I rode my banister horse at the age of thirteen. My father had joined me on my pillow saddle as he often had. We picked up where we'd left off the last time we had played cowboys. Here we were, gaining on the rustlers, and, as I lowered myself closer to Thunder's mane so we could ride like the wind, I called back to my father to hang on tighter, because we had to jump over a giant gorge. My father reached through my arms to hang on tight like he always did when we played this game, but just as he flattened his hands over my chest, he suddenly yanked them away as if they'd been burned. At first I thought he was pretending that the rustlers had shot him clean off our horse. But no, he headed down the stairs mumbling that he had something important to do. The game was over, and that night at bedtime it was my mother who came to tuck me in. I didn't think to ask why her and not my father, but after that night he never again came into my room and neither of us ever again rode my banister horse.

I talked to Alana about this, years later, and we had a good laugh about it.

"Fathers," she'd said. "They can't handle the thought of their daughters turning into actual women. And those are the good fathers. There are plenty who are not. You hear about it all the time."

I've decided not to tell Olive this story about our father, about how I felt so punished for growing up. It strikes me that his rejection of Olive robbed her of a father altogether.

Olive takes a deep breath and so do I. The night air is rich with the smell of spring rot. "I come up here sometimes," she says. "To talk to him. To thank him actually."

"For Kyle House, you mean?"

"For finally letting me into his life," Olive says, looking intently at me, "through you ... Patricia."

She places her hands upon my shoulders and in her eyes I can see how desperate she was for my father's love. My father who, it turns out, was so foolishly stubborn, just like me. Tears sting my eyes and I fight them back, clearing my throat to ask, "So what do we do now? About our men, I mean."

We begin to walk, her hand over my shoulder until the path grows narrow and now I am walking ahead as she says from behind, "I think that until we're actually face to face with them we don't have much choice but to wait it out, the same way we've been waiting out the storm these past three days."

The storm. I've been so oblivious, really, to any storm but the one raging in my own heart. I've been oblivious to so much lately.

Then, as if she has read my mind, she says, "I don't know what

I would have done if you hadn't come over to stay with me."

I'm relieved we are back to normal, almost. "Oh, come on, you found Rena the next day and then there were those linemen."

Olive snorts, "That's right, the linemen."

"You have to admit they were kind of cute."

"I noticed that you thought so."

"Me? I'm not the one who traipsed them all through my 'private parts' as Rena put it."

"Rena is one funny duck, don't you think?"

Then I do something that surprises me as much as it does her. Just as we clear the aspens and tramp towards Kyle House I lay my hand on her shoulder. "You know, Olive, I don't think you should give up on you and Arthur. You might end up going back to Toronto too."

"Are you kidding? And leave the most fucking beautiful place in the world, man?"

It's my turn to laugh to hear her quoting Alana. "All I know is that I refuse to move back to Toronto. Maybe we'll miss each other once we're both where we want to be. But you know, sometimes a girl just has to take a stand."

"But what about the sex?" I nudge her like a guy would. "Wouldn't you miss all that tickling with the feather?"

"I told you about that, did I?" We've reached the door to the summer porch. She places her thumb on the latch and turns to me, a sheepish smile crossing her face. "That happened a long long time ago and it's never happened since."

She presses down on the door latch. "At least you still have that with Ray."

After all the damp and dark of outdoors, stepping into the kitchen is like returning to life. Everything is bathed in warm yellow candlelight. Over in the corner the fire in the cookstove glows through the side vents. Gayl jumps up from her chair and comes to hug me. "What were you doing outdoors?"

"Just doing some thinking," I say, hugging her back.

"Ma," she whispers, her breath soft on my ear. I have a feeling she's had a few glasses of Olive's wine just by the way she's not letting me go. "It's not you I want to get away from. It's just that I want to live in town."

I pat her shoulder and we stand like this, her arms around me feeling solid. My daughter has turned out to be so strong. She'll finish her schooling and do better than spend her whole life standing on a cold cement floor in a factory. Maybe Ray and I haven't done so badly by her after all.

My eyes find their way to Bear over there on the kitchen couch and the rest of me marches right over there like I have every right to him. He looks like he's almost scared of what I might do next as I plunk down on the couch and lift his arm so that it drapes around my shoulders. But then I jab him with my elbow and the look that runs between us is as natural as it always has been.

Here comes Alana carrying a glass in her hand that she thrusts out at me.

"Cognac," she says. "The best thing for fainting. You wave it under the nose until they come to their senses."

"Great," I say. "Except that I didn't faint."

"Maybe not, but have you come to your senses?"

"What's the big deal?" I say, coughing from the smell of cognac. "I only went for a walk."

"You seem to be doing a lot of that lately," she says, sitting on the other side of Bear.

"Alana?" I say, swallowing another mouthful. "Thanks. I'm sorry. Stuff got weird."

She softens at my words. I can see it in her face. I look straight into the eyes of my old friend hoping she'll read all that I've been feeling. Maybe one day she will explain it all to me. Bear chooses this moment to place us both in headlocks.

"My two favourite ladies in the entire world!" he shouts as a blinding light comes from the camera that Olive has suddenly stuck in our faces.

"Wait a minute, wait a minute. Let me get one more!"

I can just imagine these same photos that will be passed around for years to come. They'll sit in an album bearing the title of "April Storm at Kyle House, 1994." Everyone in these photos will forever look grateful to be in the warmth of Olive's kitchen.

28. The Lifeboat

I OPEN MY EYES to the blackness of the room just as the bed-room door slowly opens. When I was a kid, I'd watch the door from my bed, my eyes convinced it was actually open-ing. The only way to return the door to its original position was to blink. I try blinking the door shut now, but it keeps opening, and now I know it's for real because there's a sudden draft in the room. I sense, rather than see, that someone has stepped over the threshold. When I hear the reassuring thump of Suzie's tail against the floorboards I'm relieved to know that at least it is not a ghost. Whoever it is tiptoes around to the other side of the bed trying not to make too much noise.

What if it's Ray? For a second my heart feels like it might break into song or something. I'm about to whisper his name into the darkness when I remember him saying he wouldn't get home until the weekend.

It could be Olive coming in to get another blanket from the closet. Or Kyla looking for one of her stuffed animals. It had better not be Rena looking to cozy up. You never know with Rena. What about Bear? Suzie doesn't whine that way for just anyone. Does he really expect to crawl under my covers? I'll tell him, sorry, Bear, but I'll still hold him in my arms like a friend in need of warmth.

I hear the sound of a pair of pants dropping to the floor and I hold my breath as the old springs squeak beneath this figure crawling into my bed.

I know now who this is. Obviously, Suzie does too because she scrambles out from under the bed.

I twist in my nightgown to stick my cold nose into Ray's warm neck. "How did you find me?"

"You know I'll always be able to find you," he whispers back, his hands moving up to my face.

"But how did you know I'd be in this room?"

"Bear."

"Bear?"

"When I came through the back door into the kitchen, I saw this arm rising up from the couch and pointing to the ceiling. I took it as a sign."

Ray kisses me now. He kisses me like he's hungry. I return the kiss with all the passion of a woman teetering on the edge of a cliff. But then I remember my promise to myself and I wrench myself away from him. I whisper that while it's all very well to have him crawl into my bed, there is something we need to discuss before we go any further. Now it's his turn to pull away and in spite of the covers over our bodies I feel a chill between us.

I'm thinking, okay Trish, you've set the stage. Everything that's been banging around in your head has to come out. Be strong and say ... what? "Ray," you could say, "there was a flue fire and I was afraid to tell you because you are right to think I am careless and irresponsible." Or you could say, "There was a flue fire and the house was cold and I planned to walk over to the Four Reasons, but instead ended up at Hog Holler where I tried to fuck your best friend." You could say, "Ray, my love, you were so right when you said we've come to the end of the chapter about us. I think we should call it quits."

I take a deep breath because I fully expect at least one of these things to slip out of my mouth, but something else tumbles out instead. "I want you to quit the salt mine and come home," I say. "To me."

The only one who seems to be breathing in the room right now is Suzie. The silence coming from Ray feels like torture.

Then he exhales in a sort of whistle and says, "I want to come home too."

"Really?"

"But there's something else besides my job that I need to quit."

"What's that?"

"Drinking," he says. "I want to quit drinking."

"Good for you," I say. "So quit."

I hear him swallow. "It's hard for me to quit drinking if you're still drinking."

I look to where I figure his face ought to be. "So you decide to quit drinking and you won't come home unless I quit drinking too?" I can feel my back come up along with the need to say that I'm not the one with the problem.

But then he says, "It's something we'd both have to work on."

Something clicks in my thinking. Ray is telling me that he wants to work on us. Now it's up to me to decide if *I'm* willing to work on us.

I know I didn't say that out loud, but Ray must have heard me anyway because he says, "I've been thinking about fixing up the house. We could make it real nice."

Right. And where does Ray think we'll get the money to do that since he'll be without a job? Now's not the time to get all practical though because I have this sudden image of just Ray and me and something that feels like a future. In this future we're cracking open the door to the barn and going to work on that skeleton of a dingy he and my father started to build, the one that's been sitting there in the dark ever since.

I'm about to tell Ray my idea just as he decides to touch my cheek and pokes me in the eye instead.

"Ow."

"Sorry."

I tell him, "It's not like us quitting drinking is going to solve everything that's ... you know, wrong with us."

"But it would help me to quit if you were to quit too."

"I don't know about that," I say. "But I guess we could try."

Everything is quiet, as if even the furniture is listening to us in the dark.

"Okay then," he finally whispers. "Let's start there."

I'm not sure how he has managed to find my mouth in the darkness but his lips are now on mine. His breath warms my face and he presses his body hard against mine the way he has done forever. His hands sliding under this nightgown feel exactly as they always have, warm and generous and in need of me. I ache for him in ways I don't remember feeling before this night.

So here we are, Trish and Ray, joined together for about the millionth time and we're trying to be as quiet as possible in a squeaky iron bed in a house full of people. I feel like we're riding out a storm at sea where the strength of it gathers and swells until I'm sure the whole house must be shaking too. It's like this bed is our lifeboat.

Acknowledgements

I am very grateful to the following people for reading this novel in part or entirety at various stages of its development. Their insights and opinions were greatly valued in the shaping of the work. Thanks to Hannah Ayukawa, Judith Berry, Terence Byrnes, Sarah Gilbert, Anna Turner, and Juliet Waters. I also want to thank my brother Robert Barnes for his sharp editorial eye, Ed Hubbard for his technical advice, Bärbel Knäuper for a timely suggestion, and Cathy Moss for her continued interest and encouragement throughout the years. I am especially appreciative of Luciana Ricciutelli at Inanna Publications for choosing to recognize my work and for bringing it to life. Finally, thank you family members, for showing me the way.

A variation of the chapter "Instant Sister" was published in the anthology, *Telling Stories: New English Fiction from Quebec*, under the title "How I Met My Cousin Biz" in 2002.

An excerpt from the chapter "Flue Fire" was published in the fall issue of *Matrix Magazine* in 2010.

Photo: Jens Pfeiffer.

Connie Barnes Rose is a native of Amherst, Nova Scotia. She moved to Montreal where she met her husband and where they raised their two daughters. She earned a BA in Creative Writing in 1992 and an MA in English from Concordia University in 1996. Her collection of linked short stories, *Getting Out of Town*, was published in 1997 and short-listed for the QSPELL Award and the Dartmouth Award. Since then she has taught creative writing at Concordia University and at the Quebec Writer's Federation. She continues to live with her husband in Montreal and still manages to return to Nova Scotia every summer.